Also available from
Jodi Thomas

RUSTLER'S MOON
RANSOM CANYON

ebook novella
WINTER'S CAMP

JODI
THOMAS

LONE HEART PASS

HQN™

HQN™

ISBN-13: 978-0-373-78921-4

Recycling programs for this product may not exist in your area.

Lone Heart Pass

Copyright © 2016 by Jodi Koumalats

This edition published by arrangement with Harlequin Books S.A.

For questions and comments about the quality of this book, please contact us at CustomerService@Harlequin.com.

® and TM are trademarks of Harlequin Enterprises Limited or its corporate affiliates. Trademarks indicated with ® are registered in the United States Patent and Trademark Office, the Canadian Intellectual Property Office and in other countries.

www.HQNBooks.com

Printed in U.S.A.

LONE HEART
PASS

CHAPTER ONE

Jubilee Hamilton
November 2009

THE GEORGETOWN STREET in front of Jubilee Hamilton's office looked more like a river of mud than a beautiful old brick lane.

"Why does it always have to rain on election day?" she asked the life-size cutout of her candidate.

The few volunteers left in the campaign office were cleaning out their desks. The polls hadn't been closed an hour, and Jubilee's horse in the race had already been declared the loser.

Or maybe she was the loser. Two months ago her live-in boyfriend, the man she'd thought she'd someday settle down with and have the two-point-five kids, had said goodbye. David had called her a self-absorbed workaholic. He'd accused her of being cold, uncaring, thoughtless, self-centered.

When she'd denied it, he'd asked one question. "When's my birthday, Jub?"

She'd folded her arms as if to say she wasn't playing games. But this time her mild-mannered lover hadn't backed down.

"Well," he stared at her, heartbroken.

When she didn't answer, David asked again. "We've been together three years. When is my birthday, Jub?"

"February 19," she guessed.

"Not even close." David picked up his briefcase and walked toward the door. "I'll get my things after the election is over. You won't have time to open the door for me before then."

Jubilee didn't have time to miss him, either. She had an election to run. She worked so many hours she started sleeping at the office every other night. Sometime in the weeks that followed, David had dropped by the apartment and packed his things. She'd walked in on a mountain of boxes marked with *D*s. All she remembered thinking at the time was that she was glad he'd left her clean clothes still hanging.

A few days later the *D*s were gone and one apartment key lay on the counter. There was no time to miss him or his boxes.

Jubilee had thought of crying, but she didn't bother. Boyfriends had vanished before. Two in college, one before David while she lived in Washington, DC. She'd have time for lovers later. Right now, at twenty-six, she needed to build her career. As always, work was her life. Men were simply extras she could live with or without. She barely noticed the mail piling up or the sign on the door telling her she had six weeks before she had to vacate the premises.

Then the rain came. The election ended. Her candidate had lost. She'd lost. No job would be waiting for her at dawn. No David would be standing in the door of their apartment this time, ready to comfort her.

Her third loss as a campaign manager. *Three strikes, you're out*, she thought.

She walked through the rain alone, not caring that she was soaked. She'd given her all this time and she'd ended up with nothing. The candidate she'd fought so hard for hadn't even bothered to call her at the end.

When she unlocked the door to the apartment that now looked more like a storage unit than a home, she wasn't surprised the lights wouldn't come on. David had always taken care of minor things like paying the bills.

She sat down on one of the boxes and reached for her phone before she realized she had no one to call. No friends. No old school buddies she'd kept up with. All the numbers in her contacts were business related except the three for her family. She scrolled down to the Hamiltons.

First number, her parents. They hadn't spoken to her since she'd missed her sister's wedding. Jubilee shrugged. Really, how important was a bridesmaid?

Destiny's wedding was beautiful anyway. Jubilee saw the pictures on Facebook. Had she attended, as the too tall, too thin sister, she would have only crumbled Destiny's perfection.

She moved down the list. Destiny. Her sister, six years older, always prettier, always smarter, never liking having her around.

Jubilee ran through memories like flashcards of her childhood. Destiny had cut off all her hair when she was three. Told Jubilee she was adopted when she was five. Left her at the park after dark when she was seven. Slashed her bike tires when she was ten so she couldn't follow along.

Oh, yeah, Jubilee thought, *don't forget about telling me I was dying when I got my first period.* The whole family was laughing as she'd written out her will at twelve.

The flashcards tumbled to the floor in her mind along with any need to talk to Destiny whatever-her-last-name-was-now.

If big sisters were measured on a scale of one to ten, Destiny would be double digits in the negative.

She moved down to the next Hamilton on her contact list. Her great-grandfather. She'd lived with him the summer she'd been eleven because her parents wanted to tour college options with Destiny. They'd all waved as they dropped her off at Grandpa Levy's with smiles as if they'd left a bothersome pet at the pound.

Two weeks later they'd called and said they couldn't make the trip back to Texas to get her because of car trouble. A week after that there was another school to consider. Then her father wanted to wait until he had a few days off so the trip from Kansas to Texas wouldn't be so hard on the family.

Jubilee had missed the first two weeks of school before they made it back, and she hadn't cared. She would have stayed on the ranch forever.

Grandpa Levy was ornery and old. Even at eleven she could tell the whole family didn't like him or want the worthless dry-land farm he'd lived on since birth. Levy talked with his mouth full, cussed more than Methodists allow, only bathed once a week and complained about everything but her.

Jubilee's parents barely took the time to turn off the engine when they picked her up. The old man didn't hug her, but his knotted, leathered hand dug into her shoulder as if he couldn't bear to let her go. That meant more than anything he could have said.

She never told anyone how wonderful Grandpa Levy had been to her. He gave her a horse and taught her to ride, and all summer she was right by his side. Collecting eggs, birthing calves, cutting hay. For the first time in her life no one told her what she was doing wrong.

Jubilee stared at his number. She hadn't talked to him since Christmas, but the moment she'd heard his raspy voice, she'd felt like the eleven-year-old again, giggling and telling him things he probably cared nothing about. Her great-grandfather had listened and answered each rant she went through with comments like, "You'll figure it out, kid. God didn't give you all those brains for nothing."

She wanted to talk to him now. She needed to say she hadn't figured anything out.

Jubilee pushed the number and listened to it ring. She could imagine the house phone on the wall between his kitchen and living room ringing through empty bedrooms and hallways that always smelled dusty. He lived in the two rooms off the kitchen and left the other rooms to sleep, he claimed.

"Answer," she whispered, needing to know that someone was out there. Right now, tonight, she could almost believe she was the only one left alive. "Answer, Grandpa."

Finally, after twenty rings, she hung up. The old guy didn't even have an answering machine, and he'd probably never heard of a cell phone. Maybe he was in the barn or over near the corral where the cowhands who worked for him lived from spring to fall. Maybe he'd driven the two-lane road to town for his once-a-month trip. If so, he'd be having dinner at the little café in Crossroads. He was probably ordering two slices of Dorothy's pie right now.

She wished she were there in the booth across from him.

With the streetlight's glow from the window, she crossed to her fireplace and lit the logs. Strange how after more than a dozen years she still missed him when she'd never missed anyone else. She had lived years with her parents and remembered only slices of her life, but she remembered every detail of that summer.

As the paper-wrapped logs caught fire, the flames' light danced off the boxes and blank walls of her world. She found a half bottle of wine in the warm fridge and a bag of Halloween candy she hadn't been home to hand out. Curled up by the fire in her dark apartment, she began to read her mail. Most of the time she would fling the envelope into the fire without opening it. Ads. Letters from strangers. Catalogs filled with stuff she didn't need or want.

One by one she tossed the envelopes into the fire along with every hope and dream she'd had about a career as a campaign manager.

In the last stack of mail, she noticed a large white envelope hand-addressed to her. Curiosity finally caught her attention. The postmark was over a month ago. Surely it wasn't something important, or someone would have called her.

Slowly, she opened the envelope.

Tears silently tumbled as she saw the top of the page. She began to read Levy Hamilton's will. Word by word. Aloud. Making herself feel truth's pain.

The last page was a note scribbled on a lawyer's office stationery.

Levy died two months ago, Miss Hamilton. We were unable to reach any family, so I followed his request and buried him on his land. When he named you his sole heir of Lone Heart Ranch, he told me you'd figure out what to do with the old place. I hope this will get to you eventually. I'll see you when you get here.

Jubilee turned over the envelope. It had been forwarded twice before reaching her.

She laid the will aside and cried harder than she'd ever cried for the one person who'd ever really loved her. The one person she'd ever loved.

After the fire burned low and shadows slowly waltzed as if circling the last bit of light, she thought she felt Levy's hand resting on her shoulder. His knotted fingers didn't seem ready to let her go.

At dawn she packed the last of her clothes, called a storage company to pick up the boxes and walked away from her life in DC with one suitcase and her empty briefcase.

She'd go to her parents' house over the holidays. She'd try to find the pieces of herself and see if she could glue them together. But together or not, she'd start over where the wind never stopped blowing, and dust came as a side dish at every meal. She may have only lived there a few months, but Lone Heart Ranch might be the only place where she'd ever felt she belonged.

CHAPTER TWO

Charley Collins
February 2010

"Set 'em up, Charley. We'll have another round." The kid on the other side of the bar was barely old enough to drink, but his laugh was loud and his voice demanding. "It's Valentine's Day and none of us have a date. That's something to get drunk over."

Charley Collins swore under his breath. The drunks had had enough, but he'd be fired if he didn't serve the college boys, and he couldn't afford to lose another job. This dark, dusty bar wasn't much, but it kept food on the table and gas in his pickup.

"Aren't you Reid Collins's brother?" asked the only one of the boys who could still talk without drooling. "You look like him. Taller, maybe a little older. Got that same reddish-brown hair he's got. Red River mud-color if you ask me."

Before Charley could say anything, another drunk shook his head wildly. "No brother of Reid would be a bartender." He burped. "Collinses are rich. Deep-pocket rich. They own more land than a cowboy can ride across in a day."

Charley moved down the bar, hoping to slip out of being the topic of conversation. He hated the way they'd been talking about women all night, but that was better than listening to a conversation about him.

The sober one continued just loud enough for Charley to hear.

"I heard Reid had a big brother a couple of years older than him. Papa Collins disowned his oldest son. I remember Reid saying his dad ordered an armed guard to escort his brother off the ranch like he was some kind of criminal. Davis Collins told his own son that if he ever set foot on the land again, he'd have him shot for trespassing."

Charley picked up the box of beer bottles and headed outside. He'd heard enough. He needed air.

It took several steps before the noise and smell of the bar cleared, but he walked all the way to the alley. After he set the bottles down by the trash, he stared at the open land behind the Two Step Saloon and took a deep breath. He needed clean air and space and silence. He was born for open country, and he had no idea how he'd survive working in a beer joint and living above it in a tiny two-room apartment.

Every time he swore things couldn't get worse, they did.

Staring at the full moon, he felt like cussing or drinking his trouble away. But cussing wasn't a habit he needed and he couldn't afford the liquor.

He couldn't quit and he couldn't run. Not without a stake to start over somewhere else. Charley had a feeling that *somewhere else* wouldn't fit him anyway. This part of Texas was in his blood. He belonged here even if it did seem half the people for a hundred miles around were trying to run him out.

Like a miner taking one last breath before he climbed

back into the hole, Charley filled his lungs and turned around.

He saw a woman in the shadows near the back door. She was tall and perfectly built even in silhouette. Long dark hair circled over her shoulders in the breeze like a cape. For a moment he hoped she was a ghost. Lately he'd been a lot less afraid of spirits than women.

When he was five feet away he made out her face— not that he needed more than the outline of her body to know who she was. "Hello, Lexie. You miss the turnoff to the ladies room?"

Her laugh was low and sexy. She was in her thirties now, but nothing about Lexie had slipped from the beauty queen she'd been. He'd seen her come in an hour ago with some guy in a business suit and fancy boots that had probably never touched dirt.

"I followed you out, Charley." She waited like a spider waits for a fly to land on its web. "Anyone ever tell you you're one hell of a handsome man? Tall, lean with bedroom-blue eyes. I was trying to concentrate on my next husband, but all I could do was stare at you. You got that mixture of Prince Charming and Bad Boy down pat. I can tell how good a man is going to be in bed just by the way he moves and, honey, you are walking sex appeal."

Charley thought of arguing. She must be blind. He was two months past due for a haircut, four days late on shaving, and he'd slept in the jeans and shirt he had on for the past two nights.

"Yeah, I've heard that lie before," he answered her question. "My last stepmother told me how irresistible I was about an hour before my father disowned me."

Lexie moved closer. "Must have been one wild hour."

He wasn't about to go into detail. Half the town probably already knew. He'd been screwing up his life since high school. Frogs had more sense than he did when it came to knowing the opposite sex. He'd been in his last year of college when his father, the powerful Davis Collins, finally had enough.

For once, Charley had been back home for a few days over Christmas break. He'd decided to stay at the Collins ranch headquarters and try to at least have one conversation with his father about his plans after college. Charley had studied and dreamed of taking over managing pasture that had been in his family for a hundred years. He was one semester away, and his dad was ready to hand over the work so he and his latest brainless bride could travel.

She'd been his dad's fourth wife, young enough to be Davis Collins's daughter. Charley had never turned down a pretty woman's offer, and he didn't turn her down when she came to his room wearing nothing but the bottom of her silk boxer-length pajamas. She hadn't even said a word, just closed the door and smiled.

The rest was common knowledge. His old man found them together and kicked him off the ranch. He had everything in Charley's room, as well as his horse, packed up and loaded in a trailer. Collins had a few of his cowhands deliver the load to Charley's address at the university.

Charley's accounts and credit cards were closed before New Year's Day. He had to drop out of school and find a full-time job. So, he abandoned his dream of graduation and came home to Crossroads, Texas, where his few true friends still lived. They offered help, but after a while, he had to step away. He had to figure out life on his own. There comes a time when even working a lousy job and living in a dump is better than charity.

Only Lexie whatever-her-name-was-these-days wasn't offering charity tonight.

"What are you doing in town, Lexie?"

"Trying to get rid of my aunt's rundown dump of a house. You know anyone who'd want to buy it? The place is huge."

"No." He knew neither one of them cared about any house. They were just passing time.

"What time do you get off, Charley? We could have some fun after midnight. My sweetie has to head back to Dallas in a few minutes and I'll be all alone."

"Thanks for the offer, but I'm not interested." He unwound her arm from around his. "Maybe some other time."

He almost ran to the open door, pushing himself back into the noise and the smells; they were a lesser kind of hell than what she was offering.

Charley stayed busy at the bar and didn't see her leave. He just looked up and saw the table where she had been was empty. Lexie was a kind of poison he didn't need.

A few hours later, the bar was quiet and all the drunks were gone. He washed the last of the shot glasses and headed upstairs. When he passed the bar owner, Ike Perez, Charley nodded a good-night.

"Tell Daniela to hurry on down. I don't want to wait on her." Perez sounded gruffer than he really was. In truth, he'd been one of the few in town to even give Charley a chance. There was lots of one-day part-time seasonal work, but he needed something regular. This job came with low pay for weekend work and a place to live.

Charley tapped on his own apartment door. Fifteen-year-old Daniela, rubbing her eyes, pulled the door open. "I know," she mumbled. "Papa is ready to go."

"The little princess asleep?" Charley asked as he passed the girl who'd probably already reached her full height of five foot three. Daniela was young, but she made a good babysitter.

"Yeah. I got a new strategy." Daniela giggled. "I let her watch TV until she nods off. Otherwise she never stops talking. That kid has an imagination that won't quit."

Charley handed Daniela her backpack. "Thanks." He passed her a ten—half his tips for the night.

"No problem. I'd rather be here than home helping Mama cook for the weekend." She clomped down the stairs as he closed the door. "Good night, Mr. Collins. See you next weekend."

Charley tugged off his boots and tiptoed into the little bedroom. A tiny nightlight lit the room just enough for him to see the bump in the bed. Carefully, he sat down beside Lillie and pulled her small body close, loving the smell of her. Loving the soft feel of her hair.

"Good night, pumpkin," he whispered. "I love you to the end of forever."

Lillie stretched as her arm circled his neck and whispered, half-asleep, "I love you too, Daddy."

He rocked her small body until he knew she was asleep again, then moved into the living room. Taking the blanket and pillow from behind the couch, he tried to make his long legs fit into the small space.

In the silence, he smiled. Of all the mistakes he'd made in his life, Lillie was his only blessing. Five years ago his father had been furious when he'd learned Charley's girlfriend was pregnant. Eventually, Davis Collins had accepted them getting married, but he'd never invited Sharon or Lillie to the ranch. Davis Collins had never even seen his only grandchild.

A year after Lillie was born, Sharon left Charley, saying motherhood wasn't her thing. Charley had another fight with his dad when Davis found out Charley planned to keep the baby. He'd agreed to pay tuition and nothing more. Davis had simply said, "She's your mistake, not mine."

So Charley worked thirty hours a week and carried a full load. Sharon's parents, the other grandparents, agreed to keep Lillie on Charley's rare visits to his father's ranch.

Charley had survived almost two years taking care of Lillie alone. He'd almost made it to the end of college, when he'd have had his degree and could have forgotten about any family but Lillie. He'd thought his father would turn over the ranch to him and move permanently to Dallas. Maybe Davis would even accept Lillie, eventually.

Then Charley messed up again. But he'd had no thought of sleeping with his father's brainless fourth wife until she walked into his room and his brain shut off.

Charley climbed out of his makeshift bed on the couch and walked to the fridge to get a bottle of water.

The floor in the apartment creaked so loud he was afraid it might wake up the little princess.

Neither the water nor two aspirin could take his mind off his mistakes. He remembered that at first he'd hoped his father would cool down. After all, Davis himself bragged about sleeping with other men's wives. Even after his dad kicked him off the ranch, Charley thought he'd go back to school and finish his last semester. But no money came in for tuition. He scraped all he could together, but Lillie got sick. Between doctor bills and missing work, he couldn't make ends meet. He took incompletes, planning to return to college as soon as he got on his feet. But there was Lillie to take care of, and a kid can't live in the back of a car and grow on fast food. And then his car was towed.

He finally gave up trying to survive and stay in school. He borrowed enough to buy an old pickup and made it back to Crossroads. Now Lillie was five and he was no closer to finishing the last semester. No closer to getting his life in order.

He stared at the ceiling as though it would give him an answer to the problems he faced, but no answer came.

He'd sworn off women for good. He'd probably never live down what he'd done with his stepmother even though his father was now married to wife number five. Folks in this town had long memories. So he got up every morning and did the jobs he hated because of Lillie.

He climbed off the couch again to check on her, something he did every night no matter how tired he was.

After pulling the cover over her shoulder, he went back to his bed.

That first year, he remembered, she'd cried for her mother. Charley made up his mind that she'd never cry for him because he planned to be near and no matter what mistakes in life she made, she'd never stop being his daughter.

In the stillness over the bar, Charley counted the jobs he had lined up for the next week. Day work on two ranches for one day each, hauling for the hardware store on Wednesday, stocking at the grocery any morning he could.

His ex-wife's parents, Ted and Helen Lee, helped with Lillie when they could. They'd take her to kindergarten on the mornings he had to leave before dawn, and pick her up on the days he didn't get off work early enough. But every night, Charley wanted to be the one to tuck her in.

Sharon's folks were kind people. They hadn't heard from her in over a year and that had been only a postcard saying she was moving to LA.

The old couple didn't have much, but they were good to Lillie and him. Some days Charley thought the kid was their only sunshine.

He smiled as he drifted to sleep. He had a very special standing date come morning. Sundays he'd make pancakes with Lillie and then they'd saddle up her pony and his quarter horse and ride down into Ransom Canyon while the air was still cold and the day was newborn. They'd ride and talk and laugh. He'd tell her stories his grandfather told him about the early days when longhorn cattle and wild mustangs ran across the land.

When they stopped to rest, she'd beg him for more stories. Her favorite was all about the great buffalo herds and how, when they stampeded, they'd shake the ground.

She'd giggle when she put her hand on the earth and swear she could feel the herd headed toward them.

Charley would laugh with her and for a moment he'd feel rich.

CHAPTER THREE

Jubilee
February 22

DAWN WAS BARELY up over the Lone Heart Ranch when Jubilee Hamilton heard the first knock on the downstairs back door.

"Go away!" she yelled and pulled the covers over her head.

How inconsiderate, she thought, pressing her eyes closed as if she could force herself to go back to sleep. Didn't anyone in this flat, worthless country understand that she was in the middle of a nervous breakdown and she didn't want to be bothered?

"Open the door, lady!" A man, obviously standing just below her window, yelled.

"No," she answered.

"All right. I'll leave the groceries on the porch. They'll be rotting by noon."

"Groceries?" She sat up. "Food?" She'd left her parents' house three days ago eating nothing but carrot sticks and protein bars before she finally stopped at the little town called Crossroads to buy food. The grouchy grocer had hurried her, saying it was almost closing time.

She'd been too exhausted to hurry or care what

time it was. When she checked out, the grocer interrogated her until he found out she was Levy Hamilton's great-granddaughter, then he rattled off directions he'd called "the short cut" to Levy's place.

She ended up lost for a few hours on back roads with no signs or even mile markers. When she finally pulled onto the ranch, she discovered she'd also lost the groceries. The back of her car, where she thought she had put them, was empty.

That had been two, or maybe three days ago. Since then she'd been crying, talking to herself and wandering around a big old house packed with things no one would even bother to sell in a garage sale. She'd rationed M&M'S the first day. Eaten peaches from the only can on the shelf the second day, then decided to sleep until starvation took over.

Nightmares of her Christmas with her parents would wake her from time to time. Her mom dispensing advice endlessly. Her father comparing Jubilee to her perfect sister. And Destiny dropping in like the evil fairy to show off. As if rich husband and new car weren't enough, she brought in adorable twins. Destiny always was an overachiever.

Days of hiding in the room where she grew up finally ended with her mother's morning lecture coming with a list of jobs in the area. "You have to have a goal," her mother had shouted. "It's not normal not to have goals, Jub, and right now my goal in life is to make sure you get one."

Jubilee could think of only one goal. Leave. Which she did. She packed her suitcase and drove away with her mother still lecturing from the front steps. She'd put off her trip to the Lone Heart Ranch long enough.

"What's it going to be, lady?" The cowboy interrupted her unpleasant memories.

Jubilee's left leg caught in the covers as she fell out of bed.

"You all right?" he shouted.

"I'm coming," she yelled back as she rummaged through her one travel bag for anything clean enough to wear.

If she died, someone would have to wash clothes to bury her. She didn't even have clean socks. Everything she owned, except a suitcase of dirty clothes, had been packed in a moving pod in November.

"Food," she said again as she grabbed at something, anything, to wear, fearing the cowboy and the groceries might disappear. Real food. Green vegetables. Fruit. Sweets. She stumbled to the window as she tugged on clothes. "Where'd you find my groceries?"

"You left them in the basket at the store in Crossroads two and a half days ago." The man bellowed, sounding angry. "They stored them in the cooler thinking you'd return. When you didn't, the manager hired me to bring them out."

She straightened, putting on an old army green raincoat as a robe and a worn pair of socks she'd found in one of Grandfather Levy's drawers. One had a red band around the calf and the other had blue stripes, but who cared.

When she leaned out the window, all she saw was the top of a worn Stetson. "I forgot them? I just thought they evaporated while I was lost, or fell out when I hit the hundred bumps in the road. I didn't come back for them because I don't think I could remember how to get back to town. I drove hours before I stumbled on this place."

The cowboy looked up and she swore he growled. "Could you tell me your life story later? I'd like to set these groceries down."

He lowered his voice, but she heard him add, "Lady, you're only twelve miles from town, not lost in the Amazon jungle."

She moved down the stairs and slowly neared the door, picking up an old umbrella as she tiptoed. The raincoat didn't reach her knees, but it would have to do.

He must have gotten tired of waiting because he yelled, "You are Jubilee Hamilton?"

She opened the door a few inches and stared at a handsome man dressed in boots, jeans, a worn shirt and a cowboy hat. "How do you know that?"

He smiled at her. "You left your credit card at the store, too." He studied her a minute, then asked, "You want these groceries or not? If you do, you got to open the door a little wider. If you don't, I need to be getting back to town."

She lifted her umbrella. "How do I know you aren't here to rob and rape me?"

He looked down at the ugly mismatched socks with a hole in the right big toe and then up to what she was sure was wild, dirty blond hair. "It's tempting, lady, but I've sworn off women. Maybe some other time. As for robbing you, I could have already done that. I've got your card."

Jubilee slowly opened the door. "I own this farm, you know."

He carried in the first bags. "I figured that and it's a ranch, not a farm."

"Whatever." She let her head bobble.

"Old Levy died several months back." The cowboy didn't bother to look at her. He just headed to the kitchen. "Heard someone say his big-city great-granddaughter now owned the place and all the land around. When I saw Hamilton on your card, I had a pretty good guess as to where to take the groceries even before the manager told me. You look just like Levy."

Jubilee straightened. "I do?" She remembered her grandfather as bent over, bald and so tanned he looked as if his skin was leather.

"Yeah. Crazy." The cowboy still hadn't turned around to face her so she wasted the nutty cross-eyed look she made just for him.

She followed him to the kitchen. "You knew my great-grandfather? You know this place?"

"Sure. I used to come out and help the old guy. He wasn't able to do much, but he didn't mind telling me how. He paid good wages." The stranger went out for another load.

She followed like a puppy. She was still too tired to make her mind work. Leaning on the umbrella, she simply watched.

When he brought in the last load, he removed his hat and nodded politely just like his mother must have taught him. "I'm Charley Collins. I'm sorry for your loss. I'll miss the old man. He was always straight with me."

"What kind of work did you do for my great-grandfather?"

The man called Charley shrugged. "He ran about

fifty head. I helped brand in the spring and round up in the fall. Last year I helped him plant his spring hay crop. By the time we harvested, he was too weak to climb into the cab of the tractor. I made sure the hay got into in the hay barn."

The good-looking man watched her. "You have any idea how to run a ranch of this size, Mary Poppins? It's not big, but there's plenty to do."

She shook her heard. "Nope. Why'd you call me Mary Poppins?"

"It was either that or Paddington Bear. With a rain coat, an umbrella and those ugly socks, you could go either way on Halloween." The slow grin came from a man who probably knew just how it might affect her. If he'd had new clothes and boots that weren't scuffed, he could have been a cover model.

She frowned back. *Nice try, cowboy, but forget it. I've been vaccinated against good-looking men.*

His face became serious. "The work's never done on a place like this. When you're not farming to provide grain for winter or checking on cattle, you're mending fences and repairing equipment. If you run cattle, they'll need checking on every day. The fences need constant repair, and every time it rains part of them will wash out and your workload just doubles."

"I was afraid of that." She scratched her wild hair, feeling as if something must have crawled into it and set up house while she slept.

The guy just stared at her as if she was a baby kitten trying to walk on water. "You know, lady, you're about four months behind already. You might want to think about selling the place and going back to the city. It would take a dozen men to get this place ready for spring in time."

"I'm staying." Lifting her chin she met his blue-eyed stare. She didn't have to tell this stranger she had nowhere else to go. He'd probably figured that out already.

"Then I wish you luck, Miss Hamilton."

She shook the cobwebs out of her brain and took a step toward her only chance. "Would you work for me? I'll pay whatever he paid you. To tell the truth, I'm not sure where to start but I've got to make this work." Even if it cost her all her savings.

"I don't know," he shook his head. "It's a long way out here, and I only have one, maybe two days a week open. I don't think one day a week would make much difference in this place and to come out on weekends I'd have to quit my bartending job. If I did that, I'd lose the free apartment that comes with it."

Jubilee's mind cleared enough to realize he was negotiating, not turning down her offer.

"There is a house over by the corrals. When I was a kid, a hired hand and his wife lived there. I don't know what kind of shape it's in now. If you'll work for me five days a week, I'll pay you five dollars more an hour than Levy did and throw in the house." She knew she had to make it fair because no one else was probably going to take an offer to help farm on a place in the middle of nowhere.

She didn't know much about this man, but he was honest or he wouldn't have brought the groceries and her credit card. He was a hard worker if her great-grandfather used him regularly, and he knew the place.

"Does the school bus stop anywhere near here?"

He surprised her with his question. "I have no idea. Do you have a family?"

"A daughter." He didn't look happy about the offer. "If I worked for you, I'd take off time to get her to school, and when she's here, I'd work around the headquarters so I could keep an eye on her."

Jubilee looked around the yard. There was enough work within shouting distance to keep him busy for months.

"Fair enough."

"I'd need to stable my two horses in the barn." He glanced over his shoulder. "At least it's in good shape."

"No problem. There are a dozen stalls."

He studied her. "Make it ten dollars more an hour and you got yourself a foreman, not just a hand. I furnish my own horse and gear. I'll charge for a fifty-hour week, but I'll work until the job is done. I'll also hire men when needed and you'll pay them the going wage."

Jubilee thought of mentioning that ten more an hour seemed very high, but what choice did she have? Her savings were solid. Her car paid for. She might as well put it all into the pot. This chance was the only game in town.

She nodded.

He put his hat back on. "I'll move in late this afternoon and be in for breakfast tomorrow morning. We'll talk about where to start."

"Breakfast?"

"That was the routine with Levy. We planned over breakfast and I worked until the job or the day was finished. Any problem?"

"No."

"You can cook?"

"No, but how hard can it be?"

He smiled, and she realized how young he was. Maybe a year or two younger than she. But she didn't miss the steel in his stare. He hadn't had an easy life and she guessed he wouldn't trust easily. That was fine with her, since she felt the same.

"I'll bring a few boxes of cereal and milk," he said as he moved off the porch. "You make the coffee. Tomorrow we'll set a plan."

She met his stormy blue eyes again. "Will you help me make this place work? It's kind of my last chance."

He nodded once. "I'll help you, but you got to wear normal clothes, lady. Folks around here might cart you off to the hospital for dressing like that."

"I'll remember that, Mr. Collins," she said, trying not to react to his insult. She thought of adding that she didn't do friends, so don't even try. Maybe they should keep the relationship formal? She wouldn't tell him too much and he wouldn't try to advise her on wardrobe choices.

What would be between them would be purely professional. She had a feeling he wanted it that way, as well.

As he drove away, Jubilee went back to bed, remembering how early her great-grandfather had served breakfast. Her last hope, before she fell asleep after eating half a dozen pieces of fruit and the entire bag of cookies, was that she wanted breakfast to be closer to brunch when they talked each day. Surely he'd agree to that; after all, she was the boss. She should be able to set a few rules.

CHAPTER FOUR

Thatcher Jones
February 23

THATCHER JONES RACED down the neglected dirt road as if he was an IndyCar race driver and not still too young to get his license. A rusty old sign marked the beginning of a ranch called Lone Heart. What had once been a heart-shaped brand hung lopsided on the marker.

He eased his boot off the gas a bit. He and his 1963 Ford pickup just might make this run before the rain hit. No one was at the ranch anymore; it should be easy to get in and out without anyone noticing.

Thatcher had been keeping an eye on a nest of rattlesnakes under the back cattle guard on this ranch for four months. Now there were new folks moving in near the pass and he was about to lose two hundred dollars if he didn't act fast. To add hell to fury, a storm was blowing in from the north even though the day was hot for February.

The sheriff's cruiser pulled out in front of him from nowhere. Thatcher cussed a streak of swear words.

He slammed on the brakes, leaned out the window and yelled, "Hell, Sheriff, get out of the way. My brakes are no good."

Sheriff Dan Brigman didn't budge and, judging from Thatcher's experience with the law, he knew that Brigman wouldn't change or move no matter how much he yelled.

He pushed on the brakes with both feet but had to pull off into the bar ditch to avoid a collision.

Once the beat-up old Ford finally clanked to a stop, Thatcher piled out of his truck with a stranglehold on the top of a grain sack.

"You trying to kill us both, Sheriff?" Thatcher shouted, challenging the lawman, even if he barely came up to Brigman's shoulder. "I ain't lived fourteen years just to die in a fiery crash with a cop."

The sheriff crossed his arms and said calmly, "What you got in the sack, kid?"

Thatcher had been told a dozen times not to hunt snakes off his own land, but listening wasn't one of his talents. Neither was honesty. "I got cow chips. The Boy Scouts are doing a demonstration down in the canyon about how folks used to burn the dry ones so they could keep warm in the winter. This ain't nothing but fuel for their fire."

Brigman glanced at the bag and Thatcher prayed it didn't start wiggling.

"I've told you, son, hunting rattlers is not something for a kid to be doing."

"It's cow shit, Sheriff. I swear."

Brigman shook his head. "It's shit all right. Tie that bag off and put it in the bed of your pickup. You're not old enough to drive, and you're out here in the middle of nowhere hunting rattlers in an old truck that might not even make it back to your place. I can think of a dozen ways I might find you dead."

"I'm old enough to drive. I don't have to sit on the blanket anymore to see out, and hunting ain't dangerous. I've been doing it since I was ten. You just got to jitter when you reach for them so you're a blur to the snake and not a solid target."

"Who told you that?"

"My grandpa. He was a jittering fool, he'd been bit so many times." Thatcher winked, giving away his lie.

"Get in the cruiser." Brigman didn't crack a smile. "I'm taking you home. But Thatcher Jones, I swear this better be the last time I see you on any road in this county."

The boy walked toward the officer's car. "You said I could drive the back roads out past County Road 111."

"Yeah, but I'm guessing you had to cross at least four other county roads and one highway to get this far from your place."

"You ain't got no proof of that, Sheriff." He knotted the sack, tossed it in the pickup bed and climbed into the front passenger seat of the cruiser, hating that it was starting to feel familiar. "You can't arrest me unless you see me do somethin'."

"That's why I'm taking you home."

Thatcher ran his dirty fingers through even dirtier brown hair. He hadn't even made it to the Hamilton ranch. Hell, the snakes would probably be six feet long before he could get back. He sighed, knowing Brigman wouldn't change his mind. "We stopping at the Dairy Queen before you drop me off back home, Sheriff?"

"It's standard police procedure, kid. Double meat, double cheese." Brigman started his car. "How's your mom?"

"She died again last week."

Brigman glared at him but didn't say anything.

"She was at the tent revival over the Red into Oklahoma. Preacher pays her a hundred dollars every service to keel over and let the Holy Spirit save her. Not a bad gig. She only gets twenty-five for talking in tongues and fifty for coming in on crutches."

The sheriff frowned.

"It ain't against the law, Sheriff." Thatcher saw it more as a sideshow and his mom did the entertaining. He changed the subject before the sheriff started asking more questions about his mom. "If somebody steals my truck, Sheriff, I'll have you to blame."

Brigman smiled. "If they do they won't be hard to find. They'll be dead on the road after they open that sack you got in the pickup bed. Bitten by cow chips is an odd way to die."

They drove in silence all the way to Crossroads. Thatcher figured if he said anything the sheriff would start another lecture. Brigman could lecture the wheels off the fiery chariot.

Just as the lady handed them burgers through the drive-up window, lightning flashed bright and thunder rolled in on the wind. "Storm's coming in early," Thatcher said more to himself than the sheriff. He, like most farm folks, lived his life by the weather. It always surprised him that town kids woke up like chickens and headed outside without knowing or caring what was happening in the sky above. If rain or snow started, they took it personally, as if it was their individual plague and not the way of things.

"How about we eat these in my office, son?" Brigman turned toward Main Street.

"Not a bad idea, Sheriff. I seen the way you drive in the rain."

A few minutes later, they raced the storm to make it into the county offices before they were both soaked.

They moved past Pearly Day's front desk in the wide foyer to Brigman's two-room office. Pearly'd gone home and apparently left her candy bowl unguarded.

She was the receptionist for all the offices housed in the two-story building and also passed as the dispatcher in Crossroads. When she left at five she patched all 911 calls to her cell. If anyone had an emergency they didn't yell "call 911," they yelled "call Pearly."

Brigman cleaned off a corner of his desk for Thatcher and set the food in front of him. "I need to check my messages. Go ahead and eat."

Thatcher attacked his hamburger while the sheriff listened to his messages. Nothing much of interest. A lady's voice shouted that her dog was missing and she thought someone had stolen it while she was at bingo. A man left a message that he thought the bridge south of Interstate 40 exit near Bailey might flood if it rained more than two inches. Some guy called saying he'd locked his keys in his car and complained that the only locksmith in town wasn't answering either his office number or his cell.

One call sounded official; it was about drug traffic suspected on the interstate. That was no big news, Thatcher thought, there was drug traffic going on in the back hills where he lived. Folks called the rocky land that snaked along between the canyons and flat farmlands the Breaks. The ground was too uneven to farm more than small plots, too barren to ranch in most spots. But deer and wild sheep lived there along with wild pigs and turkey. And, Thatcher decided, every crazy person in Texas who didn't want to be bothered. Outlaws had once claimed the place, but now it was populated by deadbeats, old hippies and druggies. If the sheriff even knocked on trailer and cabin doors in his neighborhood he'd need a bus to bring in the wanted.

Thatcher watched the sheriff making notes as he finished his burger. Rain pounded the tin porch beyond the office windows, making a tapping sound that was almost musical.

He saw the sheriff open a letter, then smile. It couldn't have had much written on the one sheet of paper because after a few seconds Brigman folded it up, unlocked his bottom drawer and shoved the letter inside.

Thatcher decided it must be some kind of love note because if it had been a death threat then Brigman wouldn't have smiled. Only who'd write a man like him a love note?

The sheriff was single and would probably be considered good-looking in a boring, law-abiding kind of way, but Thatcher still didn't think the note was a love letter. Sheriffs and teachers in a little town were like the royal family. Everyone kept up with them. So maybe the note was a coupon or something.

Brigman glanced up as if he just remembered Thatcher was there. "Your mother will be worried about you. Wish she had a phone."

Thatcher nodded, but he knew she wouldn't be worried. His ma had a rule. The minute the first raindrop fell, she started drinking. When he got home, she'd either be passed out or gone. One of her boyfriends worked road construction, so any time it rained was party time for him.

While the sheriff made a few more calls, Thatcher unwrapped the second double-meat, double-cheese burger. After all, greasy hamburgers were no good cold. He'd be doing the sheriff a favor by eating it while it was still warm.

About the time he swallowed the last bite, the main door in the lobby flew open. Thatcher leaned back in his chair far enough to see a man and three kids rushing in past Pearly's desk.

Brigman stood and stepped out of his office, but Thatcher just kept leaning back, sipping his Coke and watching.

"Sheriff," the man said, his voice shaking from cold or fright, Thatcher couldn't tell which. "We're here to report a murder."

The three kids, all wet, nodded. One was a boy about eight or ten, the other two were girls, one close to Thatcher's age.

"Bring the blankets from behind my desk," the sheriff yelled toward his office.

Thatcher looked around as if Brigman might be ordering someone else into action, but no such luck. He let the front legs of his chair hit the hardwood floor and followed orders.

By the time he got the blankets and made it to the lobby, the man was rattling off a story about how he and his kids were walking the canyon at sunset and came across a body wrapped in what looked like old burlap feed bags.

Thatcher grew wide-eyed when Brigman glanced at him. "Don't look at me," he said in a voice so high Thatcher barely recognized his own words. "I'm just collecting cow chips. I didn't kill nobody."

The sheriff rolled his eyes. "Pass out the blankets, kid."

While the man kept talking, Thatcher handed every dripping visitor a blanket. The last one, he opened up and put over the girl who was probably the oldest. She was so wet he could see the outline of her bra.

He tried his best not to look, but failed miserably. Her breasts might be small, but she was definitely old enough to fill out a bra.

"Thank you," she said when the blanket and his arm went around her.

"You're welcome," he answered as he raised his gaze to the most beautiful green eyes he'd ever seen.

Until that moment, if you'd asked Thatcher Jones if he liked girls, he would have sworn he never would as long as he lived. When you're the poorest and dumbest kid in school, no one has anything nice to say to you and most girls don't even look your direction. During grade school he'd been kicked out several times for fighting, but now, since he was no longer in grade school, he'd decided to ignore everyone and skip as many classes as possible.

But this girl just kept smiling at him like nothing was wrong with him.

He didn't want to move away. "Did you see the body?" he whispered.

She shook her head. "I saw the sack. It had brown spots on it. Blood, I think. My dad didn't let us get too close."

Thatcher thought of all the blood he'd seen in his life. He'd killed animals for food since he was six or seven. He'd washed his mother up a few times when one of her "friends" beat her. He'd watched his own blood pour out with every heartbeat once when he'd tumbled out of a tree, but none of that mattered right now.

"I'm sorry you had to see such a thing," he whispered to the green-eyed girl.

"He was murdered," she said so low only he could have heard her.

"How do you know? He could have committed suicide. Folks have done that before, or died in accidents down there in the canyon."

Her eyes swam in tears. "Do people who die from suicide or accident stuff themselves into sacks?"

Thatcher nodded. "Good point."

Then the strangest thing happened. Right in the middle of the sheriff calling in backup and Pearly coming in to take statements, and the storm pounding so hard against the north windows that he feared they'd break…right in the middle of it all, the girl reached out and held his hand.

As if she needed *him*.

As if in all the chaos he was her rock.

AN HOUR LATER, Thatcher stood in the drizzle and watched the sheriff working the crime scene. He'd been told, since he'd insisted on coming along, that he had to hold a big light down the trail toward where they found the body. Nothing else. Just hold the light, as though he was nothing more than a lamppost.

The county coroner had come in from Lubbock

County to pronounce the dead guy dead. Which Thatcher thought was a bit of overkill. He stood thirty feet away and he could tell the guy was dead.

"I'm going to list the cause of death as undetermined," the coroner shouted loud enough for Thatcher to hear him.

He thought of yelling down that the huge dent in the burlapped man's head should be a pretty good hint as to how he died. What was left of his face looked more like the Elephant Man than anyone Thatcher had ever seen.

"Get back in the cruiser," Brigman yelled as he started up the path.

"Yes, sir," Thatcher answered without moving. This was far too interesting to crawl back into the car. He wasn't sure he could do the sheriff's job, but he decided to check into becoming a coroner. It didn't look that hard.

As men lifted the body and began the slow journey back up the canyon, Thatcher watched and tried to figure out why someone would leave a body in Ransom Canyon. Wouldn't any old bar ditch do?

A beefy deputy from Lubbock County stepped up behind him and flashed a beam of light in his face. "What you doing here, kid?"

Thatcher smiled. "I was called in to help with the investigation. What are you doing here, deputy?"

"You're Thatcher Jones." The lawman said his name as if he was swearing. "You got anything to do with this?"

"Nope. How about you, Officer Weathers?" Thatcher made a habit of always remembering any lawman he met. When he'd seen the tall deputy once in Brigman's office, Weathers had been wrestling two drunks and hadn't had time for an introduction.

About the time Weathers reached for him, the sheriff stepped between them. "You know Thatcher?"

The deputy nodded. "He…"

"Don't tell me," Brigman interrupted. "I can already guess and I've got my hands full right now."

Thatcher grinned at the deputy and followed Brigman to his car. Once they were inside, he whispered, "I'm staying in your county from now on, Sheriff—that deputy scares me. I don't mind cops who come in small, medium and large, but somebody supersized that guy."

Brigman laughed. "It's comforting to know you're selective about where you break the law. Weathers is a good man. Anytime I need him, he's always got my back."

CHAPTER FIVE

Jubilee
February 24

THE RAIN STARTED an hour before sunset, just as it had the day before, and kept falling until full dark. The land, long dry, didn't seem to know how to take in all the moisture. Tiny lakes formed for as far as Jubilee could see. Water was suddenly everywhere, if only an inch deep.

She swore a storm had never roared like this one. Lightning so strong she felt the whip of fire in the air. Thunder rumbled, shaking the earth and sky. Nature seemed to be running full blast to tell the world that the months of drought were over.

Jubilee had spent the day listening for the sound of a truck, hoping her boxes of clothes, favorite books and office supplies would arrive today. Since her first year of college she'd always kept a home office. No matter what a mess her world was in, everything had its place in file folders or drawer organizers.

Only between noon and the storm she'd only seen one car, a sheriff's cruiser, driving down the road in front of her place. She wasn't sure if it made her feel safer to know her ranch was part of his route or not. Surely very few vehicles headed her way, except the moving truck that was supposed to come today, of course.

Jubilee never realized how little she had worth moving. The old pots and pans she'd had since her freshman year in college had gone to Goodwill a year ago when she moved in with David and he had a fully stocked kitchen. He'd furnished every room of their apartment except for one table. The used dining table she'd bought fit perfectly in the corner. It was so wobbly she had to prop it up with a book under one corner, but he'd thought it rustic.

When she'd left Washington, it simply went to the trash.

In the end, she'd had fewer than a dozen boxes to move.

The memories of a life she'd thought mattered lingered in the shadows of her mind like gray ghosts. If she could have she would have tossed them out, as well. How could she have lived twenty-six years and had so little worth keeping? For the five years since college, nothing mattered but her job, and in the end, it didn't really matter, either.

She was one of those people whose name could be wiped off the whiteboard of life and no one would notice. David hadn't called since he moved out months ago. Her parents hadn't bothered to check to see if she'd made it safely to Texas. If she disappeared, there would be no one to fill out a missing person report.

Jubilee guessed if she'd been able to mark her growth with lines on a doorframe, her chart would be heading down, not up. When she'd left what she'd thought would be a brilliant career, not one person had dropped by to shake her hand. No farewell cake. Not even a card.

As she stood in the doorway of her great-grandfather's house that was now her only home, she wondered if things could get much worse. The man she'd hired as foreman on the place had said at breakfast—cereal and milk—that he'd finish moving in today and they'd walk the land tomorrow. But, with the downpour turning everything to mud, she doubted they'd be able to start for a week.

Not that it mattered. She'd planned her last life and look how it had crumbled. Why bother to plan this one?

Maybe she should take the opposite of her mother's parting advice and go goalless for a while. She had forty thousand dollars in her bank account plus what she'd inherited. She could coast, at least for a while. Maybe she'd simply wait until a goal bumped into her for a change.

She had no idea what she was doing out here in Texas. For all she knew the foreman, Charley Collins, was the local serial killer. He might not have stolen her card; murder might be his thing. *Think about it, Jub,* she almost said aloud. *What are the chances that the man delivering groceries and working at the local bar knows how to run a farm?* Correction, he'd called it a ranch.

He did have his own horse, though. She had no idea if that was good or bad. What was a guy doing with a horse when he lived over a bar? Logic probably wasn't his strong suit. He was easy on the eyes, though. The kind of guy who broke every heart he passed.

Only not hers. Three of her four serious boyfriends had told her she didn't have a heart. Majority vote.

After breakfast, her new foreman disappeared for most of the day, then drove up midafternoon with his pickup full of boxes. He was pulling a trailer filled with a huge horse and a cute pony.

Since she had nothing else to do, Jubilee interrupted her breakdown long enough to watch him move into the little house by the corral. He had an easy way of moving, like a man comfortable in his own body.

She'd thought of going outside to stare at him or even help, but all her clothes were three wearings past dirty. The man in worn boots and a patched shirt had actually frowned when she'd greeted him at breakfast wearing a clean pair of old Levy's socks and one of his long-sleeved shirts tied at her waist. Just to be proper she used a pair of her great-grandfather's brand new boxer shorts as her shorts.

Charley looked as though he'd never seen the fashion.

She'd tried to explain that almost everything she owned was packed, but she doubted he'd like her navy suits any better. Three pairs of jeans and half a dozen tops were all the casual clothes she owned. And they were spotted with drippings from meals on the road or wrinkled beyond wearing.

Tomorrow morning she planned to ask him to turn on the water to the washer out back. Levy probably turned it off every month after he used it, and who knew where the dryer had run off to? Jubilee had a faint memory of the old guy hanging his laundry on a line somewhere.

She'd watched Charley unhitch his trailer and park

it beside the barn, and then he'd left again just before
the rain started. Jubilee finally moved out on the porch
and studied the storm. At this point in her day of doing
nothing, she wasn't sure her life was afloat. No career. No friends. No family who would speak to her.

She wasn't even sure if this ranch was a blessing
or a curse. If she hadn't inherited it, she would have
had to pull herself up and start over. Now, she could
just hide out for a while.

Slowly, her mind began to dance with the storm
as the sky darkened, and her troubles started to drift
away. She watched the rain form tiny rivers in the
ruts that Charley's truck had made. The sound of the
horses in the barn blended with the tapping of rain
falling off the roof into dead flowerbeds. Even as the
world grew black except for the one light in the house
by the corral, she refused to move or turn on a light.

She needed the night to surround her. For once she
wanted to wrap up in the nothingness of her world.
She wanted to be invisible for a while.

The rain finally slowed to a silent dribble. The
storm was over. But still Jubilee didn't move.

Truck lights turned toward her place. The white
pickup her foreman drove rocked back and forth as
it moved toward her on a road in desperate need of
repair.

When he stopped beside the corral and cut his
lights, she knew he couldn't see her even if he looked
her direction.

She watched his tall frame unfold. He stood in the
lingering rain and raked his rust-colored hair back before putting on his hat. Within seconds his shirt was
plastered against his body. Even in the low light she

could tell there wasn't an ounce of fat on the man. Just from the way he moved around the truck told her he was solid rock-hard muscle. Tall and lean and beautiful as only a cowboy can look.

She smiled. He's definitely not too bright, she decided. No raincoat. No umbrella. Hopefully he'd know more about running a ranch than he did about coming in from out of the rain.

He opened the side door to his truck and reached in.

For a moment she wondered what one last thing he'd carry inside. What had he gone back into town for on this rainy night?

He lifted something out slowly, carefully, wrapped in his work coat. The bundle leaned over his shoulder, molding against his form.

In wide, slow steps he walked through the mud. One hand tucked beneath the bundle. One hand placed in the middle as if holding his treasure close to his heart.

Jubilee stood and watched, surprised and touched as she saw thin pale arms slip from beneath the coat and wrap around his neck.

He'd mentioned a daughter when he'd asked if a school bus passed her place.

In the last blink of faraway lightning, Jubilee saw Charley Collins in a whole new light. He might not have much. His clothes were worn. His pickup old. But the man obviously had one thing he treasured. His daughter.

Charley

THE HOUSE OVER by the corral was dusty and completely empty except for a stove and old refrigerator Charley was surprised still worked. The place looked as if no one had lived in it for years but the bones of the house were solid. At one time someone had loved this place. The molding was hand carved around the doors, and cabinets were crafted carefully. The place was solid. He had a feeling it would stand any storm.

Charley worked into the night cleaning out the four-room house while Lillie slept. Ike, his old boss, had helped deliver what little furniture he had while his crazy new boss was probably taking her morning nap. The bar owner kept telling Charley that he was making a mistake accepting a job from a woman who wouldn't last six months on the land, but at this point in his life Charley figured one more mistake wouldn't matter.

With a free place to live and twice the money he usually made, he could build his savings. He could plan for someday.

He'd put up the bed before dark so Lillie would have a place to sleep when he picked her up. Charley didn't want her to see the place dirty. When she woke, their new home would be clean and her tiny play kitchen would be set up in one corner of the living room.

Finally, about 3:00 a.m. he had everything stocked and put away. The house was so sparsely furnished it didn't look like much of a home. One couch. One bed. An old dresser someone had given him a year back. A card table and four chairs for a dining table. A rocker painted white that he'd bought the day his baby girl was born.

The house was bigger than the apartment they'd been in. Two bedrooms, even though one was empty. The house had a front porch where Lillie could play and a back porch where he could watch the sunset.

After he checked on Lillie, he stood out on the back porch and smiled. Fresh air. Open space. Silence. Someday, he'd have a place like this, but for now, working here was about as good as he could hope for. No more smelly bar or worrying whether he'd have enough odd jobs to make the bills. Now, with luck, he could save most of his salary. Maybe in a year he'd have enough to pay down on a place of his own.

He'd talked things over with Sharon's parents. Now that they were both retired, they wanted to keep Lillie a few nights during the week, at least until summer. On the other days they promised to pick her up from school if the weather was bad or the school bus's rural route wasn't running.

He didn't like not tucking her in every night, but on those two days she stayed in town he could work here until dark. Putting in a couple of fifteen-hour days would make the rest of the week lighter.

The Lees had turned Sharon's old room into Lillie's playroom. Here she only had a few toys, but at their house Lillie had a roomful. This time, he'd make her room more like a little girl's room. He might have no idea how to raise a little girl, but he'd learn.

This ranch didn't have much of a chance of making it, but he planned to give it his best shot. If they could make it through the summer, they might survive, but he'd need to think of a way to have money coming in now to help cover expenses.

As he stared out into the night, he swore he saw an army green raincoat marching across the open field between the main house and the end of the corral. For a moment he thought it was a flash from an old World

War II film, then he saw long white legs and what had to be white socks.

Jubilee Hamilton. Taking yard-wide steps across the mud as if she were measuring it off.

Lightning flashed. The promise of more rain scented the air. His insane employer marched on, her damp blond hair plastered to her skull as the coat flapped in the wind.

He thought of going after her, but decided to just watch. Who knows, her kind of crazy might be catching. It was three o'clock in the morning and she was out walking. If she got hit by lightning, Charley decided he'd simply bury her and keep working the ranch.

Finally, exhaustion from a long day of moving from one kind of life to another got the better of him and Charley slipped inside, closing out any thought of his boss, as he closed the door to his new home.

An hour later in the stillness of his bed on the couch, he couldn't stop thinking about her. Something drew him to Jubilee even if he didn't want to admit it. She seemed so lost. So alone. She wasn't the kind of woman he'd ever be interested in, but deep down he wanted to help her make this place work. He'd taken this job to save himself, but he had to make it work. Not just for Lillie and him. For her, too.

Jubilee Hamilton needed to believe in something. Maybe the dream of this place working or maybe just herself.

One line she'd said earlier kept swirling in his mind. She'd said this was her last chance. Then, she'd closed up as though she hadn't meant to say so much.

He understood last chances. He'd been living in that valley so long he thought he owned the place.

Charley closed his eyes. Who was he kidding? He was no knight in shining armor. But maybe just this once, he'd give it a try. If he failed at this quest, it wouldn't be from lack of trying.

The next morning, by the time he drove back from taking Lillie to Sharon's folks' place, he'd decided not to mention having seen Jubilee Hamilton out walking. If she was crazy, she'd deny it. If she wasn't, she might think he was spying on her.

He rushed into her kitchen, in a hurry to get started working. He was surprised to see that she'd made oatmeal and toast. The coffee even smelled drinkable today.

"Morning," he nodded as he waited for her to sit down. She was dressed pretty much the same as yesterday, but she'd added a moth-eaten sweater. She'd also combed her hair and tied it in an ugly little knot that looked like a bulldog's bobbed tail. It crossed his mind that she must have to work at it to look this homely.

She handed him his coffee and sat down across the table. "So before we get started, I have a few things that need doing."

He leaned back, sipping his coffee.

"Can you turn on the water to the washer out in that little shed behind the house? I need to do laundry."

"I can show you how," he answered. "It'll need to be turned off if there is any chance of freezing."

"Fair enough." She passed him one piece of toast. "Next, I want to plant a garden whenever the time is right. A big garden with all kinds of vegetables."

"Did you ever grow anything?"

She shook her head. "No, but how hard could it be?"

"I've got a few books packed away on gardening that my mother used to make me read but we could ask Donald at the feed store. He'd know what would grow best here." Charley grinned when her eyes lit up. "I could run a line from the horse trough in the corral to water it regular."

"Great. A garden would save money on food, but I doubt it'll make any money to bring in."

He nodded. "Probably not, but it might if we ran a row of watermelons. I was thinking of boarding horses in the extra stalls. It would bring in steady money. You'd provide the feed and I'll do the work. We could use the income as operating money for the headquarters."

"Sounds like a good idea."

Before he could tell her more, a blast from a truck horn ended the conversation.

"My stuff!" she yelled and ran outside waving, as if the lone truck on the lone road might miss the lone house.

Charley ate his breakfast of half a bowl of oatmeal and one piece of toast and then he ate hers. He refilled his bowl with cereal and downed it while he watched the trucker set a dozen boxes on the porch. The truck still looked full when the driver closed the doors and headed away to the next stop.

After refilling his coffee, Charley walked to the front door and watched her running from box to box, opening all her treasures as if she hadn't seen them in months. From what he could see, she had a box of high heels, two boxes of books, one of pillows and blankets, and the rest seemed to be clothes. She carefully lifted one box and carried it into the crowded room off the kitchen that had probably once been a parlor but that Levy had used as a bedroom.

After she set the box down as if it held glass, she ran back to the other boxes.

"Wait for me," she said as she grabbed a few things and ran past him and up the back stairs.

"No problem," he said to himself as he began picking up the boxes and moving them into the kitchen. He had no idea where the stuff would go, but inside seemed a better place than outside.

Ten minutes later she emerged in gray slacks, low heels and a white silk sleeveless blouse that moved like cream over her slim body. If she hadn't still been wearing that dumb knot on the back of her hair he might not have recognized her. She was tall and slim, but she was nicely curved in all the right places—if he'd been noticing, which of course he wasn't.

"I'm ready." When he just stared, she added, "I know I'm not dressed to ranch, but this will have to do until I can wash my jeans."

"You look fine." Charley was surprised how much he meant it. "We'll be out all morning; you'll need a hat and a jacket to cover those arms."

"I'll be fine." She picked up a tiny red purse and slung the gold chain strap over her shoulder.

"Unless that's a first aid kit, you won't need it. We're going to drive over your land, not go shopping." Charley grinned. For the first time, she looked like the city girl he knew she was. All polish. No practical.

"Right." She didn't drop her purse. "I'll leave it in

your pickup," she said as she followed him out into the sunshine. "I never go anywhere without a purse."

When he opened the pickup door, she smiled at him. "Thanks for taking in the boxes."

"You're welcome." He liked the way she talked when she wasn't yelling at him. She had a nice voice. The kind of low voice that a man wouldn't get tired of listening to.

For the next hour they drove every trail on her land. He tried to fill her in, but he had the feeling he was talking to himself most of the time.

"This is good pastureland. With the natural spring you could run fifty head out here easily, maybe more. If you want I could buy a few calves. We might have to feed them until the grass greens, but it won't be long."

"How much per head?"

"Three hundred, this time of year. By the end of summer they'll be worth a thousand or more."

She looked at him then. "That's a great profit."

"Not as much as you think. We'll need to supplement-feed some of them. Then there would be shots and tagging. That'll cost you. We might lose a few before we sell them."

She was silent for a few minutes, then said, "Buy sixty head. If we lose five we'll still make enough to buy a hundred next time and have a nice profit. Would this next pasture also hold a hundred head?"

"It would over the warm months if we get plenty of rain." He was surprised at her quick logic. The lady might not know ranching, but she understood numbers.

"Then we go with the hundred. I've got enough

to make the investment and I understand Levy has a ranch account with the bank."

Charley was impressed with her quick calculation. He had no idea what background she came from. "I'll make the buy before the end of the week."

She nodded once and went back to silence.

He continued talking, "You got a gravel pit over there across the road. Always a source of quick money if you need it, but once it's gone, it's gone. We might want to save it for emergency money. The flat few acres up ahead are good for farming, but it's dry land."

The second question came, "What's dry land mean exactly?"

"It means without rain you don't have a crop. Most years crops need irrigating, but it's expensive to buy and maintain."

Again came the question of how much. If Charley hadn't been saving every dime he could to realize his dream of owning his own ranch, he might not have been able to give accurate answers. As it was, he knew down to the penny every cost.

Charley kept talking about what they could do with money or without. She must have enough money to pay him, but he doubted old Levy had left her much else. Maybe she was planning with her own money. The Lexus she'd parked near the house couldn't have been more than a few years old and the clothes she wore now weren't picked up at a dollar store. If the lady had money to invest, this ranch could be a great deal more than Levy ever planned.

"You going to take notes?" he asked.

"No," she answered. "I'll remember. I'll set up my

office tonight and make some charts. I like to see the progress."

"I agree." This was what he'd studied to do. If he'd been able to do it on his family ranch he'd be counting cattle by the thousands. Here the numbers would be small, but for the first time since he'd left college, he could do what he loved, even if it was with someone else's money.

When they stopped near the edge of a narrow canyon that crawled along one side of her land, he asked her if she'd like to see the Lone Heart Pass that the ranch had been named after.

The sun was getting warmer. He walked with her to within a hundred yards of a column of rocks maybe thirty feet high. "There is no easy way into the canyon for miles except for this pass. It's like a rock hill split in two a few million years ago and left a passage. If we were on horseback we could go one at a time, slow and easy, through to the pass, but it spooks some horses to be all closed in by the walls."

She took a few steps on ground that suddenly turned rocky and uneven.

His hand shot out to grip her arm to steady her. The feel of her skin beneath his fingers was hotter than he'd expected it to be. One touch made him aware of her as a woman. Before, he'd thought of her as lost, crazy, way out of her depth. Now, with the silk blouse clinging to her, Charley felt as if he was really seeing her for the first time.

Like the land around her, there was a beauty about Jubilee that most people didn't see at first glance. Not that he was interested, he reminded himself, but still, he could notice her.

Looking toward the passage, she asked, "Can we walk in? I'd love to see the canyon on the other side."

Charley shook his head. "Not in those clothes or shoes. It's beautiful, but it would take us an hour or so to walk through then get back to the truck." He could see already that her bare arms were blistering and the climb just to get to the pass opening would ruin her slipper shoes.

An instinct to protect her rose in Charley, surprising him, but she was no damsel in distress. The only way he could help her was to show her how to make this ranch grow.

She turned to face him. "Take me to town, then. Show me the way. If you have things to do here, I'll drive back in and buy what I need later, but I need to learn the road." Her chocolate brown eyes met his and he saw determination in her gaze. "I want to be ready to start work tomorrow. It's time we started making something of this place. I'll need the right kind of clothes and shoes to do that." She frowned as if suddenly fearing her own words. "Can you buy me a horse?"

"I'll make a few calls," he answered. "Can you ride?"

"Of course."

She'd answered too fast to be telling the truth. He grinned. "I've heard tell that brown eyes never lie," he said.

She faced him square with her lying brown eyes looking a bit angry. "I can ride."

She might be crazy, but nothing about Jubilee Hamilton was lazy.

As they walked back to his truck, she added, "Mr.

Collins, I'll buy your lunch when we get to town. I'm starving. My breakfast seemed to have evaporated."

He wasn't sure if she was kidding or not. The lady was hard to read. "I'll accept the offer for lunch, but call me Charley."

"Fair enough. My family calls me Jub."

He opened her passenger door. "If you don't mind, I'll call you Jubilee. Jub seems more like a drink than a name."

When he climbed into the driver's seat, she was busy rummaging through her tiny purse that couldn't hold more than three or four things. She didn't look at him.

For some reason, he thought he'd won a round, but Charley had a feeling it would be a long time before they knew each other well enough to even be friends. They were as different as two people could be.

Ten minutes later when she asked for the vegan menu at Dorothy's Café, Charley had to fake a coughing fit to keep from laughing.

CHAPTER SIX

Thatcher
February 27

LAUREN BRIGMAN, the sheriff's daughter, stared at him
with those sky blue eyes, as if he was toad-level in
her world. She was all dressed up in her Texas Tech
University jacket with silver buttons and he looked
as though his whole body served as the tester kit for
paint samples. Somehow in two hours he'd managed
to drip more paint than he got on the walls. The sheriff would think long and hard about hiring him again.

But he didn't care. He couldn't stop looking at Lauren's beautiful long hair. Something must be wrong
with him. He couldn't think of five girls' names at
school but all at once he was aware, first of the girl in
the rain the other night, and now of the sheriff's only
child. At least the girl whose father found a body in the
canyon was his age. Lauren was way too old for him.

But Thatcher didn't care. A guy his age didn't get
to talk to a girl in college very often, so he was happy
to be in the sheriff's office with her even if she didn't
appear to be.

He felt smarter just being in the same room with
Lauren. He heard someone say she'd never even got

a B in her school career. Neither had he, but Thatcher knew he was coming from the other direction.

She might be six or seven years older than he was, but she'd never been mean to him. That meant something to him. Since grade school, every time he saw her, Brigman's daughter had at least nodded at him. Most of the other kids treated him as if he was a pound dog who'd escaped.

He did his best to act as though he barely noticed her while he painted the far wall of the sheriff's office. This was his job for the morning and the sheriff must have assigned her duties, as well.

Every now and then she'd glance up as if she'd just remembered that she was supposed to be watching him while she filed. He didn't accept the idea of having a babysitter. Hell, he'd been his own man since he was six or seven and his mom started making a habit of disappearing every weekend. Sometimes the weekends seemed to run together before she came home. He never minded being alone.

But this morning Lauren's silence was starting to bug him.

"How old are you, Lauren?" he asked without stopping his work.

She didn't look up from her computer. "Twenty-one. That must sound pretty old to you."

He ignored the fact that she thought of him as still a kid when he was taller than she was and almost fifteen. "I guess that's not too old to still be minding your old man. I was just wondering how many days of school you missed to be stuck here in your dad's office on a Saturday."

She smiled. "I didn't miss any school. In fact, much

as I hate to think about it, I'm almost finished with college. It's a place where no one makes you go to class—you just go because you want to. Whole new concept for you, Thatcher."

He groaned, feeling a lecture coming on. He figured all the Brigmans must share some mutant gene that made them give advice the minute their mouths opened.

She laughed as if she'd read his mind. "I just came in this weekend to help Pop with the filing. My dad's a great sheriff but somehow the folders never move off his desk and into the right filing cabinet. County said they'd hire him a secretary, but he's always saying he'd have to clean up and organize first."

Thatcher set his paintbrush down and took his third break of the morning. "You know, come to think of it, twenty-one *is* old. My mom was married and had me by then." When Lauren didn't answer he added, "You're real pretty so I'm guessing it's the fact your dad meets everyone at the door wearing a gun that keeps men away."

Lauren nodded. "That's it. How about you, Thatcher? At the old age of almost fifteen you're probably looking for a girlfriend, right? Maybe already have the lucky future Mrs. Jones picked out?"

Leaning on the corner of the desk, he crossed his arms. She was probably talking down to him, like a lot of townsfolk did, but he needed a few answers and she might know enough to help him. "I thought that girl whose dad found the body in the canyon a few days ago wasn't so bad looking." He shrugged. "Or she might have been cute if she hadn't been all wet and shaking like a coyote with his ear shot off."

"You see a lot of coyotes with their ears shot off?"

"I seen a few."

Lauren closed her laptop looking as if she didn't believe him. "The girl with her father that night is named Kristi Norton. Her dad took over as the new high school principal on Monday. He and his wife grew up around here. I think Kristi is your age, so you should have seen her in school."

"I ain't been to school lately. That's why I'm here today. I made the mistake of telling the sheriff that I was too embarrassed to go to school because I didn't have lunch money. I was thinking he'd loan me some, but instead he offered me a job. If I'd turned it down, he'd know I was lying and there weren't no telling what he'd do. I swear the past few years I seem to have my own guardian cop and I ain't sure if he's from heaven or hell."

"Tough life, kid," Lauren said as she went back to filing. "I'm basically here for the same reason. My father doesn't believe in loaning money, not even to his only daughter. For once, before I get out of college, I'd like to go somewhere for spring break besides Crossroads, Texas. Maybe a beach."

"What about your mom?" Thatcher moved over to the coffee pot and mixed half coffee with half milk. "Did she run off or something?"

"My folks are divorced. Mom would give me money, but it comes with strings. She's in that do-I-still-look-like-I'm-in-my-early-thirties stage. If I told her I wanted to go to the Gulf for spring break, she'd probably buy the exact same bathing suit and go with me."

Thatcher nodded but had no idea what she meant.

He wasn't even sure what she meant by divorce. "My mom has been common-law married four times—all the guy does is move in and she starts calling him her husband. Then, when he moves out, she considers herself common-law divorced. She claims it's cheaper that way, but I never called a one of them Dad. I figured, judging from my mom's taste in men, that I'm better off not knowing who the bastard was that fathered me."

Lauren's light blue eyes stared at him. "You've got to go to school, Thatcher. I think, somewhere beneath all the dirty hair, there just might be a brain."

No one had ever said that to him. He wanted to tell her that he made two thousand three hundred and fourteen dollars last year selling snakes, and almost eight hundred selling eggs to farms too lazy to bother with chickens.

But he didn't say anything because one of his mother's boyfriends told him if he told anyone he was selling snakes or eggs the government would come after him for taxes.

"Lauren, could I ask you a question?"

"If it's about how to impress Kristi, I'd say start with a haircut, a bath and clean clothes. You've already got the brains and that cute smile."

"No, it's not that," Thatcher said as he stored the information away for later. "Could you tell me where the grid is? Mr. Fuller told me once that I lived off it."

Lauren laughed. "You mean old Mr. Fuller who retired years ago?"

"Yeah. He came in to substitute when Mr. Franks ran off with Miss Smith-Williams back before Thanksgiving." Thatcher scratched his head. "That was strange. Mr. Franks was old and mean and Miss Smith-Williams always seemed confused. Couldn't even pick a last name. And, no matter where she was—her class, the hallway or the parking lot—she'd jump when the bell rang. You'd think after teaching high school for twenty years she'd get used to it ringing."

Lauren giggled. "Wonder where they are now?"

He winked at her. "Probably on a beach where there are no bells to ring or kids for Mr. Franks to yell at. I can see them wearing matching bathing suits and listening to country swing."

Lauren winked back at him. "You might want to keep that vision to yourself."

They both laughed.

He leaned over the desk and figured it was time to risk another question. "See that bottom drawer of your dad's desk?"

"Yes." She was back to working.

"You have any idea what he keeps in it?"

"Papers, I guess."

Thatcher knelt down and tugged on the handle. "Then why is it locked?"

Now he had her attention. She swiveled around and also tried the drawer. "I don't remember him having a locked drawer. He has a safe to keep evidence in. Why would he need a drawer?"

Thatcher shrugged. "Letters from a lover. Weapons. Drugs. Body parts."

She frowned. "My pop doesn't have time for lovers. He carries his weapon. Drugs would be locked in the safe and body parts would smell."

Before he could ask any more questions, the phone on the sheriff's desk rang.

Lauren answered, nodded a few times and said yes once, then hung up.

Thatcher moved closer.

She'd turned eggshell-white.

"What?" he said.

Lauren stood slowly. "The coroner has the report ready on the man they found dead in the canyon. He's faxing it over. He said he wants my pop to see it immediately."

"So call him up and tell him." Thatcher might not have a cell phone, but everyone else in the world seemed to.

"I can't. He's down in the canyon looking for clues. No cell service in that tiny sliver of canyon behind Lone Heart Pass." Lauren looked worried as the fax machine spit out three sheets of paper. "I have to get this report to him. I know there's nothing down there, but going to where someone died gives me the creeps."

Thatcher set his cup in the sink and washed his hands. "Don't worry about anything, I'm going with you." He lowered his voice, trying to sound older. "This is official police business and you might need backup."

"But…"

He moved a few feet, blocking her exit. "The sheriff told you to keep an eye on me, didn't he?" Thatcher saw the truth in her eyes before she had time to think of a lie. "Well, the only way to watch me is to take me with you."

She grabbed her purse. "Then come on."

Thatcher exploded. "Wow! We're on a job. Do I get a gun?"

"No," she shouted as she bumped his shoulder on her way out.

"Well, fine," he yelled back. "But we're picking my truck up on the way back. The last bit of paint is probably rusting off right now from being left out in the rain."

When she didn't answer, he tried asking another question as they reached the small parking lot beside the county offices. "Any chance I could drive your car? I could use a little practice with something that I don't have to shift."

"No," she answered as she climbed into the driver's side.

Lauren started the car and shoved the gear into drive before he had a chance to close the passenger door.

Thatcher didn't care. He was on official police business. This was exciting. He might have to rethink becoming a coroner.

CHAPTER SEVEN

Charley
February 27

THE MORNING WAS COOL, but Charley could feel spring coming as he saddled his horse, Dooley, and prepared to ride out. The calves he'd bought yesterday at the auction would arrive after lunch and he wanted to cross the pasture on horseback a few times just to make sure there were no surprises. A leftover round of wire or a nest of snakes could kill a calf. He had the feeling Jubilee couldn't take much of a loss.

One bite from a rattler on a horse or cow's neck could cut off the windpipe and suffocate the animal. There would be nothing a cowboy could do to help.

He also wanted to check the quality of the water. Sharon's parents had taken Lillie to the farm and ranch show in Amarillo, and on this rare Saturday without her, he planned to put in an extra five or six hours of work. He knew his daughter would have fun with her grandparents, and he needed every daylight hour he had to get this place ready for spring. He was making progress, but not fast enough. On Monday he'd hire men to help him work the cattle but today he was working on his own.

Grinning, he remembered Jubilee mentioning twice

yesterday that she was glad it was Friday. She wouldn't be helping him today. City people might take off Saturdays and Sundays, but most farm and ranch folks kept working. *Livestock don't know it's the weekend.*

He'd spent more time explaining things to her this week than working. He should have added in the bargain that he would get paid double for every day she helped. Yesterday, when he'd gone in for breakfast, he noticed she'd turned what had been a living room/bedroom for Levy into an office. Calendars, maps and goals for each month were taped to the walls.

The woman was as much a puzzle to him as she'd been the first day when she'd stormed out in her raincoat and socks. Bossy one minute and completely confused the next. She was her own private merry-go-round of emotions.

What made it worse was that he felt the need to help her, watch over her. She seemed adrift, without any friends or family. As far as he knew, not one person had called to check on her. Now and then he had to fight the need to just hold her and tell her it was going to be all right. She didn't have to fight so hard or always put on such a brave face.

Only Charley wasn't sure he believed that himself. He knew what it was like to have few friends and no family that cared. Sometimes being brave was the only choice because the other alternative was too dark to think about.

Jubilee did look good in her jeans and boots, though. He'd give the crazy lady that. And she always took the time to stop and talk to Lillie, even if she barely spoke five-year-old.

He'd found them sitting in the middle of Jubilee's

dirt garden one afternoon. They were laughing about all the strange vegetables they could grow if plants mixed.

"If an apple married a carrot," Lillie had said, "I'd call it a carropple."

Jubilee made several suggestions for new plants and that night she brought over a tower of vegetables for Lillie to eat with her supper.

Her being kind to Lillie mattered to Charley.

The second day, when Lillie mentioned to Jubilee that her daddy was sleeping on the couch because there was no bed in his room, Jubilee insisted they go shopping in the upstairs rooms of her house. Four bedrooms were completely furnished and looked as though no one had slept in any of them for over fifty years. Plus, extra furniture lined the walls of the attic.

When the three of them moved furniture out of the old place, Charley looked around. The big old house wasn't in bad shape even if it did seem haunted with a hundred years of memories.

The fifth bedroom, the one over the kitchen, was obviously Jubilee's. She must have decorated it when she'd lived with Levy as a child. It looked as if she hadn't changed a thing.

When they started lugging the bed frame into his place, Charley complained all the way, but that night he stretched out in a full bed and slept like a rock. When he tried to thank Jubilee the next morning, she brushed it off as nothing, saying she'd had fun with Lillie.

As he led Dooley out, saddled and ready on Saturday morning, Charley noticed Jubilee walking in the dirt she called her sleeping garden. This time she had the book in her hands he'd given her. The woman was always planning. More than a dozen times over the week her quick mind had surprised him and, though he wouldn't admit it even to himself, he found that sexy as hell.

He waved and thought of reminding her to put on sunscreen, but he reconsidered. He hadn't minded two nights ago when she'd knocked on his door and asked him to cover her back with aloe vera lotion. She'd worn a sleeveless blouse with tiny straps that morning and blistered both her front and back all the way down to the top of her bra line.

For a moment he'd just stood there staring at her bare shoulders.

"Well?" she said. "Would you mind helping me?" She'd obviously taken off her blouse and bra and wrapped herself in a towel.

He couldn't stop staring. The towel was low enough to show off not only the sunburn, but the white line below where no sun had touched. With each intake of breath a tiny bit of creamy breast seemed to push up from beneath the towel.

"I'll help. Sure." He tried to sound simply polite.

She handed him the lotion and turned, lifting her hair off her red shoulders.

He poured the lotion in his palm and slowly spread the cream over her skin. Back and forth from just below her hair, down her neck, over her shoulders and down to where the towel blocked his progress down her back.

If he didn't know better he'd think his soft caress was absorbing the heat from her skin, for he felt as though his entire body was growing hot.

When she turned and his hand moved over the tops of her breasts where the skin was burned the worst, she let out a whispered cry.

Charley wasn't sure if he'd hurt her or if she was simply reacting to the feel of his touch.

Lillie pushed her way between them. Taking the lotion away from him, she claimed his rough touch made Jubilee jump.

The five-year-old had taken over the doctoring, even insisting Jubilee stay for ice cream as part of her treatment.

Charley tried to apologize, but when he looked at her talking to Lillie, smiling at her, letting Lillie be the doctor, he couldn't seem to form words.

The feel of her warm skin lingered on his hands but he'd done his best to ignore it the next day. No women in his life, he reminded himself. If he ever did need a woman, he'd pick someone like Lexie, who'd know from the start that there would be no strings, no commitment, no future. He'd been fighting to get his footing since his dad kicked him off the ranch and made sure his college days were over. He'd worked and saved and done his best to raise Lillie. Nothing would stop him. No woman would ever get to him again.

Not even one with skin like silk and breasts that promised to be irresistible.

Don't get involved, he reminded himself—so often that it started echoing in his mind.

If he'd had any doubt that Jubilee wanted it the same way, all he had to remember was yesterday morning. When he'd asked how the sunburn was, she'd said "fine" as if drawing a line of what should not be talked about. The rest of breakfast had been formal, all business. He'd eaten his burned eggs and almost-raw bacon without another word about her body.

Of course, he couldn't help it if now and then his body went rogue with memories of its own. The way she'd felt. How he could feel her breath brushing against his throat as he leaned closer. The soft cry that could have been pleasure or pain.

Yesterday morning, all that seemed to have vanished with the dawn. Maybe he'd just imagined how good it felt so close. Maybe he was simply starved for a woman and had seen a request only for help as an invitation.

He had looked across the table. All business.

"Fine," Charley had finally echoed under his breath when she got up to get her notepad. He wanted it that way, too. The last thing he needed to do was get involved with her on anything but a business relationship. She'd told him while they were eating lunch a few days ago that she'd lost both her job and her lover, whom she didn't really love anyway.

She was the definition of mixed-up. He hadn't asked any questions, but now he wished he had.

"Someone's coming," she called to him as she closed her book and walked across her sleeping garden toward him.

He noticed the cloud of dust flying behind a little compact car. "Looks like the sheriff's daughter's VW Bug. Don't know anyone in town who drives a yellow one except Lauren."

Jubilee raised an eyebrow. "You know everyone's cars in town?"

"No, but I know Lauren's. She's had that one since she left for college. She and my little brother are friends, or at least they were the last time I talked to Reid. He's a year older than her but my dad said once that they dated some." Charley clamped his lips together. Too much information, he decided. Jubilee wouldn't care. Why did he always feel as though he needed to explain everything about not only the ranch, but also the town, to her?

It occurred to him that maybe he talked so much because he wanted to learn more about her. Or maybe he simply liked that low voice of hers that was starting to whisper through his dreams. Who knows, maybe if she knew the place and the people better, she'd stay.

As the car turned into the dirt drive, Jubilee commented, "I didn't know you had family in the area."

"You didn't ask and the answer is no, I no longer have family in the area. None that claim me anyway." He could hear the bitterness in his words, but he didn't plan on explaining. Let everyone for a hundred miles around believe whatever they wanted. He was the bad seed in the Collins clan. He'd gotten one girl pregnant and she'd left him with a kid. He'd slept with his stepmother. He'd never amount to anything. He was blacker than the blackest sheep.

Charley clenched his jaw to keep the swear words from spilling out. He'd prove them all wrong even if it took him a lifetime.

Before Jubilee could ask more questions, Lauren jumped out of the VW and hugged Charley. "It's good to see you," she said. She was laughing, though for some reason she looked a bit nervous. "I've missed your being around campus, Charley. You're my favorite Collins, you know."

He guessed Lauren was trying to tell him she

wasn't one of the ones who judged him. He didn't know her well, but she'd always been kind. He'd been sad when he found out she'd dated Reid. She deserved better.

"It's good to see you, too." That was it, he thought. The limit to their conversation since they'd been toddlers.

The last time he'd seen Lauren was the day he packed to leave college. She'd been much more of a kid then, it seemed. Tall, slender, her hair blowing across her face wiping away tears. She hadn't asked questions then, she'd simply looked sorry for him.

"I wish you could stay," she'd said even though they seldom saw each other on campus. "It isn't fair. You only need to finish one semester."

Charley hadn't explained. He figured she'd heard the stories. "Don't worry about it. No big deal." He'd lied. "I'll come back when I have time."

Now he needed to think of something to talk about before she started asking questions. She'd had over a year to think of a few. The last thing he wanted to do was talk about ancient history.

With his arm still resting on Lauren's shoulder, he turned her toward his boss. "This is Jubilee Hamilton, old Levy's great-granddaughter. I'm helping her get the place up and running again."

To his surprise, Jubilee was very professional. Shaking hands. Saying she'd seen the sheriff's car drive by a few days ago and looked forward to meeting him.

Charley didn't miss the gentleness, a true friendliness, in Jubilee's welcome. She'd been like that with Lillie, too. Maybe he was the only one alive who brought out her anger? Or maybe it was men in general—after all, every boyfriend had left her, she'd admitted. Which he found hard to believe, remembering the feel of her skin.

Charley tried to get his mind back in the present.

"What brings you out here, Lauren?" he said as he noticed the bone-thin kid Thatcher Jones trying to get out of her tiny car. He reminded Charley of a long-legged spider. "Did you bring the boy out to pick up his truck? I saw it parked down the road in the bar ditch."

"Something like that." Lauren glanced back as if she'd forgotten Thatcher was there. "He's riding shotgun on my mission."

Charley waved at the kid and Thatcher waved back. He'd seen the boy around. They'd never talked, but they were on waving terms.

"I'm looking for my father." Lauren straightened as if finally getting to the reason she'd driven out. "Hikers found a body in the canyon a couple of nights ago. My dad said he'd be north of Lone Heart Pass this morning looking for clues. I've got information he asked for and thought the pass might be the quickest way to get it to him."

Charley got the picture. Lauren needed his help, but she didn't want to give more away than necessary. "You could go down into the canyon behind the museum, but I'd pack water if I were you. It could be a long walk. Or I could saddle up another horse and take you through the pass. I'm stabling several extras here and I figure the owners would be happy if I got them out for a little exercise. Once we ride down the hiker trail, we'll probably be within sight of the sheriff if he's still in the canyon."

"Would you?" Lauren smiled, but like always, she seemed a bit shy. "I'd appreciate it if you'd go with me, Charley." She gave him that you're-almost-like-my-big-brother look she used to shoot him when she visited the ranch. Reid, who was more her age, and his friend Tim O'Grady usually ignored her at parties and roundups. Charley would always end up saddling her horse, or talking to her for a few minutes.

"Sure. Glad to help," Charley answered, knowing he'd be working later into the night to make up the time.

The Thatcher kid's voice cracked with excitement. "Mind saddling two horses, Mr. Collins? Like Lauren said, I'm traveling with her."

Charley turned and saw the boy walking tall and serious. Charley gave the kid his due. "Happy to. I can always use another man who can ride." He offered his hand. "The canyon can be tricky."

"Glad to help." Thatcher shook hands. "Might as well. I've been helping Lauren at the sheriff's office all morning."

Charley had an idea there was far more to the story, but he didn't ask.

"I'm going, too," Jubilee announced. "Just give me a minute to get my new boots on and find that hat with the strings on it."

"But…" He tried to think of a reason for her not to tag along, but saying that his ears could use some rest from her constant questions didn't seem polite.

Her stare locked on him. "I'm going." She turned around so fast he had no doubt the discussion was over.

Charley fought down a groan. He'd be willing to bet his boss hadn't been near a horse in years. He'd bought a gentle one for her while he was at the auction buying cattle and she'd yet to touch the mare.

Five minutes later, when the others climbed into the saddle, Jubilee walked to the wrong side of her mount.

"This side," he whispered.

"Of course. I knew that." She circled around.

She seemed so determined. He whispered a few instructions as he placed his hand on her backside and shoved her up into the saddle.

She stared down at him with angry eyes. Before she could comment, he slid his hand along her leg and shoved her boot into the stirrup. "Try to hang on to the reins, Jubilee."

Now she looked too angry even to speak. Which Charley decided wasn't a bad idea.

When he passed Thatcher, he whispered, "Stay close to the lady and make sure she doesn't fall off."

"Will do, boss," Thatcher answered as he saluted.

As Charley expected, the kid rode as if he'd slipped from the birth canal directly onto a saddle.

On the mile ride to the pass, Lauren and Thatcher stayed on either side of Jubilee, giving her pointers, but she bounced up and down all the way. Charley had a feeling her shoulders wouldn't be the only things red tonight.

As they entered the pass, Charley looped a lead rope from her horse to his saddle horn. Within minutes they had left the morning sun and ridden into the cool darkness of the passage. The walls on either side shot toward the heavens, and a slice of light slid down the rock, showing off the beauty of the stone that had stood silently against the weather for more than a million years.

When anyone spoke, the words echoed off the passage walls, bouncing back and forth like dueling chimes.

Every time Charley glanced back, Jubilee looked terrified. Her hands had a death grip on the saddle horn and her eyes were wide. But her back was straight and she didn't cry out or demand they stop.

"You're doing fine," he offered, but she didn't look at him.

Lauren's calm voice whispered from behind them. "I remember how frightened I was when I rode through this pass for the first time. The night was cold, but I wanted to see the moon cross the opening above. There is a legend that if you see the full moon while in the pass, your heart's wish will come true. Only that night I was too scared to wish for anything, even though my Pop was with me."

From behind her, Thatcher added with a laugh, "I'd be scared if the sheriff was with me right now. I get the feeling he's worrying his brain trying to come up with one more thing I'm doing wrong."

Charley laughed, remembering when he was in his teens and felt the same way about Dan Brigman. Only since he'd been back from college, somehow they'd become friends. Dan had even asked him to help out a few times, manning a road block one night, rounding up drunks after a barn party and, once, directing traffic at a funeral for a ninety-year-old O'Grady. They'd had ten family cars that day. Charley didn't want to be a deputy, but he didn't mind being the sheriff's friend.

After several minutes of silence, Jubilee whispered from just behind Charley, "It's like we're walking among ghosts in here. Like we don't belong. Like this is a passageway only for the gods."

"Trust me," Charley whispered back. "If anyone were in here with us, ghost or human, we'd know it. I heard once that outlaws used this pass to disappear into the canyon."

Thatcher didn't help the tension by adding, "This would be a great place for snakes to hide. If it were warmer, we could probably find a whole nest curled up sleeping the day away."

When no one commented, he added, "You know the young ones can be as deadly as the big ones. I saw a rattler not yet a foot long kill a pup once. Bit him on the nose."

When no one joined the conversation, Thatcher started whistling softly.

Everyone took a deep breath when they made it to the other side. The small canyon, no more than a few hundred feet deep in this spot, opened out with colors ribboning the rocks and the first brush of wildflowers along the base.

Lauren and Thatcher took the lead, winding down to the bottom of the canyon so they could follow the shallow creek. From there they could look up and spot the sheriff easier.

Charley held back until Jubilee rode even with him. "You did good in there," he encouraged. "Don't worry about snakes. I've never seen one in the passage."

"Thanks. I wasn't worried about snakes. Or wishes, for that matter," she said, her lips still white around the edges, showing her lie. "Only one thing I do need to say to you before we go any farther. Don't put your hands on me again. I can manage on my own."

"You got it, lady," he snapped as he nudged his horse ahead of her without looking back to see if she followed.

All he'd done was help her up. She acted as though it was an assault. With his luck, she'd have him arrested when they found the sheriff.

A few moments later, Lauren yelled, saying she'd spotted her father.

Sheriff Brigman was riding toward them on a huge bay Charley recognized as part of the Kirkland stock.

Lauren handed him an envelope and the sheriff instructed her and Thatcher to walk their horses down along the stream to search for anything that didn't look as if it belonged in the canyon. Then Brigman headed up the trail.

Charley waited, halfway between the bottom stream and the top ledge of the passage. He knew he needed to stay close to Jubilee no matter how much she wanted him to keep his distance.

Glancing back, he saw her slowly picking her way down to where he waited. The sheriff reached him first and Charley was glad of the opportunity to ask a few questions with no one around.

"Morning, Sheriff."

Brigman touched his hat in greeting. "Thanks for bringing Lauren down. Knowing her, she filled you in."

"She did, but she didn't seem to know how the guy died. Natural causes, or something suspicious?"

Brigman tapped the file against his leg. "Coroner said he was in his late sixties or early seventies, signs of a hard life, lots of old scars and tattoos, no dental care, probably heavy drug use at one time." He looked straight at Charley. "But someone had to be with him. Someone wrapped him in the burlap sacks. Maybe they didn't kill him, but the man did not die alone. So, why didn't whoever was with him simply turn him over to the police? The only reason I can come up with is that whoever was there either killed him, or caused his death."

"Any hint as to cause of death?"

"Blow to the head. Caved the side of his skull in." Brigman paused as if thinking through the crime. "Strange thing is the coroner said it looked like someone beat him after he was dead. Bruises, cuts, even dents all over him. A little blood soaked into the burlap, but not as much as would have if the heart had still been pumping. Some of the cuts must have happened after he'd been wrapped and tied up like a mummy."

"That doesn't make sense." Charley knew the kick of a horse could easily break bones or crack a skull, but why would someone put a dead man in sacks and then beat on him? Or, why would anyone leave his body here in the canyon?

Both men swung from their saddles as Charley asked, "Exactly where did you find the body?"

The sheriff pointed to a small ledge twenty feet to the left of them. It was not more than six feet wide or deep. "He was laid out on his back like someone put him on display. I saw no trail of how he got there because of the hard rain that hit the other night. Mr. Norton, the man who found him, said he remembered seeing drops of blood around, but it was all washed away before I got here."

Brigman paced, thinking aloud. "The trail is too

narrow for a four-wheeler, so whoever brought him here had to have carried him."

"Or brought him out here alive. Killed him. Then beat the body bloody and left before the rain even started."

"Possible," the sheriff agreed. "Or he could have used a horse to transport the body. If so, he would have been on Hamilton land. He would have used the pass. Any other way in would have been too public for too long. Someone would have seen him."

Charley shook his head. "I've been working for Jubilee Hamilton for a week. I can't see the entrance to the pass from the headquarters, but I was working outside. I would have heard anyone crossing the land pulling a trailer. On horseback he might have stayed in the trees that run along the windbreak almost to the pass entrance."

Brigman frowned. "The man hadn't been dead more than a few hours. He was probably left in the canyon about twilight. Most of the hikers would have been gone by then. Norton grew up around here; he knew the trail so he'd let his kids stay late in the canyon."

"So no clues?" Charley tried to think why someone would kill an old man and leave his body out here by a trail hikers used. He must have wanted the body found. Maybe he wanted to make some kind of statement?

Or whoever did this was planning to come back and bury the body when the rain stopped. There were spots where the ground was soft—easy to dig a grave. There were caves, too. This unfortunate fellow probably wasn't the first body buried out here.

Charley remembered that about ten years ago a

science class looking at rocks had found a skeleton buried with handcuffs like they'd been on the man when he died.

"One clue," the sheriff said as he pulled a plastic bag from his vest pocket. "When we moved his body, this was underneath. One joint."

"Drugs?" Before Charley could say more, his boss's horse brushed his shoulder.

He turned and lifted his arms in an offer to help her down, but the last thing she'd said about not touching or helping her crossed his mind. Patting her mount, he lowered his hands, hoping the sheriff didn't notice the coldness between him and Jubilee.

Charley simply stood, holding the reins as she tried to swing out of the saddle with at least an ounce of grace.

The horse shifted, widening his stance on the uneven ground. Jubilee's body slammed against Charley as she lowered. The full impact of her moving against him shook him. He forced calmness far beyond what he thought possible as her soft parts moved against him, reminding him he may have sworn off women, but he wasn't immune to them.

As her boots crunched against the rocky ground, the horse moved away, and Charley felt the loss of her pressed against him like a sudden blow.

Jubilee had the nerve to look at him as if their accidental brush had been a conspiracy. As though Charley and the horse had planned the whole encounter.

He held open his palms as if to say he had nothing to do with it. At least this time, if she accused him of anything, he could use the sheriff as a witness.

Only when Charley glanced at Brigman, the sheriff looked as though he felt sorry for him, rather than planning to come to his defense.

Charley swore to himself again he'd have nothing to do with any woman. Even the crazy ones had the ability to mess with his mind.

He told himself she could stay or go. He didn't care. All that mattered was the job and he needed this one to last long enough to save a little more money.

CHAPTER EIGHT

Lauren Brigman
February 27

LAUREN SHADED HER eyes as she looked up toward her pop. The beauty of Ransom Canyon surrounded him, framing the man in his element. He was tall and broad-shouldered. His Stetson and boots grounded him to this place. A man the town depended on. A sheriff well respected. A father she could always count on.

Only today he looked as if he had the worries of the world on those shoulders. Something was bothering him. The problem seemed deeper than one body in the canyon. He seemed to be waiting, a lone man standing on guard against a storm he knew was coming.

Thatcher's comment about the locked drawer worried at the corner of her thoughts. Was it possible her father carried a secret? All her life she'd thought him an open book. If he didn't tell her something, it was police business. She'd never known him to harbor a secret. Maybe it was nothing. She'd ask him about the drawer and he'd explain it. Simple as that.

Charley and Jubilee were over by Jubilee's mare, but her father had turned toward the ledge where they'd found the body.

She'd glanced over the coroner's report. She felt

as if she knew everything her father did about the case, but he looked deep in thought. The pieces didn't fit. Too many clues were missing. She could almost hear him saying, *Put the details together and it'll all make sense.*

Thatcher rode toward her father. When the horse couldn't move fast enough on the uneven trail, he jumped down and crossed the rocky slope like a mountain goat. "Sheriff." His one word echoed off the canyon walls. "I think I found a clue."

Lauren rode to them. She reached her father as he slowly unfolded what looked like an ad from the local grocery store. The paper was dirty, with dried mud flaking from it as Pop opened it carefully. It had been in the sun and weather several days because the once brightly colored ads were faded. There was writing on the corner, but it was too smeared to make out more than a few letters.

"It's a clue, right?" Thatcher was moving back and forth with excitement like a metronome.

The sheriff slipped the paper in a plastic bag. "It might be. I'll take a look at it back at the office, but Thatcher, it's probably only a piece of trash someone left."

"I know. You got to look down a lot of rabbit holes before you find supper."

Lauren laughed. Sometimes she swore Thatcher had grown up a few centuries before her, even though he was younger than she was.

After they left the canyon, Lauren took Thatcher to his junker of a pickup and waited to make sure it started before she drove back to town.

The kid hadn't stopped talking all day. He must have

thought she was close enough to his age to make them buddies. In truth, Lauren could barely remember being in her midteens. She wanted to tell him how painful the next few years would be. She couldn't imagine him fitting in. School was full of cliques and groups, but there probably wasn't a snake-killing-dirty-hair gang. Dante would have added another level of hell in *Inferno* if he'd known about high school when he'd written his poem.

She decided to go back to the county offices and work, hoping Pop would drop back by his office, but he was probably too busy. As sheriff, this place was his responsibility, and someone had dropped a body off in his county. Or worse, they'd killed an old man and left him on display. Lauren had a feeling her pop wouldn't sleep until he found the answers.

About seven, she locked his office and headed home alone. As she drove down the incline to the lake, she couldn't stop smiling. Somehow this little lake community next to Crossroads always seemed to welcome her. The winding road. The sparkles on the lake at sunset. Home.

Everyone her age talked of leaving, but not Lauren. She had a strong feeling that when she finished school she'd be back living here. The only problem was, what would she do?

Lucas Reyes crossed her mind. She'd had a crush on him since she was fifteen, and now, six years later, he still lingered in her thoughts and dreams. When they'd seen each other at Tech, all Lucas could talk about was stretching his wings in some big city. He'd be a lawyer. He'd wear suits. He'd be rich before he was thirty.

"Another reason we'd never work," she whispered

to herself as she pulled in front of her home. "He had dreams and I can't find mine." No matter how many bricks he piled up between them, Lauren had the feeling she'd always long for Lucas. Tall, good-looking, brilliant Lucas who made his dreams come true but somehow never wondered what her dreams might be. They'd talked of someday but the bond between them now was as thin as thread.

If they were meant to end up together, shouldn't they spend time together, talk often, share dreams?

She opened a can of soup and ate half while flipping channels. Back at school she never had time to watch TV. There always seemed to be something else to do.

Curled in her favorite fuzzy blanket, she drifted off, only to dream of the old man wrapped in burlap. She'd only seen the pictures of the wrapped body, but somehow he haunted her.

Somehow, the dead man blended with her memory of being trapped in an old house that was falling down around her. She'd been Thatcher's age when the accident happened, but that night had never left her.

She'd never forget the panic, the dust filling her lungs so thickly she could barely scream as the floor crumbled beneath her feet. In that second she saw Reid Collins jump out the window, heard Tim O'Grady's body crashing down below and felt Lucas's hand close around her wrist. For a moment she'd swung in the air, then, slowly he'd pulled her until she was balanced with him on a few inches of wood that had held. He'd folded her tightly against him, this boy she barely knew then. Their lives had blended that night, for her anyway. They'd become friends. Somehow in the horror of that night they'd bonded. She owed Lucas Reyes something, and even if they'd grown apart in college, Lauren knew that someday she'd pay him back for saving her life. A blood oath. Sometime she'd save his life. She'd repay the debt.

When she jerked in her dream and woke up, Lauren knew it would be hours before she'd trust sleep again. She walked out on the deck, facing the lake, and tried to shake off how helpless the dream had made her feel. She was twenty-one, in her last year of school, but she had that feeling of standing on two inches of wood just as she had at fifteen. Only now she had no one holding her. No one telling her which way to jump. Her mother wanted her to get a master's in business; her father was hoping she'd pick law school.

If she could talk to Lucas, he'd tell her what to do. He was three years older and had always seemed wise. Only he'd graduated. She didn't even know his address now. Not that she'd seen him often when they were both in school. Lucas Reyes was always in a hurry and rarely had time to even talk on the phone.

The lake in winter always seemed lonely, Lauren thought, as she picked her way along the rocky shoreline. Even after the few rains this month, the water level was still down.

"Lauren." Someone whispered her name.

She turned and saw a lone figure in a hooded jacket. A cane rested against his side.

She didn't need much light to see her best friend. Tim O'Grady had grown a beard over Christmas break and she couldn't help thinking he looked like a young Hemingway. Maybe he was. He'd told her he'd finished his second novel, but he'd never let anyone read a word.

When she'd asked what it was about, he'd simply said "Life."

Moving across the uneven ground, he used his cane for balance.

She stood still as he walked toward her. As always, when she saw Tim, a part of her saw the goofy, red-haired six-year-old trying to cheer her up. She was five and had just moved to the lake with her father.

"What's a girl like you doing in a place like this?" His voice seemed to blend with the wind that tickled against her throat.

She giggled. "You still using that old pickup line, Tim? No wonder you're out here alone." She couldn't tell if he smiled.

"Heard you were home this weekend." His voice seemed low, as if he hadn't talked to anyone in days. "I'm guessing it's no fun at Tech without me there."

She agreed. "You're right. No fun since you graduated. Why don't you come back and sign up for grad school? I haven't had a cheap chicken fried steak since you left."

He shook his head. "I'm too busy."

Lauren wanted to ask about his writing, but Tim never talked about it, or worse, he made jokes about what he was doing.

She offered a hand to her friend and they walked to the water's edge. "Do you come out here every night?" she asked, thinking she could smell whiskey on his breath.

"Pretty much. I have trouble sleeping. Occupational hazard all writers suffer, I've been told." Tim laughed more at himself than at anything funny. "Tell me what's happening at Tech. I miss living in the bee-hive."

"Nothing."

"And your roommate, Polly, how is she?"

"She's dating an engineering major, but every time I get back from home she asks about you."

Tim shrugged. "We weren't meant to be, Lauren. A one-night stand that somehow lasted a few weeks."

Lauren nodded. Tim was the kind of guy who had a hundred first dates and very few second. He rarely took anything seriously.

Tonight, with a watery moon bobbing on the water, she felt as though they were dancing around a conversation, not really having one.

"What is it, Tim? What's wrong?"

He let go of her hand and just stood there looking straight at her as if she was part of the landscape and not his oldest friend.

"Tell me," she whispered.

"I'm working on a new book. I moved out here to the lake after my parents took off to paint in France for a year. I was thinking it would be my refuge, my writer's retreat. Only, lately, the story in my book is taking me over. I can't crawl out. It's like the novel is real and my life is the make-believe."

Lauren cupped his face. "Tim, have you been drink-ing?"

"Always. At first to slip out of reality for a while and set my imagination free, but lately, it's been the other way around. I'm living in the book and some-times feel like I might forget to breathe in real life."

Lauren felt a sudden cold and didn't know if it was

coming from the lake, or from her heart. She put her arms around Tim and held on tight. Nothing he said made sense but she knew he was in trouble.

She held him for a long time, thinking of how they used to swim together in the lake as kids, how he showed her around when she came to college a year after he. She remembered the long talks they'd had at night, sitting out on a rock that rested halfway between his parents' house and hers.

Without a word, she slipped her hand in his and took him up to the house.

He was eating the last of the soup she'd made for supper when her father came in the door thirty minutes later.

"Hello, Sheriff." Tim clanked his spoon into the empty bowl. "Haven't seen you for a while."

Dan Brigman pulled off his service weapon and locked it in the safe in the entry closet. "Hello, Tim. Heard you were writing a mystery this time."

Neither Tim nor Lauren were surprised that Pop knew what was going on. If Tim told one person in town what he was working on, the whole town knew. That was Crossroads. A town too small to hold a secret.

"Yeah, but I'm having trouble with the plot. No mysteries ever happen around here."

Lauren handed her father a cup of coffee and whispered, "Sorry, Pop, your supper vanished."

He nodded and turned to Tim. "I got a mystery for you."

Lauren saw Tim's entire body come to life. Pop had hit the "I'm interested" button in his brain.

For the next hour Pop told him all about the body

left in the canyon, even showed Tim the notes. They went through every possible theory of what might have happened. Tim was fascinated.

"Strange thing is, you'd think the body would be easy to ID. About seventy years old, tattooed, drug user. No arrest record. No match on a driver's license."

"Details," Tim encouraged.

"Average height, slim build. The few hairs he had on his head were dirty white. Two heart-shaped tattoos on one arm, both with the names inside blacked over by what looked like a homemade job. One wrist tat that was faded but looked like it said Surrender to the Void. A joint under his body. Any of that fit together?"

"Sure," Tim leaned forward to the edge of his chair. "The guy's had two broken hearts. Hated the loves bad enough to have them scratched off his hide. Also he was single when he died. Men that age, who have a wife, tend to round out from good meals. As far as the writing on his wrist, maybe the old guy was an early space jockey. Sounds like something a pilot might say."

Tim kept following his thought pattern as he pointed at the sheriff. "You're thinking it's unlikely some drug gang would hire a man that old, or kill him somewhere else and drive all the way to Crossroads, navigate a dirt road toward that spot in the canyon, walk him down in the dark, kill him, beat him up and then put him on display."

"Right. That would put the pieces together in order, but a gang wouldn't go to so much trouble. They'd just bury him or toss him in a Dumpster."

"So if drug dealers didn't kill the guy, who did?"

Tim was taking notes on the back of an envelope he'd pulled from the trash.

"I have no idea." Pop laughed. "If he lived around here, folks would know him. Someone would have reported him missing."

Tim shook his head. "He could have lived alone. Maybe even grew his own pot. There are a few little settlements out by the Breaks where folks who want to be invisible live. I've seen them at the fair and the trade days where people sell their junk so they can buy someone else's junk. Most live alone in one room cabins or old trailers."

Lauren's head was starting to hurt. "If he lived out in the middle of nowhere alone, then who killed him? Someone wrapped him in the bags. Someone took him to the canyon. Someone killed him."

Tim stood and began to pace, reminding her of her father. Pop could never think or lecture unless he was on the move.

"He's a local. He has to be." Tim pointed at her as if he was expecting her to write his words down. "But we're not looking for one man. We're looking for at least two. The ID of the body and the man who wrapped him up."

"And probably killed him," Dan added. "And when did this investigation become a 'we,' Tim?"

"Deputize me, Sheriff. I can help. I've spent the last year doing research. I've read every detective book in print. I'm starting to solve mysteries in my sleep."

Dan shook his head.

"I can dedicate twelve hours a day digging through files and county records. Driving back roads. Talking to people. The folks out there in the Breaks will identify with me. I'll grow the beard longer and paint on a few tats." Tim took a deep breath. "I'll even go by every tattoo parlor within a hundred miles. I got nothing else to do."

Pop glanced at Lauren and she knew he could read her mind.

He turned back to Tim. "All right. I've got a secretary job open at the county office. You can have it for a month, but you're not a deputy and don't even think you can carry a gun or interfere with police business. You're just there to help with research. I have a feeling we'll be digging a long while to solve this case."

"I'll be in the office at dawn." Tim put his hand over his heart as if he were being sworn in.

Pop smiled. "I'll be there at eight with the key. Try to get some sleep, Tim, and shave that beard. Believe me, it won't help people trust you and if it gets any longer, folks will think you probably have fleas."

Tim saluted and Pop swore as he headed for the kitchen.

Lauren walked out on the deck with Tim. "Are you sure this is what you want?"

"This is what I need. Reality." He pulled her close. "Thanks, Lauren."

Without hesitation, he leaned down and kissed her soundly on the lips.

A moment later when he straightened, he shrugged. "That wasn't bad, L. Maybe we should do that again, sometime. I'll let you know when it's about to happen so you can react next time."

She pushed hard on Tim's chest. "I'll think about it when you save yourself, Tim O'Grady. You're lost right now and I miss my friend." She scrubbed her lips. "Pop's right, you need to shave. Give up kissing till you do."

"Sounds like a promise." He winked and turned toward the back steps. "I'll keep you in the loop on the investigation. What I'm allowed to divulge to nonprofessionals, of course."

Lauren rolled her eyes, but it was too dark for him to see. Her father may have just created a monster. With Tim's imagination, there was no telling where this investigation might be headed.

She walked inside and found her father eating a tomato and cheese sandwich. "Why'd you give Tim a job, Pop?"

"The kid needs a direction," he muttered between bites.

"He's not a kid. He's a man."

"Yeah, but he doesn't know it yet," Dan answered. "He doesn't know who he is and sometimes heading in a direction, even the wrong one, can help a man figure it out."

Lauren laughed. "When did you get so smart?"

He smiled. "About the time your mother left me. Before that I was an idiot. Just ask her."

CHAPTER NINE

Charley
March 3

THE FEED STORE loaded his farm supplies in half the time Charley thought it would take. Today was his day to pick up Lillie from school. If he drove back to the ranch and delivered the grain, it would be time to turn around and come back to town to get her, so he decided he'd stop in for a cup of coffee at the Evening Shadows Retirement Home.

Everyone in town knew they had an "open door, coffee pot's always ready" policy. The retired teachers welcomed former students as friends.

In the two weeks he'd been working at the Lone Heart, he was surprised how quickly the place had changed. The days were hard and long but he liked seeing progress. Working for a day or two on ranches didn't give him that chance. He also had to admit he liked the fresh air and the silence when Jubilee wasn't trailing behind him asking questions.

His family had settled this part of Texas over a hundred and fifty years ago. The sandy soil and open sky had mixed in the Collinses' bloodline. Managing a ranch, even if it wasn't his own, made him proud.

He was helping Jubilee, but he was also improving the ranch, and that mattered. The land mattered.

He'd hired several men to work fences with him the past few days so he'd barely seen Jubilee. Since she'd felt the need to tell him never to touch her, their meetings at breakfast had been cold. Which was fine with him. This was just a job, he kept telling himself. The last thing he wanted was to get involved with any woman.

Someday, he'd have his own place. Thanks to the free rent and the fact he'd talked her into paying him almost twice what he usually made at odd jobs, his dream didn't seem so far away. From the time he'd come back to Crossroads, he'd decided to work five days a week to pay the bills, but if he worked Saturday or the weekend nights tending bar, that money was stake money. He'd put it away to buy his own place.

Working the extra time didn't seem so bad when he thought about how his savings were slowly growing.

Lately that was the only dream he allowed himself to believe in.

Now the barn was stocked with hay, and he'd contracted to stable four more horses. Folks on the edge of town loved keeping a horse or two for their kids, but when the animal needed extra care or doctoring, the big pet became way too much trouble. The vet had recommended him, and Charley hoped the extra money coming in would buy her a few more months to make Lone Heart Ranch pay.

As he pulled in front of the village of little bungalows Charley couldn't miss the new sign. Evening Shadows: a planned community for retired teachers. The place used to be an old motel called Canyon View

Cabins. The cabins had long ago been turned into one-bedroom bungalows. Each of the twelve residents had their own little front porch, but most walked to the office lobby and spent their afternoons visiting or napping in the sun.

The old name had always bothered him because there was no view of the canyon. The cabins were in the center of town and faced the main highway through Crossroads. The lack of canyon view or the traffic never seemed to bother the retired teachers.

The place didn't look much like it had when he was in high school, thanks to the manager, Yancy Gray. He'd fixed up the original tiny houses and built four more bungalows, plus, he'd made the office an inviting all-glass activity room with a front seat view of the town.

Over the past year of delivering groceries as one of his odd jobs, Charley had gotten to know most of the teachers well. He'd even been a pallbearer when the retired principal, Mr. Hall, passed on. The much-respected teacher and principal had wanted only former students to carry him on his last journey.

Mr. Browning, the newly retired AG teacher, had bought Mr. Hall's small house at Evening Shadows. He had a daughter a few hours away in Amarillo, who wanted him to live with her, but he wanted to stay with his friends. Charley thought maybe it was the fact that these people had taught together for so long, they were like veterans of a war civilians didn't understand.

Unlike some places in town, Charley was welcomed by all at Evening Shadows. As he walked into the sunny activity room, Cap Fuller stood to shake his hand. He didn't let go until he'd pulled Charley to an empty chair beside Mr. Browning.

Charley knew them both well and had loved being in their classes years ago.

Before the men could start talking, Mrs. Ollie rushed over with a cup of coffee for him. She leaned close and Charley thought she'd smelled like apple pie all his life.

"Morning, Charley Collins," she whispered. "You getting into any trouble with the girls lately?"

"No, Ma'am. I've sworn off women." He felt fifteen again, remembering when she'd caught him kissing some cheerleader behind the stage one afternoon. She'd given him "The Talk" that day about how a young person's body can head down the wrong path and refuse to listen to his brain.

Looking back, Charley decided he should have taken notes on that lecture.

Mrs. Ollie straightened. "I'm glad to hear that. A good-looking man like you needs to be careful. Watch out for the girls."

Cap Fuller laughed. "I know what you mean. I've always had the same problem."

Everyone within hearing distance laughed. Cap was short, old, bald and almost toothless.

Mrs. Ollie waddled off and Charley began asking questions. He needed advice and the retired teachers were a brain trust. Within twenty minutes they'd not only answered questions he had about exactly how much land to farm, how to build onto the barn and where to put a new well, they'd offered to drive out and orchestrate the jobs.

As he walked away, he was feeling as if he might

just be able to make Jubilee's plan work without having to sell gravel off the east slope. Gravel was always good for fast money, but once it was gone, it was gone.

When he glanced up toward his truck, he frowned. Lexie leaned against the right fender of his pickup. For once, she looked a little wilted. Her hair didn't seem so perfect and, in the sun, he could see lines around her heavily made-up mouth and eyes. The wind must have brushed away some of her beauty-queen polish. Before long she'd only be a barroom beauty where the lights were low and the men looked at her through a whiskey glass.

"Morning," he said as he walked past her, heading straight for the driver's door.

"Wait," she snapped. "I want to talk to you about something."

"I'm in a hurry." He could think of nothing they might have in common.

"I just have one question." She did her best to look pouty.

He was trapped. All the old folks were probably watching. He couldn't be rude to her. "All right. One question, and then I have to go pick up my daughter."

Lexie walked around to his side of the pickup as she talked. "You may know that my aunt died last year, leaving me her huge old house here in Crossroads."

Charley didn't know, or care. Lexie was years older than he, so he hadn't known her in school, but then everyone in town knew her as Homecoming Queen and runner-up for Miss Texas. He knew of her just as she probably knew all about him.

"What's your question?"

She shot him an irritated look that wilted even more

of her beauty. "Well, my soon-to-be husband wants me to redo the place as a kind of weekend getaway. I thought you might be the man to handle the job. I'll be dropping in and out, but I need someone to oversee the makeover."

Charley opened his pickup door and turned to find her as close as a shadow behind him. "Not interested, but thanks for the offer." With one hand on the door and the other on the steering wheel, he had nowhere to go.

She rested her perfectly manicured fingers on his arm and leaned close. "Drop by any time and I'll show you the place. There are eight very empty bedrooms. You might change your mind. If I don't find someone fast I'm going to sell the place."

She drew in a breath and her blouse brushed his chest.

Charley just stood there like a man hypnotized by the rattler on a snake.

Without warning, she struck. Closing the distance between them, she pressed her mouth against his. Then, just as suddenly she stepped away and laughed. "We'll finish this talk later, cowboy. I always get what I want in the end."

He climbed in and slammed the truck door. If he didn't get out of sight quickly, Mrs Ollie would be out to give him "The Talk" again.

He had a feeling a weekend getaway home was not what Lexie was talking about getting when she mentioned him dropping by. The idea of having her for a boss made him rethink his relationship with Jubilee, who looked like an angel compared to Lexie. If all Jubilee asked for was a hands-off policy, it was fine with him. Even having her following him around didn't seem so bad compared to Lexie.

By the time Lillie came out of her school, Charley had already written down a dozen things he needed to talk to Jubilee about tomorrow. He had to wash any thought of Lexie or the kiss from his mind. He didn't want it there. Everything about the woman bothered him. Even the way she called him "cowboy," as though he was a breed she was inspecting to buy.

While his daughter told him about her day, Charley silently swore to make more of an effort to get along with his boss. Jubilee Hamilton might be crazy and quick to anger, but at least she wasn't a pariah. He could work with crazy. Maybe even forgive her for yelling at him when he'd touched her. Who knows, maybe she had a guy like Lexie always trying to handle her.

He and Jubilee shared a common goal. She paid him good money, was nice to Lillie and didn't ask personal questions. Everything he learned on her ranch would serve him well when he started his own place. Plus, if he screwed up this job he might have to work for Lexie.

Charley rubbed his knuckles across his mouth, wishing he could wash away the taste of lust from Lexie's lips.

As the afternoon waned, he stayed near the house. Fixing the fence in the corral, walking the boarded horses as Lillie rode each one. While he worked on the barn door, Lillie played with three baby rabbits she'd found by the back of the barn. Something must have killed the mother. They were wild at first, but by nightfall she almost had them eating out of her hand.

About sunset he spotted Jubilee walking in her invisible garden. She didn't look up at him, but he had a feeling she was aware he was near.

Funny, he thought, how now and then he had the urge to simply hold her. It wasn't passion or love. Charley felt as if his boss was probably as lonely as he was. He knew all the signs. She never got any mail, though she insisted on going to check it every other day. As far as he knew no one had called the house since she'd arrived. She didn't even carry her phone most of the time and the light in her office burned late every night as if she didn't want to go to bed.

Jubilee had no one on her side. No one fighting for her to win.

She tried so hard to learn everything as if she expected him to disappear any day. If he could just hold her for a while, he'd tell her he would stay. He'd help her build her home.

But she wasn't open to a single touch.

CHAPTER TEN

Thatcher
March 5

ON FRIDAY MORNING, Thatcher Jones got up at six, took a bath, washed his hair, ate a piece of leftover pizza he found in the refrigerator and headed off to school.

Not, he decided, because of any fear of the sheriff, but because he wanted to see what Kristi Norton looked like in dry clothes.

As he parked his pickup where the dirt road met County Road 111, he watched the sun rise and waited for the school bus. He thought about Kristi for the hundredth time. He doubted he'd be able to see her bra in dry clothes and he was pretty positive she wouldn't hold his hand, but still, he needed to see her again.

Since the night of the storm when her family had found the body in Ransom Canyon, she'd slowly become more fantasy than reality in his thoughts. If he went another week without seeing her, he might not recognize the real girl when he did finally bump into her.

The bus almost didn't brake as it passed his stop. The driver was fifty feet down the dirt road before she could stop.

"Hell," Thatcher yelled as he climbed on. "Is this

part of Phys Ed class that I have to run to chase the damn bus down!"

The driver had her headphones on. She just waved him in.

Thatcher looked around. Two kids in middle school were trying to make out in the very back seats. From the looks of it they had no idea what they were doing, but Thatcher was no expert. In the middle of the bus were half a dozen older girls, probably fifteen or sixteen. They appeared to be trading makeup as they all talked at once. The few others scattered about were either reading or sleeping—in other words, trying to be invisible.

Not wanting to draw attention, Thatcher sat down in the second seat beside a tiny little girl who looked too young to be on the bus.

She stared up at him without fear as she raised one finger. "If Mizz Tiffee had heard you, she would have kicked you off of the bus for cussing."

He glared at the fairy of a girl. "You are not even old enough to go to school, so why are you on this bus?" He was surprised she knew enough words to talk in sentences.

"I am five and a half. I'm in kindergarten. There is no cussing or fighting on this bus."

Great, Thatcher thought, the tiny kid knew more about the bus rules than he did. "What's your name?"

"Lillie Collins. If you bother me in any way, I'm supposed to scream and tell Mizz Tiffee."

Thatcher frowned. "What if you bother me?" He noticed a sign behind the driver that said Your driver is Miss Tiffany today.

Tiny Lillie turned her pigtails from one side to the

other and finally said, "Then you scream and tell Mizz Tiffee."

"Good plan." He glanced back. There were at least ten seats between them and all the other kids. "You don't know anyone on this bus, do you, Lillie?" It was March and he'd never seen her ride before.

She shook her head. "When we lived in town, my daddy took me to school, but my daddy says we live too far out for him to do it everyday so I have to ride the bus sometimes. I don't have a momma." Big tears floated in her eyes.

"Don't worry about it, kid. I don't have a dad."

"You don't?"

"Nope." He smiled at her. "You want to know something else?"

She nodded.

"I don't have any friends on this bus, either. How about you and me decide to be friends? When I get on the bus, I'll wave and say 'Hi, Lillie,' and when you get off you tell me to have a nice day."

She thought about it for a minute, than said, "I don't ride the bus on Thursdays and Fridays. I stay in town."

Thatcher shrugged. "That's all right. I don't usually go on those days anyway."

When the bus pulled to a stop between the high school and the grade school across the street, he got off first and smiled as she yelled for him to have a nice day.

Miss Tiffany took off her headphones and told Lillie that she had to walk her into her classroom. Thatcher watched them go. When the little fairy glanced back at him, she looked as if she was about to cry. He made a funny face and Lillie smiled. Then, she waved until she disappeared behind the doors.

Thatcher grinned, making up his mind to keep an eye on Lillie when he could. If anyone picked on her, they'd answer to him.

As the first bell sounded, he heard laughter coming from a few feet to his left.

Thatcher turned. Standing there, smiling, was the reason he'd come to school. Kristi Norton. Her hair was long and curly and her clothes were dry, but there she was, the girl of his dreams.

"Hello, Thatcher," she said moving closer. "I figured I'd run into you eventually. The school's not that big."

He just stood there. He'd lost the ability to talk. Hell, if he didn't act fast his muscles would die on him soon. Brain activity was already questionable.

Kristi didn't seem to notice that he'd turned into a short flagpole. She giggled and took his hand. "We'd better run or we'll be late."

Then they were running up the steps and down the hall. She let go of his hand when he turned one direction and she turned the other.

"See you at lunch," she yelled a moment before she disappeared.

Thatcher stopped moving when he realized she was in the sophomore hall and his classes were in the freshman hall. He had no doubt she was smarter than him, but she was also older. She'd never talk to him at lunch. He might as well stop dreaming about it happening.

As he walked to his first class, he swore under his breath. No one seemed to notice. No one talked to him anyway. As usual, he was simply a nobody who walked the halls.

Maybe Kristi just wanted to make fun of him at lunch. He'd always been that odd kid who didn't fit into any group, didn't have any friends. Why should this day be different?

He didn't watch TV, or have a cell phone or play any games. He could count the number of movies he'd seen on his fingers. He always missed the first week of school because the teacher would have them write about where they went on vacation. His mother never worked anywhere long enough to get one and if she did ever take a vacation he doubted she'd take him along.

Kristi would probably act as though she didn't know him next time. No, that didn't make sense; she could have done that before school.

Maybe she wanted to be his girlfriend. After all, she did hold his hand. He'd never had a girlfriend. He had no idea how to act or what to say.

Hell, the little fairy on the bus probably knew more about it than he did. All he knew for certain was the proper way to act had nothing to do with what he saw at home.

He found his backpack and books in his locker. *Damn, damn*, he swore as he walked into his class. He'd have to stay around until lunch and see what was going on. If Kristi made fun of him, it would hurt a little, but he could handle it. If she talked to him, he'd do his best to at least nod.

He sat down in the back and decided to pay attention in class for a change. After all, Kristi might say something about what he'd learned.

The morning seemed endless. By lunch, he'd

started worrying whether he'd have the ability to eat in front of her. When he headed into the cafeteria, a line of little kids was passing by like a centipede.

"Hi, That." One of them raised her hand.

He laughed. "Hi, Flower."

Lillie giggled as she passed, but he heard her telling the little girl behind her that he was her friend.

Thatcher was still smiling when he looked across the room and saw Kristi Norton. She looked even more beautiful, if that was possible. She was carrying a tray and nodded toward a table.

He nodded back, guessing she wanted him to get his food and join her. This was hard to figure out. Suddenly, he was Columbus without a map.

A few minutes later he sat down across from her.

She smiled. "You only got pie, Thatcher. Correction, three slices of pie."

He looked down at his tray. "I like pie." He thought of adding that he liked her, too, but that might be too much. "I'll share."

She reached across the space between them and handed him half of her sandwich. "You like tuna?"

"Sure."

"Good." She nodded toward his tray. "I like chocolate."

Then, a few minutes later, he learned his first fact about girls.

If you listened, they didn't seem to notice that you didn't talk. She told him about how she liked the school and how tough it was having a father for a principal and how she loved this girl's hair and wished hers looked like that girl's. She even told him she never wanted to be a cheerleader, which Thatcher would have never thought to ask.

As they finished off the third slice of pie, Thatcher managed to say, "I like your hair just the way it is."

Right then he learned his second fact about girls. One compliment is all it takes to make them smile.

CHAPTER ELEVEN

Jubilee
March 10

JUBILEE STOOD IN the dawn darkness of her bedroom and watched Charley moving around down by the barn. He'd worked for her for over two weeks and she still didn't feel as though she knew him. What she did know was that he worked hard and never wasted time with compliments or lies. She liked that about him. Honesty was rare in her world.

At over six feet and void of fat, there was a grace in his movements, but everything else about Charley Collins's appearance bothered her. She'd spent six years dressing for success. Dressing her candidate to be polished. Measuring the worth of a man by the cut of his suit.

Charley's hair was a month or two past needing a cut. None of his clothes looked as if they'd ever seen an iron. He was the total opposite of the men she'd known in DC. She couldn't even imagine him in a suit.

When they'd first met, she'd thought he'd be hard to get along with, maybe even a little chauvinistic, but he wasn't. Oh, he was headstrong, but he was also kind. He never pointed out her weaknesses or failures. She'd spent years working with political sharks who, at the first sign of weakness, could smell blood in the water. Maybe that was why she'd always picked easygoing men to date who let her set all the rules.

Charley didn't fit into either type.

Jubilee remembered the morning she'd felt the need to tell him that wash-and-wear was just a suggestion and he'd promptly told her to mind her own business. Dressing for success evidently wasn't his thing. They talked over everything about the ranch, though, but her word wasn't law. Most of the time they argued it out, and he won as often as she did.

And he was a great father to Lillie. This down-on-his-luck drifter who didn't own a bed to sleep in was the best father she'd ever seen. He was strict, had rules he expected even a five-year-old to follow, but no one could miss the love in his eyes when he looked at his daughter.

Jubilee had to wonder what it would have been like to have grown up with that kind of love.

She moved closer to the window as first light crept across the land behind the barn. "You're not like any man I've ever known," she whispered to his shadow circling the still dark barn. "If ever there was a man who wasn't my type, you're him. Bossy, headstrong, impatient." All the other men she'd gotten to know well enough to sleep with were calm. Nothing was ever worth fighting over. They'd always simply left. But not Charley; he'd argue his point of view to the end and she had a feeling that if he did leave, he'd have plenty to say on his way out.

The man was exhausting, but she knew without any doubt that she'd never be able to get this place in shape without him. The first few days she'd had to fight to get him to show her how everything was done, but finally they'd begun to work as a team. Their breakfasts were strategy sessions using both their strengths.

As she tugged on yesterday's jeans and shirt, Jubilee decided he was rubbing off on her. She was becoming a bum. No more silk blouses. No navy or black suits. No heels. The people in the campaign office wouldn't recognize her now.

She barely recognized herself in the mirror. She'd started braiding her hair to keep it out of the way. Her face and arms were tanned and freckles brushed across her nose. Though she tried to remember to wear a hat, her hair now had streaks of sunshine in the color her sister had always called dirty blond.

After pulling on her boots, Jubilee brushed her teeth and headed down to make breakfast. After a week of cereal, she'd figured out how to make pancakes. It really wasn't that hard—just shake the plastic bottle, add milk, shake again, and pour. Bacon was even easier. Buy precooked and microwave it for twenty seconds.

Of course she had to buy a microwave first, then mattress covers, rugs, pillows, shower curtains, towels and bedspreads for all the bedrooms no one used. The little touches upstairs made the house seem brighter. At night, when she couldn't sleep, she'd bring down antiques from the attic and decorate each room in which it looked as though Levy hadn't stepped foot since she'd left that summer years ago.

She'd found trunks of beautiful quilts and handmade lace that was spider-web fine. She'd discovered a box of dolls with porcelain faces and hands.

Levy had showed them to her that summer and said she could have them if she still played with dolls.

When she shook her head, he'd handed her a hundred-dollar bill and drove her to Walmart. "Buy what you need. If you're too old for dolls, I have no idea what you want."

"Can I fix my room up?" she'd asked.

"Anyway you want, missy. You're the one who has to sleep in it."

At eleven years old, she'd bought the wrong size sheets, way too many washcloths and enough shampoo to last years. But she'd had great fun decorating her room with old blankets and furniture she'd found scattered around in the house.

Now she could decorate the entire house. She was home.

A noise from the barn pulled her away from being Martha Stewart.

She reached the porch just as Charley ran out of the barn and headed to his house.

"Lillie!" he shouted as if calling an alarm.

Jubilee took off toward him but he reached his front door at a full run. Something was very wrong.

She almost made it to their porch when he rushed back outside, his daughter on one arm and a rifle on the other.

He stormed toward Jubilee, but his voice was surprisingly calm. "Take Lillie inside your place. There's something in the barn I'm going to have to deal with before I come back to get her."

Jubilee opened her mouth to ask questions, but the look in his eyes frightened her more than his words. She took the girl and tried to keep panic from spilling into her words. "Sure. We'll make pancakes."

Jubilee talked to Lillie all the way back to her

kitchen. The little angel had eaten breakfast with them twice before. Usually, when she stayed on the ranch, she was up earlier and Charley fed her before he drove her down to the ranch gate where she caught the bus. Today something had kept Charley in the barn longer than usual.

"Are you really cooking pancakes?" Lillie asked.

"Do you like pancakes?"

"Yes, with blueberries inside and strawberry jam on top."

"I might need some help." Jubilee had never tried them with blueberries. After all it wasn't in the recipe on the box.

A few minutes later, as she poured the pancakes out on the hot grill, Lillie dropped the blueberries in the batter as they cooked.

Jubilee tried to relax and enjoy the fun, but her whole body was tense, waiting to hear a shot. She'd seen Charley carrying his rifle before. Once in the pickup when they were out on the back pasture, and once when he was cleaning it on his porch on a night Lillie had stayed in town. He'd told her it was simply a tool that was around every ranch, but she still didn't like seeing it.

Now all kinds of possibilities of what might be in the barn ran through her mind. A coyote, maybe, or a mountain lion. They had seen tracks of a lion in the mud near the pass. A snake, maybe. Or the killer of the man someone had found in the canyon might be hiding out in the loft. After all, he hadn't been caught.

The awareness of how isolated they were out here settled over her like a wet blanket. She'd never even heard the phone ring. Even if someone could find the place, whoever was hurt would be in grave danger. And if a killer was on the property, they'd have to deal with him themselves.

By the time they had breakfast ready, Jubilee wasn't sure who was keeping whom calm. Lillie made her laugh with her story of the dangers of the playground and how a third grader had told her the janitor was really a zombie.

When Jubilee moved a foot away to reach for milk, Lillie flipped a pancake on the floor and said that it had escaped.

Jubilee saw the mischief in her sparking eyes and decided to play along.

Finally, Charley stepped through the door. Slowly, as if it were simply a routine, he lifted his rifle and slid it onto a shelf above the door's frame.

"Everything all right?" she said as she tried to meet his eyes, but he was looking only at his daughter.

He nodded to Jubilee. "Breakfast ready?"

She smiled. "I had help this morning. Your daughter is a great cook."

Lillie was busy spreading jam on her pancakes and rolling them up with one slice of bacon in the middle. "I had to show her how to make pancake rollups, Daddy."

Jubilee passed him a cup of coffee and they all sat down as if they'd done so for years. Halfway through the meal Jubilee realized something. Charley was a different man around his daughter. Kind, funny, loving. The hardness about him had vanished.

She thought about how her father had been when she was growing up. He considered mealtime as a captive opportunity to lecture and criticize. Jubilee was his favorite target. If all was right with politics on the six o'clock news, her father would turn his attention to what was wrong with his youngest daughter. The meal and the lecture usually ended with him telling her to try and be more like her sister.

But Charley had Lillie laughing when he made a face as he bit into a blueberry. "Who put blueberries in my pancake? Everyone knows I hate blueberries."

Lillie giggled. "They just fell in there, Daddy. It rains blueberries sometimes."

Charley kept complaining as he finished his breakfast making up all kinds of stories about how blueberries might kill him. Lillie just laughed.

Finally, he stood and faced Jubilee. "Thanks for the fine breakfast."

His first compliment ever, she thought.

"I'll take Lillie to school. I'm afraid we missed the bus this morning." He met Jubilee's gaze. "We'll talk when I get back. Looks like rain coming in from the north. You might want to stay out of the barn until I get back."

She offered another idea. "How about I ride along with you? I need to stop by the post office and pick up my mail. If it rains we might get more done in town than here. We can talk while we run errands."

"Suit yourself."

A few minutes later with Lillie between them, they flew down the back road while Lillie told them about a boy she met on the bus called That.

"Any chance his name might be Thatcher?" Charley asked as he pulled up at the school.

"It might be." Lillie climbed over her father with backpack and lunchbox in hand.

Charley ignored all the elbows and knees as he kissed her forehead and said, "Tell Thatcher to drop by after school. I'd like to talk to him."

"I will, if I see him." Then she was running toward the door.

Jubilee smiled. "She's precious."

"Yeah, she is."

"Would you mind it if I asked where her mother is?"

Charley didn't look comfortable, but he answered, "We got married not long out of high school. I thought I could go to college and be a father. Turned out, she was the one who didn't want to be tied down at nineteen. She lasted almost a year, then she left me for parts unknown."

"She left Lillie, too?"

He stared out at the schoolyard. "Said she wasn't the type to be a parent. Claimed she never wanted kids, though she'd never mentioned it before." He stared at the door where Lillie had disappeared. "Surprisingly, I did, from the moment they put Lillie in my arms. I couldn't turn away from her even if it meant going to school, working two jobs and staying up with her at night. I seem to do a great job of screwing my life up, but one thing I try to get right. Loving Lillie."

Jubilee knew that if he'd been taking odd jobs when they met, he must have been struggling. But he worked hard, and now she saw the reason.

Jubilee whispered as if Lillie might still be able to hear, "What was in the barn?"

"A bull snake," he answered softly. "Until I got a good look, I feared it might be a rattler. Biggest one I've seen in years."

She shivered. "Did it matter what kind it was? I hate snakes. How'd you get rid of it? I didn't hear a shot."

"I wouldn't shoot it. I just trapped it. Bull snakes eat mice. They generally don't bother cattle or horses except in barns. They'll make the horses nervous. I thought I'd give it to the kid, Thatcher."

Jubilee smiled. "I'm sure his mother will be tickled to hear the boy has a new pet."

Charley, for once, smiled back. "I don't think she'll mind. From what I hear she's dating a man who could pass for a bull snake."

Jubilee thought of asking him if he dated, but somehow that was far too personal a question. Besides, she knew the answer. From what she'd seen the past few weeks, Charley was either working or with his daughter. The man had no time in his life for anyone else. Maybe he had a midnight lover he visited now and then. Women in town would line up for that job.

"Thanks for taking care of the snake," she said, meaning every word. "Poisonous or not, it would have scared me to death."

He grinned as if he thought she was joking. "Just part of the job, boss."

He started the pickup and didn't say a word when she got out a few blocks later to check the mail at the tiny post office on Main.

When she returned empty-handed, he didn't comment, just put the truck in reverse and headed out.

Jubilee flipped the sun visor down as they turned east. Folded envelopes and pieces of paper tumbled down on her. "What's this?" she said picking up the papers.

"Notes I've made on what we need on the ranch.

Things I want to talk to you about when we get a little money coming in. I'm trying to get them in order of what we have to have first." He laughed. "I don't want to hit you with too many things at once. You might bolt. I'm guessing money is tight with you, Jubilee. Everything I buy, you ask if it was really necessary."

She had done just that. Always keeping tabs on every expense and trying to guess what came next. It surprised her that he must have been trying to calculate on the other end, only, like her, he was doing it blind. He didn't know how much he had to spend and she didn't know how much she needed to buy.

"Pull in at the bank." She pointed to the small bank across from the town's only grocery store. "I'm about to prove to you how crazy I am."

He turned in and parked as if planning to wait for her again. When he cut the engine and she didn't reach for the door handle, he shifted to face her.

She held her head high as she always did when addressing a campaign board meeting. "If we're to make this ranch work, we have to use both our strengths and I have to trust you."

He didn't move and showed no sign of looking as if he believed her.

"Levy left me over a hundred thousand dollars in his ranch account and I've got close to forty of my own money to put in. I want to put your name on the account so you can buy cattle or supplies when needed. If we're going to make this ranch work, you need to know what we've got to work with. I've figured your salary for a year. That's the low-water line. Anything above that we spend as needed."

She had no doubt her suggestion shocked him, but

he did a good job of hiding his feelings. "If we fail, I'll sell out by the end of the year and go back to DC. If we show a profit, thirty percent is yours for a bonus."

Now his face looked as stormy as the sky. His fists gripped the steering wheel so hard his knuckles turned white. "What's the catch, Jubilee? Folks in this part of the country are not long on trust when it comes to me, and this deal sounds too fair to be real."

His words told her more about Charley Collins than all the others he'd said in the weeks she'd known him. He'd been shot out of the saddle before, had dreams promised that never happened. She guessed that he'd had others not believe in him for so long he had trouble believing in himself.

"All I'm offering is a possibility. I need you to make this place work. I've overheard folks in the post office and grocery store whisper about me. They all think I'm a nitwit for even trying to make a go of a ranch. I'm smart enough to know that I don't know enough but I think I'm a pretty good judge of character. If we fail, then it couldn't have been done. If we succeed, it'll take us both working together."

A corner of his mouth rose slightly in a hint of a grin. "Maybe we're both nuts, but if you're serious, I'm in. We play this to the end and we walk away friends or we double the bank account in a year. Either way, I want to say thanks to you for giving me this chance."

For a few moments they just stared at each other, knowing that this would change things, then she lifted the handful of notes he'd stuffed in the visor. "We go over these today. We each get a vote. Fifty-fifty."

"What if it's a tie? You win, right, it's your money."

She shook her head. "It's Levy's money. If we cross on any issue, big or small, we flip for it. Fair enough."

"Agreed. I won't write a check over a hundred without calling you."

"I've already thought about that. We have to work together. We have to trust each other."

They both stepped out of the pickup and headed into the bank. In ranch terms, a hundred thousand dollars wouldn't buy much, but it might buy her a chance. She was betting it all on one man whose only reference seemed to be that he loved his daughter.

Ten minutes later they walked out, and the Lone Heart Ranch had two signers on the account. Chance walked a little taller, maybe because they both knew he'd stepped out of being a hired hand and now was a real ranch manager, even if the ranch was small.

All the way home, as thunder rumbled and lightning flashed, they talked as fast as dueling banjos. Rain started as they turned into the gate. Without any discussion, they ran toward her porch, shaking off the water like wet dogs.

She made coffee as he went over his lists. By the time she handed him a cup, he'd spread a map of the ranch out on the table.

While she studied the map, he disappeared and returned with a towel. Drifting it over her shoulder, he faced her as he tugged her hair free of the towel.

"Thanks." She'd been so excited she hadn't realized she was shivering.

"You're welcome," his voice softened slightly before he turned back to business. "We'll need a little tractor. Something to plow your garden and use in the barn. Something small enough to load in the truck if I need it out on the land."

"But we've got a huge old tractor," she commented as she sat beside him at the table and not across from him.

"It'll pay for itself in time saved." He bumped her leg with his and neither acted as if they noticed. "With twelve horses in the barn there's a great deal of shit to move. And I mean that literally. The horses' fees will give us a monthly operating budget that'll cover headquarter bills, but, if we do this right, we'll need most, if not all, of Levy's bank account to make it to the fall."

"Then we use it. I'll take care of the books for the horses being boarded to save you time, and if you'll teach me, I'll help with the care. That will save an hour of your time a day."

"Fair enough." He grinned. "You may want to take your shower after we work with the horses every morning."

"Maybe I'll just stand in the rain." She bumped her knee against his leg and they began work.

That was it, she realized. They'd become partners. Two people totally different who both swore they didn't need any help. She'd given him what he'd needed—trust—and in return she'd earned his respect. He wasn't arguing points now; he was explaining, and for the first time she was really listening.

As the morning aged they talked about all the possibilities and she found Charley was more conservative with old Levy's money that she was. Any doubt that she'd done the right thing vanished.

They made sandwiches at noon. He folded his in a

paper towel and grabbed a bottle of water as she picked up her sandwich. "I'd better head down to the road so I can be waiting for Lillie when she gets off the bus."

"Mind if I tag along?" Jubilee asked.

"You'll get wet."

She looked down at her wrinkled clothes. "So?" She folded her lunch in a towel and grabbed a root beer. "We'll have a picnic while we wait."

They laughed as they ran to his truck. For the first time in longer than she could remember, she felt young. Twenty-six should still be a wild, free time, but somehow Jubilee felt as though she'd been trying to act older all her life. As mature as her big sister, as serious about school as her dad thought she should be, old beyond her years so she'd get respect. She'd even dressed like a woman in her forties: she wore her hair up, bought practical shoes.

She shivered and he cranked up the heater in the truck. He glanced over at her. "Your hair curls when it's wet."

"Just wait. As it dries it'll frizz like I've been struck by lightning."

He drove slowly down the flooded road. "There is something I need to say to you. I've been thinking about it since that day we rode out to the pass."

"All right."

"You need to know." He didn't look at her. "When I helped you on the horse I didn't mean anything by touching you. I just wanted to get you up fast and when you bumped into me coming out of the saddle, I didn't plan that, either."

She kept her gaze on the windshield wipers splashing water back and forth. "I may have overreacted.

Could we just forget it and start over like it never happened?"

He shook his head. "We'll be working together. You're a beautiful woman. If we happen to bump into each other, I want you to know I'm not flirting."

She frowned, not knowing whether to be flattered he thought she was beautiful or irritated that he would never flirt with her.

He slowed the truck in the middle of the road a few feet from where the county road connected. "Storm's getting worse. Once we get back we'd be wise to stay inside till it stops."

A few minutes later the bus rattled down the road. Charley grabbed his rain slicker from behind the seat and climbed out. He was waiting in the rain when the bus door opened.

Lillie jumped into his arms.

Jubilee saw the kid named Thatcher standing just behind Lillie. He yelled something at Charley. Charley nodded at Thatcher and nodded toward the pickup.

Jubilee opened her door to welcome Lillie and was surprised to have Thatcher rush in, as well. Suddenly, they were all four crammed into the cab of the pickup with Lillie in her lap. Everyone seemed to be talking at once as they bumped toward home.

Thatcher told them that as soon as he heard Charley wanted to see him, he decided to catch the first bus home. No sense wasting his time in school when all he'd be thinking about was how Charley needed him.

"Things seem to happen during storms," Thatcher shouted over the thunder. "Last time it rained like this I had to help the sheriff investigate a body found in the canyon. Didn't matter how hard it rained, me and the sheriff were out there working."

Charley pulled up to his house and jumped out. When he reached for Lillie, he yelled over the rain at Jubilee. "Come on in, if you like. As soon as I take Lillie in I need to show Thatcher something in the barn before we dry off. Thought you might like to keep Lillie company for a few minutes."

Jubilee nodded and rushed into the house. She hadn't been inside since the day she'd delivered the bed. Everything was in order. For such a complicated man, Charley lived a very simple life.

The cowboy sat his tiny daughter on the couch. Thatcher waited at the door, obviously not sure if he was invited in.

"Light the fireplace," Charley said to Thatcher. "The first thing I do when Lillie gets home is to make her a snack. I'm glad you can join her for snacktime today, Jubilee. Thatcher, you and I can take care of a little business while the ladies have a tea party." He winked at Jubilee and she laughed.

Thatcher struck a match to the waiting fireplace, then followed Charley out before the room had time to warm.

Jubilee stared helplessly at Lillie. "I have no idea how to have a tea party. Can you help me?"

She giggled. "Neither does my daddy. My grandmother says a proper tea party should have tea, but I always have juice and cookies."

Ten minutes later, Thatcher and Charley joined them. No one seemed to notice the teacups had juice or that half the party guests were dripping wet. They all sat around an old trunk that doubled as a coffee table in front of the fireplace.

"That," Lillie asked, very politely, "do you have snacks when you get home from school?"

"Never have, but it seems like a good idea. I'll mention it to my mom when she gets home. She left a few days ago with her new boyfriend. He's a long-haul trucker."

"When will she be back?" Jubilee asked.

"A month, maybe more," he said as he shoved his long hair out of his eyes and reached for his fourth cookie.

Jubilee looked over Lillie's head at Charley and swore she could read his mind. He was about to take Thatcher under his wing.

Jubilee realized it didn't matter how he dressed or even if he cut his hair. Charley Collins was a good man and that was all she really needed to know.

CHAPTER TWELVE

Thatcher
March 10

AFTER HIS FIRST tea party was over Thatcher went outside to watch the rain. Lillie was playing with her dolls and Charley was talking about ranching with Jubilee, which Thatcher decided might be a year-long lecture. She was green. He'd bet five bucks she didn't know how to skin a rabbit.

He looked at the barn and smiled. Charley had trapped a bull snake that had to be six feet long in the barn earlier. One of the horses the ranch boarded had been bit by a rattler and was skittish about snakes, even the ones that didn't have rattles. Bull snakes kept the rat population down and were known to eat a rattlesnake now and then, but they still weren't welcome around most horses.

Thatcher said he'd take the snake down by the creek near his place and set it free if they would let him hunt rattlers on their place. Old man Hamilton never liked him hunting on Lone Heart Ranch. Maybe because, with his temperament, Levy considered the snakes kin. This land was bound to be rich hunting.

Thatcher grinned. He'd need the extra money now that he was buying lunch regularly. Kristi Norton was something, but having a girlfriend would be expensive. She was smarter than him, talked to him as if they were already friends and was all the way filled out to be almost a woman. Girls didn't come any better than that.

Thatcher could see new clothes in his future. She was bound to notice that he only owned three shirts good enough to wear to school.

Staring through the sheet of rain flowing off the porch roof, he thought of asking her to marry him. After all, they'd had lunch together for almost a week. But it might be too soon. He needed to start planning first, and second, he'd need money—a lot of money—if he were to get married. If it happened he sure wasn't bringing her back to the Breaks to live.

Plus there was always the possibility that she'd figure out how dumb he was and start inviting someone else to sit with her. Or, worse, the teachers would start noticing he was hanging around school more and decide to try and teach him something.

Thatcher had to stop his worrying when someone opened the screen door behind him.

"Storm lightening up?" Charley asked.

"Nope. I'm thinking that dirt road from here to the pavement is a river by now. I'd be safer to ride a horse home. I could bring him back tomorrow."

Charley shook his head as he sat down on the porch bench next to him. "I got a better idea. Why don't you just stay here? No one is waiting up for you. I've got plenty of supper to share and you won't want to eat much breakfast after you taste Jubilee's cooking."

Thatcher had to swallow hard to keep from jumping up and cheering. He'd been eating beans every night for a week. As slow as he could manage, he nodded. "You may be right. That may be a better idea. I appreciate the offer."

Both men stretched out their long legs almost to the rain and did what country folks do. They talked about the weather and horses.

Eventually the conversation moved around to the body left in Ransom Canyon. It seemed everyone in town had a theory of how it got there. Drug dealers dropping off their trash from Chicago, or a fight in some bar in Lubbock or Amarillo killed the guy and for some reason the murderer wanted the body dropped off.

"It'll probably always be a mystery," Charley finally said.

"Nope. I'm going to help the sheriff work on it." Thatcher seemed determined. "He's my friend, you know, and I can tell it's twitching at him like fleas on a backbone."

Charley laughed. "You may be right."

Thatcher leaned closer and lowered his voice. "You think a man like Sheriff Brigman has a secret? A real secret, like he'd lock away in a drawer?"

"Probably. I think any man who lives to be over thirty probably has a few secrets. Maybe more than would fit in a drawer."

"You have any secrets? Tell me one."

Charley shook his head. "If I told you, That, they wouldn't be secrets. But all things a man keeps to himself aren't bad. Some are just dreams he doesn't want to share."

Thatcher nodded and leaned against the house.

When it started to grow dark, they moved into the

house. Charley pulled a couple of bags of chili from the freezer. While they warmed, he made cornbread and then served the feast with buttermilk. It was the best meal Thatcher could ever remember having.

They all seemed to talk at once as they crowded around the little card table. Lillie made a buttermilk mustache and everyone else followed suit. Thatcher could never remember laughing so hard.

After supper they watched the fire and Charley tried to teach Jubilee to play poker. Everyone, including Lillie, was better at it than she was. But she was a good sport. When she lost her last toothpick, she offered to do the dishes.

Charley whispered just loud enough for her to hear, "That, did you notice the dry spell we've been having ended about the time Jubilee showed up?"

"What do you think that means?" Thatcher played along.

Charley leaned in as if their conversation wasn't being heard from the kitchen. "Maybe when the Lord saw Jubilee heading toward Texas He figured He'd better send the rain along. Wouldn't be fair to send two plagues at once."

"I heard that." Jubilee laughed. "Just for that crack you have to dry while I wash."

Charley complained, but he didn't hesitate.

Thatcher sat on the floor playing High Card with Lillie and listened to them talk in the kitchen ten feet away. He leaned his head against the couch and took a long, slow breath. Their low conversation reminded him of music so far away he couldn't make out all the words, but he knew it must be a good song.

When they returned to the living room, Jubilee

brought marshmallows, chocolate bars and graham crackers. Charley held up wire coat hangers he'd straightened out.

"Look, That," Lillie squealed. "We're about to have dessert."

Lillie burned her marshmallows and ate her father's. Jubilee had trouble getting the toasting down. She insisted her marshmallow be perfectly browned all around before she smashed it between the crackers. Thatcher ate so many he decided that if the marshmallows expanded in his stomach, he'd explode.

Finally, Jubilee made him a bed on the couch while Charley put Lillie to sleep. Thatcher picked a book off a small shelf just to have something to do.

"Do you like Westerns?" Charley asked when he walked back into the room.

"Never read one," he answered.

"You're welcome to try that one. It's about a guy who loves rodeo. It's by a real cowboy named Dusty Richards. I'm guessing he's written over a hundred by now and is still writing."

Thatcher, to be polite, nodded and curled under his blanket. "I'll give it a try."

"You do that." Charley laughed as if he didn't believe him. "I'm going to walk Jubilee home."

"I'll be fine," Jubilee said.

Charley shook his head. "Humor me. If you go out there in the rain alone, I won't sleep for worrying about you stuck knee-deep in mud." He lifted his slicker from a hook by the door. "I'll walk you to your porch."

"What if you fall on the way back and get stuck?"

"I'll call when I get back." He patted his pocket.

"After I grab my new cell from where I left it on your kitchen table."

He held the wet slicker up like a wilted umbrella and she joined him beneath the coat.

Thatcher could hear them laughing as they ran into the rain.

He opened the book and began to read. He knew he'd remember every detail of this night forever. This was normal. How folks acted. And this was nothing like he'd ever known.

But it was waiting for him in the future. He'd make it happen someday.

CHAPTER THIRTEEN

Charley
March 10

As they stepped off the porch into the mud Charley slipped his arm around Jubilee's waist so they wouldn't keep bumping together.

She did the same, pulling close against him.

Her tall, lean body fit nicely against his as they slowed their pace in the dark spot between his porch light and hers. Neither said a word, but he guessed she felt as good as he did about being so close.

The day together had changed things. There was more than just a trust between them. He'd grown to really like her. She wasn't crazy; she was just scared.

When they reached her porch, she sat down on the top step and tugged off her boots. "Thanks," she whispered. "Tonight was fun. Best time I've had in a long time."

"I doubt chili and cornbread can compare to a fancy restaurant, and toasting marshmallows isn't exactly a wild party."

"Oh, but it was. I think I still have a piece of marshmallow on my cheek."

He turned and brushed his thumb over the white

spot on the left side of her face. When he licked the tip of his thumb, he winked at her. "Still warm."

Her brown eyes widened in surprise, or maybe something else. He hadn't meant it as flirting, but it took all his strength to keep from closing the distance between them and seeing if her lips tasted the same as her marshmallow cheek.

Charley leaned back against the post. "Why'd you say this place was your last chance? You must have had a career in DC." He didn't know if she'd open up, but he had to give it a try.

"I lost my job. I ran political campaigns and my third candidate lost. I'd worked so many hours for years I hadn't had time to spend much money so I did have savings, but it wouldn't have lasted long. No job. No future. Nowhere to go. Then I inherited this place. Last chance."

"I get it. What about the guy you mentioned you'd lived with in DC."

"He left a few months before. To tell the truth I barely noticed. As least he was nicer than the others. He didn't stop to tell me all my shortcomings before he left."

"Shortcomings. You?"

She nodded. "I'm self-centered, controlling and incapable of love. Every boyfriend I've ever had said the same thing, so it must be true. I don't have a heart."

Charley shook his head. "Impossible."

"No. It's true. I've never known a man who didn't just walk away. Just once it would be nice to meet someone who stayed."

"Did you ever ask them to?"

She shook her head. "I don't think I have enough love to give for it to be worth their trouble."

Something about the storm and the low yellow porch light cast a spell around them. They were talking, really talking for the first time.

He wanted to touch her and the need to just hold her grew inside him every day. But, she didn't move closer, not even as she opened up, telling him about her life.

He leaned back and doubled up one leg. As they laughed and shared mistakes they'd made, Jubilee kept tapping him on his knee, or patting his leg just above his boot.

Charley watched her. It seemed she was back in grade school, the way she was hitting at him. Touching would have been too personal. It might be the start of something. But a tap was all she could manage.

He didn't move away.

When the rain slowed, he stood and offered her a hand up. "I'd better get back," he said more to himself than her.

"I know, it's getting late." She didn't turn toward the door. She just stood waiting, watching him.

"Jubilee, when you know what you want, just ask." The words were out before he could stop them. He wasn't sure what he meant, he only knew he had to say them.

At least she didn't pretend they were talking about the ranch. Her brown eyes studied him a moment before she let out a sob. "I wouldn't know what to ask for."

"How about a friend, to start? I'm thinking you could use one and I'm short on them myself."

Her nod was jerky as he pulled her against him.

For a long time he just held her like he'd wanted to do for days. At first she was stiff and jerky as if fighting down tears, then slowly she relaxed and warmed against him.

"You're worth a great deal more, Jubilee, than you think." He couldn't say the words aloud, but he thought that he wanted to add that she was worth the loving.

The men who'd walked out on her had no idea who she really was.

CHAPTER FOURTEEN

Lauren
March 13

SPRING BREAK IN Crossroads, Texas, was probably the worst place a college senior could go. The weather was still too cold to wear a bathing suit. Lauren thought about her friends who'd driven down to Galveston and the ones she knew who went on a three-day cruise to Cancún. In a week they'd come back with tans and stories to tell.

Where was she? Home on the last spring break of her college career. Her mother said she needed to study for her last semester of finals. Her father always thought she should come home. Only this year he had one more reason than usual. Apparently his new research secretary was driving him crazy. He called, begging her for some relief.

Tim O'Grady had worked for her father for over a week but Pop swore it seemed like a lifetime.

"He's a writer," she insisted. "Of course his mind thinks of 'what ifs' all the time."

"He's a few bricks shy of a full load, honey." Pop insisted. "If I'm in the office he talks to me all day. If I leave, he works out theories. One day he covered an entire wall of my office with notes and pictures. Said we had to *whiteboard* the investigation. You'd think the body in the canyon was a national crisis."

So Lauren had come home, telling herself she would babysit Tim and think about what she wanted to do after she graduated. She'd saved enough birthday and Christmas money to go to Europe for a month. A few friends wanted her to tag along with them. One even had an aunt who lived in London.

But if Pop hadn't gone along with Cancún or Galveston, he probably wouldn't be thrilled about Europe.

At this point in her life, she felt she was standing at the crossroads trying decide which way to go. So, why not be in Crossroads, Texas, while she made up her mind?

As she walked into Dorothy's Café on Main Street it entered her mind that maybe she should come home and open another café in town. Maybe work as a cook first or waitress to learn the business. She'd always liked those cooking shows. Maybe that was her calling.

Only the place was empty. Bad idea to open a café in a town that couldn't even keep one busy. It was two o'clock, but surely someone would be eating late besides her and Tim.

There he was, in the last booth closest to the pass-through window at the back. When they'd been about eight or nine, Tim's mother would drop them off and let them order and eat lunch alone on Wednesdays in the summers. That was the day she taught an art class. Then her father would pick her and Tim up an hour later and claim babysitting duty for the afternoon.

Lauren remembered how big and grown-up she'd felt that first summer of having lunch on her own. Tim always ordered a cheeseburger with double fries, but she went down the menu, ordering a different meal each time.

"About time you got here," Tim said, as he unfolded from the booth and offered a quick hug.

She didn't answer; she simply stared. Since she'd left at the end of February he'd shaved, had a haircut and started dressing like a hatless Sherlock Holmes. All he needed was a pipe. "Pop says you work twelve hours a day, Tim. Aren't you afraid of too much reality?"

"I simply work until he leaves the office. He says I'm volunteering after five, but I don't care. Figuring out how this old guy died has become an obsession. The sheriff is the same way."

Lauren believed him. Unless she was at home waiting, she'd always thought her pop would see no reason to stop working. As the only lawman in town, she guessed he often worked sixty or more hours a week.

"I'm starving. Fill me in while we eat."

Tim slid in across the table from her. "At least I stop for lunch. I'm not sure the sheriff does that."

Dorothy yelled from the pass-through window. "I told the new waitress she could go get her eyes checked, so no one is going to be dropping menus off. Don't imagine you two need them anyway. Tell me what you want and I'll pass it through. You'll have to get your own drinks."

"Will do," Tim answered, "but we're not leaving a tip."

Dorothy laughed. "Like you ever do, Tim O'Grady. I'm telling you right now, when you publish a book and get rich and famous, I want one autographed free."

"Promise." He winked at Lauren and whispered, "It's the least I can do. Growing up I learned most of my R-rated language from her cooks."

A few minutes later they ordered and Tim got their drinks from behind the counter. The door chimed and two truckers came in. The sound of swearing came from somewhere in the back a moment before Dorothy rushed out to take the truckers' orders.

Tim leaned forward and started telling Lauren all the facts he'd found about the body in the canyon. It seemed as if he wasn't holding anything back. So much for classified information.

He'd been out to the Breaks that ran across county lines to the north, near where the cap rock climbed. "Not much in the way of roads that far out once you turn off County Road 111. I'm guessing some of the people who live in the brush and scrub trees are on public land, but no one bothers them. Most wouldn't talk to me until Charley Collins suggested I take that friend of yours, Thatcher Jones, along."

"He's not my friend," Lauren answered, wondering how much trouble Thatcher had gotten into since she saw him last week.

Tim laughed. "According to him, you two would be dating, but he thinks you're too old for him."

Lauren made a face.

Tim shrugged. "Whatever. Back to me and my investigation. Thatcher knew how to talk to the people out there. It's an odd community. Reminds me a little of what I'd think an outlaw camp must have been like a hundred years ago. Some folks are just scraping by, growing their own food, hunting deer and rabbits and, I suspect, an occasional rancher's calf now and then.

They trade for what they need. I doubt any of them have filed a tax return in years, but they've got their own brand of interesting."

She could see the excitement in his eyes. Apparently, a few miles from home, he'd found that another world existed.

"You wouldn't believe these characters. They're like straight out of some book. They speak a kind of old-time talk, mixing religion and superstition. It's not just that they don't have cell phones and computers— some don't even have running water. But they know things. There I was, standing in front of them with a college education, and a few looked like they felt sorry for me because I didn't know I was standing in poison ivy or had never seen a hog hanging up to bleed out." He rubbed his eyes. "That's one sight I hope I never see again."

"Did you find any clues?" She tried to get him back on track.

"Oh, the investigation. Thatcher got a few people to say they'd seen someone who fit the dead guy's description. They claim he lives far back. One remembered the two scratched-out tattoos. Another said he thought the guy grew his own pot."

"Any of them able to ID him?"

"No luck. Only name I got on him was Hubcap. They said he paints old hubcaps and mailboxes for the fall trade days. Says he does pretty good selling them, too."

"Well, at least that's a start."

When the hamburgers arrived, the subject changed to tattoo parlors. By the time they both ordered cherry pie, Tim was talking about all the ideas for stories he'd collected, and Lauren wondered if he'd even found one useful fact that might help the investigation.

When he finally ran out of steam, he leaned back and stared at her.

She swore she could almost hear his brain running. "What are you thinking, Sherlock?"

He leaned across the table. "I was running through my list. You know, that list everyone keeps in their head about what they want to do or should do or have to do before they die."

"Okay," she answered, thinking she'd forgotten to start her list.

"When I was in school I thought I was learning to write, but I was wrong. I was just beginning. What I need to know is out there in the world. I need to live, walk in others' shoes, drink deep of the good and the evil."

Lauren had followed Tim down this rabbit hole before. It never went anywhere beyond talk. One year he'd wanted to climb Denali and cross Africa. One summer he'd read all about flying and decided that as soon as he graduated, he'd join the army and fly jets.

"So, Tim, where do you want to go now?"

"Nowhere. I want to stay right here and learn to understand people better. Why they love and why they hate. Why they stay out along the Breaks when civilization is only a few miles away. Why people stay in Crossroads when the city isn't that far."

She joined in. "Why do they live in Lubbock when New York is a three-hour flight away?"

"Right. Why do they put up with the noise of a big city when they could live on a ranch right outside Crossroads?"

They both laughed. He reached across the table and took her hand and held on tight.

"How can I help?" she asked, thinking maybe they should make up a questionnaire.

Tim stared at her. "How about sleeping with me, L?"

"What?" The question blindsided her. For a moment she thought it was part of the questioning, but then she saw the look in his eyes. He wasn't just talking or kidding. Tim was serious.

"You know what I mean. We're both adults. I want to know how it would feel to have sex with a friend. We could talk about it as we did it. No mixture of love or approval or flirting. I just want to know how it feels with no emotions involved. You're my best friend. You'd be the perfect one to do it with."

Lauren felt as if they'd been sailing along on a cruise and she'd suddenly fallen off the boat into shark-infested waters. Tim had kissed her dozens of times, but not because he was attracted to her. He was just playing around.

Suddenly, the swinging door to the kitchen popped open and Dorothy stormed out. Lauren looked up and saw fire in the old woman's eyes and had no doubt she wasn't dropping by to refill drinks.

She raised a long flat skillet and thumped it against the back of Tim's head.

He yelped and let go of Lauren's hand.

Dorothy, skillet still in hand, put her fists on her hips. "Tim O'Grady, you've said some crazy things over lunch, but your idea today beats all. Everyone says you got a creative mind, but it needs a little straightening out."

Tim rubbed his head, pulling his fingers away, testing for blood. "You're stepping in on a private conversation, Dorothy. I work for the sheriff's office. I believe what you just did was assault."

"Yeah, you go report it and see what the sheriff does when you tell him what you just suggested. Bullets are bound to hurt more than my omelet skillet. You're going to die a virgin, boy, if you think any woman in the world would fall for that crap."

Lauren was choking on her laughter. "She's right, Tim."

"I guess so." He glanced at Dorothy. "She seems to feel strongly about it." He took a deep breath accepting defeat. "I'm sorry for the suggestion, L," he turned slowly to Dorothy. "Thanks for setting me straight."

"You're welcome." Dorothy lowered the skillet. "Leave a tip. Scrambling brains is extra." She walked back through the swinging door.

The two truckers dropped bills on the table and rushed out.

Lauren laughed so hard she finally had to stop or she'd throw up.

Tim left a ten-dollar tip. As they walked out, he said, "You want to come over and see what I've done on the investigation?"

"Sure." She smiled. "Still friends?"

He looked a little surprised. "Always."

She took his hand. "You're going to be a great writer, Tim. I know it."

"How?"

"Because your mind doesn't work like anyone else's."

Tim rubbed his red hair with his free hand. "Right

now, it doesn't seem to be working at all. I may have brain damage. If I die, will you cry over my grave?"

"Of course. What are friends for?"

"Don't ask me that question. Though, I have found out recently what they are not for. So much for the idea of 'friends with benefits.' Doesn't seem to be an idea that's caught on in Texas."

Lauren started giggling again. "With Dorothy around, I don't think it ever will."

CHAPTER FIFTEEN

Charley
March 16

WHEN CHARLEY STEPPED into the kitchen, the smell of cinnamon greeted him. Jubilee was trying to cook again, and he figured he'd be trying to eat whatever she mixed up by the time it was full daylight. She was gifted when it came to decorating, though. The old place had never looked so good, but cooking just didn't seem to be her thing.

He managed to get a cup of coffee and sit down before she rushed into the room with her long blond hair flying like a cape behind her. Since she'd given up the stress of the big city, it seemed as if she was getting younger. If she kept it up, he'd be raising two girls out here.

"I forgot how many minutes it said to cook the bread," she cried as she opened the oven door.

The smell of something burning drifted through the room. "I'm guessing it's done." Charley fought to hide his grin. He reached for one of the cereal boxes that were now a permanent centerpiece on Jubilee's table along with a dozen books on gardening.

"I think it's okay." She leaned down to look in the

oven, showing her backside to him. "I'll just cut the black parts off. The bread will be fine on the inside."

He watched her, guessing she was talking more to herself than to him. He liked that she did that and doubted she was even aware her words were coming out in the open. When she talked to herself, he had the advantage of knowing what she was thinking without feeling any need to participate in the conversation.

By the time she cut off the black crust, her bread loaf was the size of a stick of butter and he'd finished his first bowl of cereal. As she headed toward the table, he stood and held out her chair as if they were at a restaurant. When she sat down, he touched her shoulder. "Not bad," he managed as he looked over her head at what had once been a loaf of bread. "You'll be a great cook in no time."

As he'd seen her do a dozen times, she straightened, forced a smile and said in what sounded like an office voice, "Let's go to work. What do we talk about first? I've got some ideas on the garden. Also, we could grow tomatoes upside down from the porch. I figured out how I can be of some help with that field you want to plant and, if you make me a list, I'll pick up..."

"Slow down, Jubilee." He poured her a cup, fearing what caffeine would do to her. This was the way she was every morning lately. Wanting to run out of the gate at a full gallop. "We've got all day. It'll save time to plan a few minutes first. I thought I'd get started on a few chores in the barn if you'll drop by the vet and pick up our new boarder. A mustang mare who is in a bad way. Doc will load her for you and I'll unload—all you have to do is drive. Slow and easy. And remember to go through the cattle guards straight on or you'll hang the trailer."

"I can do that." She cut the tiny loaf and passed him half.

She'd learned to handle the stick shift in his truck, even if she did skip second every now and then. She'd offered a trade: they'd use his truck for all the ranch work and she'd pay for his gas. She claimed it would be cheaper than cleaning her car every other day.

Charley poured her cereal as if she were Lillie's age. "Eat," he insisted, noticing she'd lost weight since she'd arrived. "We've got a few lists to make before we leave this table."

She grinned. "Anyone ever tell you that you're bossy?"

"Nope," he answered, fighting down a laugh. "I bossed my little brother around for years and he didn't hear a word I preached."

"My big sister never bossed me. She was too busy ignoring me. Once my mother mentioned me and she said 'Who?' like she'd forgotten she had a sister."

Charley didn't laugh. He got the feeling Jubilee was telling the truth. He was glad they'd settled into an easy kind of peace. They had nothing in common but the work, yet it was somehow enough. He was surprised at how much he liked having someone to talk things over with. Sometimes he felt as though he'd been alone, thoughts to himself, for as long as he could remember.

The memory of how they'd talked the night it rained drifted across his mind. That had been nice. He wouldn't mind doing it again.

Just as they finished planning, the kitchen phone

rang. "Who..." Jubilee said, heading toward the phone that hadn't rung since she'd arrived.

Charley picked up his cell from the table and turned toward the door. Whoever was on the other end probably wasn't his business. Jubilee had mentioned a few times that she'd had a boyfriend in DC. Maybe the guy was missing her and wanting her back. Once she'd finally cleaned up, she wasn't at all bad looking. She was probably something all decked out in a suit and heels. Any guy in his right mind would want her back.

Charley didn't want to think about how that bothered him. She was just his boss, he reminded himself. Maybe they were friends, but that was all either of them wanted. Getting involved with her on any other level was not an option.

The memory of the rainy night flashed once more across his mind like dry lightning. She'd felt so good pressed against his side as they jogged through the mud. And for a second or two they'd stood on her porch, rain dripping off of his slicker. They both held on to the other with their free arm. For one heartbeat neither wanted to step away. Then the moment was gone.

Her voice shook him out of a memory that had haunted him all week.

"Hello." Jubilee sounded hesitant as she spoke into the phone.

"Jub!" A high-pitched voice screamed out of the phone so loud Charley heard it from the back door.

He dropped his cell back on the table and moved closer, fearing something terrible had happened. Maybe a neighbor was hurt? Maybe the school bus crashed?

"Destiny?" Jubilee whispered, panic holding to the edges of her one word.

Charley was at her side. He relaxed. Destiny was her sister. Nothing to do with the ranch or him.

He took a deep breath and looked down at Jubilee. Fear still danced in her pretty brown eyes. His hand rested on her waist in an offer of support.

"Of course it's me!" the voice yelled back from the phone. "I've been looking for you for hours. I thought I'd get to Grandda's farm early this morning, but apparently Google can't even find the place. It is so like him to have a farm literally in the middle of nowhere. Dad always said he was a crazy old goat."

Jubilee stared at Charley and he swore he saw a cry for help in those eyes he'd grown used to watching.

He made no pretense of not having heard Destiny's side of the conversation. Leaning in an inch from Jubilee's free ear, he whispered in mock confusion, "Who is Google? And who the hell is Grandda?" Levy would roll over in the ground if he thought someone called him that. Jubilee said that when she'd lived with him he'd insisted on her calling him Levy.

Jubilee pushed him a few inches away and giggled. Her hand remained in the center of his chest as if she needed a bit of his strength when she turned her attention back to the phone.

"Where are you, Destiny?"

"I'm in some dump of a diner in some nothing of a little town." Her voice lowered slightly. "Can you believe that this town doesn't even have a Starbucks? I pulled into a place across the street for directions first. When I went in what I thought was the lobby of a business, a half dozen old men tried to tell me how to get to your place and then they all voted that my Cooper would never make the road. Too muddy. Can you believe that? You've moved somewhere too muddy to even drive to."

Jubilee held the phone with one hand as she rubbed her temple with the other. Then, as if it was her usual routine, she placed her hand back on Charley's chest and began to play with one of the snaps on his Western shirt.

He listened to the most damning description of his town that he'd ever heard, then raised his hand. His finger gently covered Jubilee's. "I'll take care of this," he whispered. "Do you want her here, or gone?"

Jubilee covered the bottom half of the phone. "She won't leave until she says whatever she's come to say. Would you go get her?"

"The horse trailer's already hitched," he answered back, making his boss laugh. "I'll bring the Cooper back, too."

Now she covered her mouth, fighting to be silent, but giggles escaped as she stepped away.

"Jubilee!" Her sister screamed. "Are you having some kind of fit?"

Charley took over. "Destiny, this is Charley Collins, Miss Hamilton's foreman. I'll be on my way to pick you up as soon as I can. Stay where you are. And have the pancakes."

As he put the phone back in its cradle he heard her yelling, "How do you know where I am? Who are you anyway? How will I know you when you pull up? Jub has a foreman?"

Charley leaned against the wall beside his boss and

looked at Jubilee still giggling. "Does your sister ever stop talking?"

Jubilee shook her head.

"Fine," he said. "She's riding in the trailer with the horse."

There was nothing professional or reserved about Jubilee's laugh. It was full-out, tummy-holding delight. She rolled slightly closer as if they were sharing a private joke and didn't want anyone to hear.

He couldn't stop staring at how cute she looked when she laughed and decided she should do it more often. He couldn't decide if he wanted to tickle her or kiss her. Either would be most improper but right now there was very little space between them.

When she finally got under control, she tried to say calmly. "All her life Destiny has always blamed every problem in her world on someone else. She even claimed her husband was too potent and that was why she has to deal with two children in diapers. The fact that she has a live-in nanny, housekeeper and cook doesn't seem to matter."

Charley was barely following the conversation. He wanted to help, but there were a few other things he'd like to do also. He swore if Jubilee pressed her hand against the middle of his chest one more time he planned to see that there was no space between them.

She kept talking as if totally unaware of how near he was. "If I don't listen to whatever problem brings Destiny here, it will only upset my sister more."

"Then I'd better go get her." He pushed away from the wall and shoved on his hat. He needed to put some distance between Jubilee and his wild thoughts. The next time she played with one of the snaps on his shirt, he might show her just how fast the shirt would come off.

"Thanks. Whatever it is must be bad if she can't take it home for Mom and Dad to fix." She patted the wall of his chest just over his heart. "You're my hero, Charley Collins. This is above and beyond your job description."

He thought of saying that taking care of this place and her was exactly his job, but he worried it might sound too heavy. They'd come a long way in trusting each other, and he wanted to keep it comfortable between them.

He needed air. He needed distance suddenly. Hell, he needed her.

He took a few steps toward the door, then turned back. "We'll get through the visit one way or the other. If you need someone to help you bury the body, just let me know."

"Once you meet my sister you'll give up on the idea that I'm a plague. Leave her car in town. We'll blindfold her. That way she'll never know the way out here."

"I've already thought of that. See you later, boss."

Half an hour later, Charley was convinced Destiny was worse than most of the plagues Moses brought. The good news was everyone in Dorothy's Café looked happy to see her go. The bad news: she was in his truck yelling out complaints faster than a greased Gatling gun fires bullets.

"Do you ever wash the inside of this thing? I think I smell something dead. Don't roll down the window. No telling what will blow in. Doesn't the air conditioner work? Does this truck even have a seat belt? I'm not putting my purse on that floor."

He glanced at her, remembering how beautiful he'd
thought she was five minutes ago when he'd walked
into Dorothy's and saw her looking so alone. Chocolate brown hair curling down to ample breasts that
peeked out of a low-cut dress that hugged her body.
She was a polished and pampered kind of beauty.

Since she started talking, she was uglying up fast.

"Nope," he answered to pretty much everything
she said.

"I didn't think so. How far to the farm?"

"Ranch," he corrected.

"What's that noise following us? I swear it's giving me a headache on top of the one I already have."

"That's the horse I stopped by and picked up on my
way to town. She's hurt real bad and not happy to be
loaded in a trailer. She's trying to kick her way out,
but don't worry, she can't."

Destiny's head snapped to face him. The anger in
her gaze was hot enough to start a grassfire. "You
mean you stopped to pick up a horse on the way to
get me?"

"Yep," he answered. "I didn't want the horse to
have to wait."

He only glanced in her direction but he swore her
eyes rolled back in her head and steam came out of
her ears. For half a country song she was silent, and
he made the mistake of relaxing.

"What do foremen do?" Her words came fast, whip-
ping through the warm morning air.

Before he could answer, she snapped again as if
one look from him might be deadly. "Oh, never mind.
I don't care. Whatever my sister is paying you is too
much, I'm sure." She huffed. "Add one more thing

to the list of problems I'll have to straighten out. My little sister is a nitwit. She didn't need a career. I told her from the first to get married to David. But no, she wanted to work. Now she's lost any chance at a career or hooking David and I've got to save her from this mess."

He rolled down his window. Nothing flying in could be as deadly as Destiny.

With the wind blowing her hair, she went back to picking on him.

He kept driving, slow and easy so the horse wouldn't be in any more pain than she already was. The sister, on the other hand, was starting to grow horns—in his mind anyway. The first thing she'd said to him was *Where is my sister?* And she hadn't got over the answer yet.

"Does this thing go any faster?"

"Yep," he said.

She waved her hand as if she feared he'd dozed off. "Well then, go faster."

He kicked it up about five miles and stared at the road. If this woman didn't stop talking she'd be toad-ugly by the time they made it back to the ranch.

"Is it always this hot?"

"Nope." It couldn't be more than eighty, but he didn't think she'd appreciate a weather report.

She fanned herself. "What do you do on really hot days?"

"Roll down the other window."

She tried that, but when the wind blew in, she screamed and rolled it back up. "My sister has moved to hell."

Charley couldn't resist. "And you came to visit."

She glared at him. Now that her once-perfect hair was slicked back by wind, he decided she wasn't beautiful at all.

She spent the next few miles ignoring him and patting on her hair. When he pulled up to the barn and pointed to the house where Jubilee waited on the porch, she glared at him. "You've got to be kidding. You expect me to walk?"

"Mud is mostly dried," he offered. "I'll bring over your luggage as soon as I take care of the horse."

"I need it now and I'd like to be let out at the house, not a hundred feet away. Do these look like walking shoes?"

"Look, lady, I'm the foreman, not the doorman. I got a horse about to die on me if I don't get her taken care of fast. I don't really give a damn what kind of shoes you wear."

He climbed out of the truck and started working on the trailer gate, mad that he'd started cussing again when he was trying so hard to break the habit since Lillie had gotten old enough to talk and repeat everything he said.

Destiny was still sitting in the cab when Jubilee walked by her window. "Hello, sister. Make yourself at home in the kitchen. I need to help Charley with the horse."

She finally stepped out of the cab. "I've never made myself at home in the kitchen, Jub, and I can't believe the horse is more important than welcoming me."

Jubilee was helping him lead the horse out. "Welcome to my ranch. I'll be with you in a while. Right now I've got work to do that can't wait for an unscheduled visit."

Charley grinned. There was that boardroom tone he'd heard Jubilee use before. Only, thank goodness, it wasn't directed at him this time.

Complaining with every step, Destiny started across the yard between the barn and the main house. Halfway there, she stopped to make a call.

Charley walked the horse slowly into the barn with Jubilee close, her hand resting on the animal's neck. She was whispering to the mare in a gentle voice.

"Watch her right side," he said low. "She's about to foal and was hit by a stray bullet a few nights ago. The doc patched her up. She'll recover from the bullet, but he isn't sure about the colt or if the mare is strong enough to deliver and live."

Jubilee's tone matched his. "Why didn't the vet keep her?"

Charley shook his head. "He's got his hands full with three others that were shot and the colt may come early. Apparently some drunks thought they were at a shooting match. Luckily it was dark and they were drunk, but still it doesn't take any skill to hit horses in a herd."

Jubilee placed her forehead against the mare's neck and gulped down tears. "We'll take care of her, won't we, Charley? You know what to do and I'll help all I can."

"I was raised around horses, then when I was in school, I worked at the AG barns. I know what to do, but none of us know if it will work. I'm going to need your help, Jubilee, houseguest or not."

"I understand. Destiny's problems can wait."

For an hour they worked, doing everything they

could to settle the horse. Finally, when they stepped out of the stall, Jubilee lowered her head against the gate.

More out of instinct than any belief he could comfort her, Charley pulled her against his chest and held her tight. This was her first time seeing an animal in such pain, but she'd stepped up. "If the bullet hit the foal inside, they both might die during the delivery. If she doesn't take a turn for the better, Doc says I'll have to put her down. You need to understand that. It's not an easy thing to watch. I've seen seasoned cowhands cry when it happens."

"Can we put down the drunks who shot her for fun?"

He looked at her big brown eyes that were now flooded with tears. "The sheriff caught them. Vet said none could make bail so they are locked away for now. Said they were all throwing up this morning and Dan was making them clean it up."

"Good. I wish we could torture them for a while."

He kissed her forehead as if she were no older than Lillie. "We could send them Destiny. Being locked away with her might cause jailhouse suicides."

She laughed, wiped her nose on her sleeve like an adorable kid then panicked. "My sister. I forgot all about her."

Charley turned Jubilee loose. She bolted toward her house and he started cleaning up. It was going to be a long day. First, he'd have to keep checking on the mare, then try to work at both his jobs for the day and probably a few of the things Jubilee planned. She'd have her hands full with the wicked sister.

Around one Thatcher Jones showed up with Lillie. He claimed that after lunch school was just too boring to sit through. He found Charley in the barn and began helping without saying a word as to why he got off the bus at Lillie's stop.

The kid was born to the land; he knew what to do. He took over jobs Charley had delayed. After he'd fed and watered all the other horses, he hauled in hay and cleaned up the stalls.

Lillie climbed into the stall with the mare and offered her a peppermint. The mare seemed to settle. The little girl sat next to her, gently patting the horse's neck. When Charley checked on her a few minutes later, she was asleep next to the downed animal as though she understood the mare needed company.

Thatcher looked over the gate. "I've seen a child calm a horse before. It's like the mare senses her. I'll keep an eye on them both, if you like."

"I do need to get everything ready and make sure I have all the supplies. If anything changes I'll be within yelling range."

Thatcher stepped into the stall.

"You want a job, kid?" Charley asked.

"No. I just want to help. I heard about the horses being shot. It happened along the edge of Ransom Canyon where a small mustang herd runs free."

It didn't take much to put the pieces together. The shooting had happened not a mile from where the bus dropped Thatcher off. The drunks were probably Thatcher's neighbors.

"You know something about this, don't you, That?"

The boy didn't raise his head. "No. Nothing that would help the sheriff. He's already caught the fellows who did it."

Charley waited.

Finally, the kid added, "From what I heard, they weren't drunk. Word is a man living far out in the Breaks offered some men free drugs. Bad drugs. I heard one of the kids on the bus say the men weren't shooting at horses, they were firing at the demons riding them."

"Why hand out bad drugs?" Charley asked, not really expecting an answer.

"Maybe the dealer don't want no one coming into the Breaks and figured shooting horses would keep them out. Several of my neighbors said there were some suits knocking on doors asking questions about who owns the land out there. Then there is the sheriff driving by asking questions about the dead guy. Add Tim O'Grady just asking questions in general. Folks out there are starting to feel nervous."

Charley offered Thatcher a bottle of water from the fridge in the barn that stored medicine for the horses and cattle. "Who'd want to buy that land?"

Thatcher shook his head. "I don't know, or care. But my mom is still gone and I don't want to be out there alone tonight. Any chance I could stay here? I'd sleep in the barn."

"You are welcome to stay and you'll sleep on the couch. Lillie and I would be happy to have you join us for supper. Jubilee's got company so we won't be seeing her. How about I drive in and get burgers then we'll take turns staying up with Last Chance?"

Thatcher pointed his thumb at the downed mare. "That what you naming her?"

"Seems to fit," Charley answered.

"I agree. If you hadn't stepped up to take care of her, she probably wouldn't have had much of a chance." The kid studied the horse. "I feel like that sometimes. Trouble's likely to find me no matter how I try to avoid it."

"You're welcome here," Charley said again. "You're safe here."

Thatcher seemed to relax for the first time, and Charley couldn't help but wonder what else the kid knew and wasn't saying. He was afraid of something, and the boy didn't look as if he frightened easily.

CHAPTER SIXTEEN

Lauren
March 17

LAUREN SPENT HER spring break helping out at her father's office. She loved it, just as she always had. To her, the sheriff's office was the center of the town. The heartbeat. Something was always happening.

Her pop used to say that the saints had to drop by and mention how good they were and the sinners had to come in to remind you they haven't done anything lately. He guessed that priests and preachers in town had the same conversations.

Having Tim O'Grady there made it even more fun. When he was in the office he was talking, and as soon as he rushed off to investigate something Pop would always whisper, "Thank God, silence."

But she knew her father. If Tim wasn't helping, he'd be gone. With every case, from parking tickets to the body left in the canyon, Tim had theories. His mind was a jackrabbit on speed.

The minute the sheriff came down from checking on the drunks housed in the tiny jail on the second floor, Tim asked, "How about letting me talk to the Dulapse brothers. I hear they want to visit the drunks."

"No."

"But Thatcher introduced me to them one day last week." Tim pleaded his case. "They weren't too friendly but still, they'd probably talk to me before they would you, Sheriff. There's more going on out at the Breaks than firing shots at wild horses."

"No," Dan Brigman said again without hesitation.

"I looked it up." Tim started pacing beside the sheriff. "I'm not sure it's even a crime to shoot wild horses. I know it's no problem to shoot hogs."

Lauren just watched from her tiny desk between file cabinets.

"I've got enough to hold them for a few days," Pop said.

"Right. That's my point. I could put the screws to them for a few hours and maybe find out more about the body we found in the canyon or where they got the bad drugs. Bad guys, dumb as they are, probably know other bad guys."

The sheriff stopped and faced Tim. "You think maybe they have a fraternity?" He didn't wait for an answer before he fired the next question. "Where'd you hear a term like 'put the screws'?"

Tim straightened. "I'm a writer. I read. Let me talk to them."

"No." Dan smiled. "Didn't you ever hear of cruel and unusual punishment?"

The sheriff walked out of the room before Tim could answer. When he must have been almost at Pearly's desk, he yelled, "Get back on the research for the dead body in the canyon."

"Will do," Tim yelled back, but the sheriff's only reply was the slamming door.

Slowly, piece by piece, Lauren and Tim put together

who the man in burlap might be. On the tax rolls for
the fall trade fair, several vendors called themselves
yard art painters. One by one Tim tracked them down
and, if they were breathing, eliminated them as his
man. Finally he only had one name and that yard art-
ist had listed his address as "Homeless."

Since the clerk said all the vendors were local and
homeless people don't carry around yard art, Tim de-
duced that the dead guy must not want anyone to know
where he lived.

He'd had little luck with the tattoo artists around
knowing anything about a tat that said Surrender to the
Void. Some kept haphazard records. A few kept none
at all. Those who did didn't know or care if they got
the full or right names. Plus, a man that age, with old
tattoos, could have gotten them in the sixties.

Friday morning, Lauren was alone when the Franklin sisters rushed in, out of breath from darting the
thirty or so feet from their store. They reminded Lauren of Halloween scarecrows you buy at the discount
store to stand in your yard. Not scary or funny.

Lauren reached for her notepad and pen as she
stood. "How may I help you, Miss Franklin and Miss
Franklin?"

While they both fought to control their frantic
breathing, Lauren tried to hide her grin. They considered themselves the town criers and followed their
calling with gusto, whether it was a cat in a tree or
a murder.

Rose Franklin, the slightly larger sister, gripped
her hands in front of her ample chest and straightened. "Morning, Lauren. Good to see you're home
for spring break and not running around in a bikini

down on the coast. There is no telling what college girls pick up in the sand."

Lauren knew better than to argue. She just smiled.

Daisy Franklin winked at her. "We always knew you were a sweet girl, dear. I remember when you were little and came into the bakery we had then. You'd pay your quarter and get your cookie without handling all the others first. Not like some of the other kids who'd touch several then lick their fingers. I should have charged them a dime a lick."

"I miss your bakery," Lauren admitted. "Hope the antiques business is going well."

"Oh, it is. We've had a real run on vinyl records lately. I still love the songs of the seventies. But we're considering another business. One that will let us combine our cooking skills and our love for antiques."

Rose looked at her sister as if Daisy was wasting time with small talk. "We've a mission, sister. No time to discuss what might be."

Lauren put down her notepad and picked up her phone. "The sheriff is out of the office right now, but I can give him a call if it's urgent."

Rose's lips pinched so hard that all that showed beneath her nose was her thin mustache. "We're not here to see the sheriff. We heard Tim O'Grady is working here. We'd like to talk to him. Rumor is he's thinking of becoming a writer."

Lauren shrugged. "Yes to both, but he's not here, either."

Daisy's eyebrows wiggled. "Do you know what he's writing? You've read some of it, haven't you? He's not planning to turn Crossroads into a Peyton Place?"

"Or worse, one of those X-rated stories where

people use whips and chains while the wives swap places." Daisy was off on another thought. "Did you ever think about why they call it wife-swapping? Why not husband-swapping? I think it's because no one ever wants to trade off a husband for potluck. After all, I've heard they take years to train."

Rose cleared her throat long and loud.

Lauren knew Rose wanted the conversation to move along. "I haven't read any of Tim's work. Why are you ladies so interested?"

Rose took over the conversation. "We want to make sure he gets a good start. Crossroads has never had a writer. He could be famous one day. Real famous. Buses might come from all over the state to drive around the town where he grew up. Reporters would flood the streets to talk to anyone who knew him before he hit big."

"So big we'd have to put a sign coming to town saying he lived here." Daisy giggled as if she was already organizing the committee. "Oh, wouldn't that be something."

"I'll let him know you want to see him the minute he gets back." Lauren decided she would go with Tim when he dropped by the Franklin sisters' shop. She wanted to see his face when the ladies told him there might be a sign.

They both nodded but Rose added, "You tell the O'Grady boy to come find us. We know a way to help him. There's a woman who can change his path from good to great just by looking in his eyes and visiting."

"I will," Lauren promised, wondering what these two had planned for Tim.

Rose nodded once. "We best be getting back to the store."

Daisy opened her mouth, glanced at her sister then reconsidered whatever she'd been about to say or maybe just knew to let the older sister have the last word.

Lauren watched them march out. She doubted they would help, but it might be worth watching.

When Pop came in a little after noon and began answering calls, Lauren slipped away from the office for lunch at the retirement home with her former piano teacher.

She'd never known too much about music, but she'd always loved visiting with Miss Abernathy.

If the Evening Shadows Retirement Home had a queen, it would be Miss Abernathy. She'd taught music for fifty years before she retired. She was one of those rare people who remembered every student she'd ever had.

The long sunny front office of what had once been a bungalow hotel now served as the meeting room. Even though Lauren was fifty or more years younger than anyone in the open area, she felt right at home. Half a dozen retired teachers, who'd known her since the first grade, crowded around to join in the visiting.

Lauren was an honored guest. Everyone filled their plates from the Saturday noon potluck and sat in a circle, each with their own little tray table. The conversation drifted from college to careers for Lauren, to happenings in Crossroads.

When talk settled on the body in the canyon, all wanted to hear details of what research Tim was doing and what the sheriff's theories were. She'd planned to say little—after all, it was an active case—but they wore her down with their smiles and experience with just what to say to make young people talk.

Lauren filled them in on what she hoped was common knowledge, ending her account with, "The man who died had a tattoo we can't figure out."

Mr. Leo, always quick, asked what it was.

Lauren wasn't sure she should tell, but then several people in town already knew about the tattoo and so did every ink shop within fifty miles, thanks to Tim. "One of his tattoos says Surrender to the Void. I have no idea what that could mean."

The room went silent. Not one of the dozen retired teachers circling her moved, or spoke or even chewed.

She looked around. Without a word, she realized they all knew what it meant. "What?"

Miss Abernathy pushed her table to the side and stood. "It's a song, dear."

Miss Bees giggled. "I remember it. It's a Beatles song about dying."

"No," Cap said. "It's about coming back."

Everyone was talking at once about reincarnation. Lauren leaned back in her chair and finished her egg salad. She suddenly felt as though she knew the burlap man. He'd loved a song enough to tattoo it on his arm. A Beatles song about coming back to life.

The dead guy no longer seemed so frightening.

CHAPTER SEVENTEEN

Jubilee
March 19

JUBILEE JOINED THEM in the barn a little before dark. Charley, Lillie and Thatcher were having a picnic in the corner of the injured horse's stall.

"How is she?" Jubilee whispered as she sat down between Charley and his daughter.

Charley looked worried. "She's growing restless even with the drugs the doc sent over. I've been talking to the vet every thirty minutes. He says he'll try to make it out soon, but he wants me to cut down on the sedatives. What might help make her comfortable won't be good if she goes into labor."

"Can't he do more? Don't they have big horse hospitals around here that we could take her to?"

"He's doing all he can, Jubilee, and no, there's nothing near."

She laced her fingers in her lap trying not to fidget. "I wish there was something I could do."

With one of his rough hands, Charley covered her fingers, as if he needed to offer warmth. "A long drive isn't something she needs right now. We'll do all we can."

She could feel Charley watching her closely as

he added, "You haven't grown up around horses, or you'd understand. This is a mustang, not a high-priced racehorse. The mare's half wild and probably doesn't belong to anyone. The vet can't find a rancher who claims her or, for that matter, any of the small herd. They probably came down from the north during the winter. He offered to pay the board bills and gave me the supplies free, but that's about all."

"You're right. I don't understand."

"You got a big heart, Jubilee." Charley patted her hands. "Must go with those big eyes."

She gulped down a sob.

"We'll watch over the mare," she whispered. "If people were horses, I'm afraid I'd be one of the mustangs."

"Me, too," Thatcher, who hadn't even looked as though he'd been listening to the conversation, added. "Ain't nobody watching over me."

"Me, too," Lillie said. "If we were horses, we'd be our own herd. Only I'd be the princess of the herd."

"You got that job, kid." Thatcher smiled at her. "The crown wouldn't fit me anyway."

When Jubilee stole a French fry, Charley offered her a bite of his hamburger. "Did you have supper?"

"Not much. Destiny said there was nothing fit to eat in the house. By the time she told me what was wrong with all the food in my kitchen I wasn't very hungry. She claimed I was lucky she had health bars in her bag. We each ate one and she went to bed."

They shared his burger and fries in silence as Lillie told Thatcher about all the princesses she'd heard of. Jubilee noticed her body relaxing as she realized she'd never felt as comfortable, as at home, as she did right now. Maybe the four of them were a herd. If so, she considered herself lucky to be included.

An hour later the mare grew more restless. Charley sat Lillie on the railing so she'd be out of harm's way to watch as the others took stations around the horse, ready to help, ready to jump out of the way. Somehow they had to get this baby horse born without the mare opening the wound on her side.

Charley smiled at Jubilee. "Ready to step into the game?"

She could see how he loved this work. He didn't care that it was hard and fixing to get messy. "I'm ready, cowboy. Let's get to birthing this foal."

Ten minutes later they were both cussing and Thatcher was the only one laughing. The mare had stepped on Jubilee's foot twice and slung snot into her hair. Charley was covered in whatever was coming out of the south end of the mare.

In what seemed like forever, the horse delivered a small colt. Everyone moved into action, knowing that the work was just beginning. Charley and Thatcher took care of the mare while Jubilee cleaned the baby's mouth out and Lillie wiped him down with a soft piece of what had once been her baby blanket.

The little girl reminded Jubilee of Charley as she talked to the newborn as if he could understand every word she said.

By the time the vet showed up they were all covered in blood and afterbirth and straw.

The lanky doc appeared as tired as Charley, but he grinned as he looked them all up and down. "Who won the battle?" he asked.

"We did." Lillie giggled. "We all helped bring this baby horse to life."

The vet didn't look too happy. "A colt I'm afraid no one but his mother will want."

"We'll want him," Jubilee said without thinking. She silently polled the others. Thatcher, Lillie and Charley nodded. "The horses can stay here if they have nowhere else to go."

The vet smiled. "Best news I've heard today."

When the doc examined the mare and colt, he told them that both mom and colt were going to be fine. I'm not so sure about you four. I'll stay with the horses while you all clean up."

Jubilee offered to take Lillie to her place for a bubble bath and the boys headed to Charley's house for showers. Everyone was laughing and slapping each other on the back and marveling at how dirty they were. Somehow, in the hours of hard work, they'd become a tribe.

Thirty minutes later, a clean Charley stepped into her kitchen with a princess gown and tiny socks in one hand and a carton of root beer in the other. "Thatcher is still washing up, but I thought I'd come over and help dress our royalty." He winked at Lillie, who was wrapped in a huge towel. She held a doll with a porcelain face and was wrapped in a hand towel.

"Who is this?" Charley asked as knelt to put on her sock.

"Jubilee gave it to me. Her name is Willow. I promised I'd take very good care of her. Right now all she has is a blanket, but I told her my granny will make her a dress."

FREE Merchandise is 'in the Cards' for you!

Dear Reader,

We're giving away FREE MERCHANDISE!

Seriously, we'd like to reward you for reading this novel by giving you **FREE MERCHANDISE** worth over **$20** retail. And no purchase is necessary!

It's easy! All you have to do is look inside for your Free Merchandise Voucher. Return the Voucher promptly...and we'll send you valuable Free Merchandise!

Thanks again for reading one of our novels—and enjoy your Free Merchandise with our compliments!

Pam Powers

Pam Powers

P.S. Look inside to see what Free Merchandise is **"in the cards"** for you!

We'd like to send you two free books like the one you are enjoying now. Your two books have a combined price of over $10 retail, but they are yours to keep absolutely FREE! We'll even send you 2 wonderful surprise gifts. You can't lose!

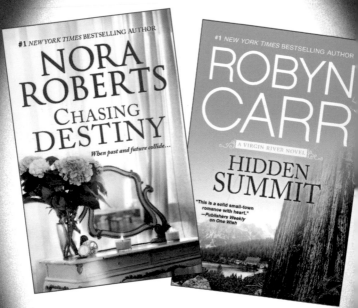

REMEMBER: Your Free Merchandise, consisting of **2 Free Books** and **2 Free Gifts**, is worth over $20 retail! No purchase is necessary, so please send for your Free Merchandise today.

Get TWO FREE GIFTS!
We'll also send you 2 wonderful FREE GIFTS (worth about $10 retail), in addition to your 2 Free books!

Visit us at:

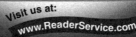

www.ReaderService.com

Books received may not be as shown.

FREE MERCHANDISE VOUCHER

❏ Please send my Free Merchandise, consisting of **2 Free Books** and **2 Free Mystery Gifts**. I understand that I am under no obligation to buy anything, as explained on the back of this card.

194/394 HDL GKCL

Please Print

FIRST NAME

LAST NAME

ADDRESS

APT.#   CITY

STATE/PROV.   ZIP/POSTAL CODE

NO PURCHASE NECESSARY!

ROM-516-FMH16

◀ If offer card is missing write to: Reader Service, P.O. Box 1867, Buffalo, NY 14240-1867 or visit www.ReaderService.com ◀

BUSINESS REPLY MAIL
FIRST-CLASS MAIL   PERMIT NO. 717   BUFFALO, NY

POSTAGE WILL BE PAID BY ADDRESSEE

READER SERVICE
PO BOX 1867
BUFFALO NY 14240-9952

NO POSTAGE
NECESSARY
IF MAILED
IN THE
UNITED STATES

"I'm sure she will." He kissed Lillie's head, then the doll's. "Be sure and thank her. You've got the best granny and papa in the world you know, kid."

"I know." She giggled. "They say I got the best daddy."

Charley looked up at Jubilee and smiled. "Thanks," he silently mouthed.

"You are welcome," she answered without a sound.

With his dark hair wet and slicked back he almost looked like a businessman and not a half-wild cowboy, Jubilee decided. A month ago she would have thought this look more handsome, but now she longed to mess the straight combed hair back into lazy curls that had never been styled. Charley Collins was growing on her just as this style of life was.

Jubilee had on clean jeans and a sweatshirt but her feet were bare as she stood over Lillie, trying to get the tangles out of the tiny girl's hair.

Charley handed Jubilee the gown and offered to make pancakes.

By the time Thatcher showed up, the first stack of pancakes was piled a foot high and the sausage was done. Everyone dove into the food as if it were a grand feast.

"Shh." Charley tried to calm the tribe down. "We'll wake Destiny."

"No way. After she does her nightly routine to keep wrinkles from crawling on her when she sleeps, my sister takes sleeping pills. She said she had to start it after the twins were born."

Charley leaned over and kissed Lillie's head. "I remember the late nights. She'd wake up and I'd rock us both to sleep."

Thatcher's fingers slowly began to walk toward Lillie's plate. "Wrinkles crawling to get you, girl."

Lillie giggled and bopped the creeping hand with a sticky fork.

As everyone laughed, Jubilee tucked her toes under Charley's leg for warmth. Charley leaned back in his chair and covered her cold feet with his hand as if it were the most natural thing in the world to do. Neither mentioned it, but she had a feeling he was as aware of touching her as she was of his warm hand moving over her cold feet.

"It's been a hard night," he started. "I couldn't have done it alone."

"Yep," Thatcher said as he licked syrup off the back of his hand. "Best time I've ever had."

"Me, too," Jubilee echoed and was surprised at just how much she meant it. When her eyes met Charley's, something passed between them that neither could have put into words. A bond. An understanding. A warmth.

A few minutes later, when he lifted a sleepy Lillie in his arms, he met Jubilee's eyes once more with a hunger that surprised her. "I'll put Lillie to bed. Thatcher and I will take shifts sleeping in the barn tonight." His gaze moved over her slowly as if memorizing this one moment and the way she looked. "I'll come wake you if there's trouble, but I think we're through the hard time."

She nodded, trying to read what else he was thinking. Nothing, she decided. He was just tired. Maybe glad the horse made it. Maybe, like her, sorry this magic time between them was ending.

Only when she crawled in her bed she could see the low light in the barn burning and wondered if he was lying in the straw thinking of her. Her mind told her to keep her distance. What they had now was good. The worst thing in the world would be to complicate their relationship. She didn't need that and neither did he.

Only her body didn't seem to be listening. A part of her wondered what Charley Collins would do if she simply went to the barn and curled up beside him.

She didn't need him. She'd never needed anyone.

But tonight, with only the midnight moon to see, she realized that maybe for the first time in her life she wanted someone.

Charley

CHARLEY STOOD IN the shadow of the barn door. He could hear the colt and the mare a few feet away, but his eyes were on the center window on the second floor of a house a hundred feet away.

Life had been good tonight. His heart had felt settled. If he believed it possible, he'd almost say that for the first time in longer than he could remember, he was happy. Only he'd learned that life never settles down and happiness is a rug that can be ripped out from under a man the minute he lets down his guard.

Charley didn't blame his bad luck on anyone but himself. But a man who doesn't learn from his mistakes is a fool.

He went over the rules in his brain. *Don't step out of line. Don't get involved with any woman. Don't hope for anything more than you got.*

He swore and turned back into the barn and said softly, "Don't dream of what might be, just learn to live with what's already been."

CHAPTER EIGHTEEN

Jubilee
March 26

BY THE END of the first week of her visit, Destiny gave up even acting interested in what was going on at the ranch. Her diet consisted of health food bars for the meals and a pound of chocolate a day for snacks. Except for an occasional cup of coffee, her drink of choice was wine. Which she drank from noon until bedtime.

Jubilee reached the point that she swore if her sister commented one more time about the dump of a ranch she'd inherited, Jubilee would drive her back to Dallas even if she had to take the pickup.

Destiny was unhappy with her life for some reason and had decided to come make over Jubilee's as her therapy.

The only thing that made her sister's visit easier was Charley. The first day, he'd started counting the number of times Destiny complained about simple things like the weather, the horses making noise, how dark it was at night and, of course, the one bathroom in a house that should have had at least three.

Charley made Destiny's visit bearable with his whispered humor and laughing winks when he knew only Jubilee could see him. It also helped that Destiny went to bed early most nights, always slept until ten and never came near the barn.

Jubilee spent her time working with Charley. They'd both taken the wounded mare on as a mission. Charley had called the horse Last Chance and she called the tiny colt Baby, which Charley swore she'd have to change. They worked together, making sure they did everything the vet ordered, even though no one had claimed the horse, therefore no one would be paying the bills.

Jubilee had grown used to Charley's low voice talking to the mare, encouraging her to live. Sometimes, late at night, when she tried to stop worrying about the ranch and sleep, she'd hear his voice in her head. Whispering for her to relax.

When she hugged both mare and colt goodbye late one morning, Charley reminded her that the animals were not pets.

"I know," she said.

"Sure you do," he added as he held the gate open for her. "You're worse than Lillie. She wants to braid their manes and put a ribbon in one braid like you did to her hair this morning."

"Do you mind?" she asked as they began the routine of setting out supplies for the next doctoring.

He shook his head. "She looked cute. Sometimes I can be staring at her and I swear I see her grow. The sheriff, who also raised his daughter alone, told me that one day he was tying her laces and the next day she was learning to drive. I don't want to miss any of it."

"Speaking of children, I'm beginning to think

we've adopted Thatcher." The kid had spent last weekend helping out, caught the bus with Lillie on Monday and returned every afternoon. He might be only fourteen, but he did a man's share of the work.

"I like having him around," she admitted.

"I told him he could stay over anytime but he said tonight he needed to go home," Charley said as he passed her with a bucket of grain in each hand. "I don't think anyone is raising him. He may look calm, but down deep he's as wild as that mustang mare. Remember that."

As they stepped into the sunlight, both seemed to mold back into their roles. He told her what he had planned to get done before dark as he pulled on worn work gloves. She took the list of supplies that needed to be picked up.

"Any chance your sister is going home for the weekend?" he asked.

"No mention of it. Besides resting, she seems on a mission to straighten my life out and I don't think she's leaving until she does what she feels she must." Jubilee shrugged. "In her way, she loves me. But, like our parents, she wants me to be more like her."

Charley smiled. "That would be a real shame."

She blushed when he winked at her. Changing the subject was her only option. "I plan to get the tomato plants today. If I hang them I can always take them inside if it looks like it'll freeze any night." She looked over at the plowed square of dirt. "I'm planting seeds tomorrow. Carrots, beets, beans, peas, corn and pumpkins for the fall."

"It's a little early," he said calmly as if agreeing to set the conversation back on a business level only.

"I can't wait. If they freeze out I'll replant." She stared at him, determined to stand her ground. She'd waited long enough. In her mind she almost believed that if she made something grow here, she might grow on this place.

"Then go ahead, Jubilee, put down roots." He smiled as if he understood. "You planning to stay till fall harvest?"

"I'm planning to stay forever." The charts in her study hinted at another story she feared. Her money was dwindling faster than she thought it would, but she wouldn't worry Charley with it. Not yet. Not until she had to.

Charley tipped his hat and turned toward the barn. She thought she saw a hint of sadness in his eyes. Maybe he didn't believe her, or maybe he wished he could be the same. He'd promised her a year, until she got the place running or went broke. But he hadn't said a word about what would happen in a year and a day.

As she drove to town, she thought about how she didn't want to worry about next year. With the mare needing care, a hundred jobs on the ranch needing doing, and Destiny hanging out upstairs all day eating chocolate and complaining, Jubilee decided she should give up thinking altogether.

By the time she reached the grocery, she had calmed down. She might even cook tonight. Something simple. It was Friday. The butcher always had smoked ribs and brisket on Friday night. She could pick up ribs and bake potatoes. The vegan diet she'd tried to follow all the time she lived with David in DC seemed impossible now. He'd been more committed to it than to her.

For a moment she wondered what he'd think about her becoming a rancher. Then, just as suddenly, she realized she didn't care. David was part of her past now.

So was avoiding sugar, she decided, as she considered baking a cake. After all, the directions were on the back of the box—how hard could it be?

The cloud on her dinner party was Destiny. If she came downstairs they'd all have to put up with her. It was hard to argue with someone who started every lecture with, *I'm just here to help you.*

Jubilee picked up the supplies Charley had ordered and the sweets and wine Destiny had insisted on, then wandered through the tiny stores of the main street. She wasn't looking for anything; she just wanted to get lost for a few hours.

Deep inside she felt she was changing, molding into someone else. She was changing on the outside, too. Her dull hair was sun-bleached and her slim body now had muscles from hard work and lots of riding. She wasn't sure she liked all the changes, but for the first time ever she felt comfortable in her skin. It occurred to her that maybe a small part of that was the way Charley looked at her. She could see it in his eyes; the man found nothing wrong with her.

She didn't need a man's approval, she thought, but she didn't mind his admiring glance, either.

That afternoon while she put away the groceries, Destiny came into the kitchen to make tea.

Her sister was in the middle of one of her complaints when Jubilee abandoned her task and headed to the barn. "I'll be back," she yelled over her shoulder. "Hold that thought."

Charley was unloading the back of the pickup.

"Thanks," she said, thinking she should have already done the chore.

"No problem. You all right?" He looked at her as if he could tell that she'd been wandering the aisles of every business in town.

She nodded. "When the mare recovers and my sister leaves, I'd like to cook you and Lillie dinner."

"You don't have to do that. We manage fine on our own." Lifting the last load he walked away.

Jubilee realized she'd somehow insulted him with her offer. He always seemed a little sad on the nights Lillie stayed in town with her grandparents. Maybe he was missing Lillie and didn't want to talk about her.

No. Something else was bothering him and obviously, he didn't want to talk about it.

This simply wasn't her day. Maybe she should just go to bed and start over tomorrow. She could take one of Destiny's pills and forget about the world for a while.

Her sister was waiting when she walked back into the house. Her day must have not gone well, either, because she had a list of suggestions for Jubilee on the counter and half of the new bottle of wine was gone.

As Jubilee listened to Destiny's carping, slowly, one complaint at a time, the real reasons she'd come to visit began to surface. The twins were far too much work. Mason didn't help her enough. It had taken her a year before she could fit into any of her clothes. No one had any idea how hard live-in staff are to manage. She hated everything about her life.

It wasn't Jubilee who Destiny had come to fix, but herself.

"What do you want me to do?" Jubilee finally asked as she pushed Destiny's untouched sandwich toward her.

Destiny was silent a full minute before she said, "I want half this ranch. I'm not happy. Maybe, if I had the money, I could start over. Mason said our great-grandfather was senile. He probably meant to leave what he had to both of us."

"You're planning to leave Mason?"

"I have to. I can't take it any longer." She made a face. "But, don't worry, I'm not coming here. This place is worse than home. So the only solution is we sell the farm and split the money. Don't you see? We'll both be much happier. You can't want to spend the rest of your life working yourself to death in the dirt."

"Ranch," Jubilee whispered as if she hadn't heard the rest.

"Whatever." Destiny moved on. "Don't you see, the money from this place will save us both."

Jubilee couldn't believe what she was hearing. "Why are you so unhappy?" she finally whispered. "You're married to a rich banker. Our parents always gave you the best of everything. You've got a beautiful home and healthy children. Why would you want or need half of this place?"

"Mason says it might sell for a million in a good market and everyone knows there could be oil. I'll bet old Levy never even had it tested. I think it's only fair that I get half when you sell." She looked as if she might cry. "I've got to start over. Mason doesn't see how stressed I am." She smiled suddenly. "Maybe I could go to DC with you. I'd help you find an apartment. Maybe stay with you awhile."

"I'm not selling this place." Destiny was a nightmare here; Jubilee didn't want to think about what she'd be like in DC.

Destiny smiled as if she thought she was talking to a child. "Of course you'll sell. You're no more a country girl than I am. It's just a matter of time before you run away from this like you run away from every career and every man who ever got close."

She patted Jubilee's hand. "Now, little Jub, you have to understand, if I have to take you to court we'll both lose, but I'll do whatever it takes to save you from this kind of life. I'm your big sister. I know what's best for you and this isn't where you need to be." She nodded slowly as if hoping the words soaked in. "Even Mom and Dad agree with me."

Jubilee dropped her supper into the sink and bolted out the back door.

She ran all the way to the barn and collapsed in the hay. Anger shook her whole body, but tears didn't come. Not this time. Destiny wouldn't get her way this time.

This one time in her life, Jubilee was where she belonged.

CHAPTER NINETEEN

Charley
March 27

IT WAS AFTER twilight when Charley walked out to the barn to check on the horses one last time before he turned in. He'd put in a hard day on horseback and stayed away from the house in the afternoon.

Only the plan hadn't kept Jubilee from his thoughts. He was attracted to her, but he had to keep his distance. This was one time he didn't want to ruin what he had built. A friendship, he reminded himself. Nothing more.

He never slept well when Lillie wasn't asleep in her bed so he usually worked late and read late into the night on those nights. A part of him wondered if, when she grew up, he would miss her forever.

The colt was asleep in the soft hay beside his mother and, to Charley's surprise, Jubilee was curled in the corner of the stall, her head resting on a blanket Lillie sometimes curled up in when she watched him work.

He sat down beside Jubilee, leaned his back against the stall boards and rested his hand on her shoulder. "You sleeping it off in the barn, boss, or did the evil sister kick you out of your own house?"

Her big brown eyes opened slowly and tried to focus. "I… I…"

He brushed her hair away from her face. "You're in the barn on your ranch. You're safe."

She frowned at him. "I know where I am, you idiot."

"The lady is awake. Want to talk about it?"

"No. You told Thatcher he could sleep in the barn. Maybe I thought I'd give it a try."

"He didn't take my offer after you handed him that stack of new clothes you bought him. New jeans and a Western shirt with pearl snaps. That and Kristi Norton go a long way in making him want to catch the bus to school."

They both smiled and she straightened so she was leaning against the stall wall. Her shoulder was almost touching his, but Charley didn't move away.

"First love." She sighed. "I remember mine. His name was Benny. I followed him around for months. I knew his class schedule better then he did. I even kept track of what he ate."

Charley grinned, thinking about her following some guy around like a puppy. "How old were you?"

"Fifteen."

"How far did he get?"

"First base." She laughed. "The moment he realized how flat-chested I was he ran. Kind of the story of my life. Guys stay around until they figure out what's wrong with me, then they disappear. No boobs. Then no trust. And finally, no commitment. I'm the kind of girl guys wonder why they ever got involved with."

"I find that hard to believe, Jubilee. I've seen how

hard you plan and work." He nodded toward the mare. "I've seen how much you care."

"Charley," she whispered as if they'd wake the horses. "Would you hug me? This is nothing to do with you or me or starting something between us. I could just use a hug. It's been a bad day."

He opened his arms and she moved against him. For a long while he did what she'd asked, he just hugged her. He'd always said he wanted a woman for a friend and she seemed to want the same thing. He could be happy with that, right? No complications.

He liked watching her move. He enjoyed teaching her about ranching and laughing with her, but she'd made it plain that their friendship would never go further. It couldn't, because if it did they'd both probably break this time. They both seemed like old veterans of a long war. One more battle would shatter them both.

All he'd ever been good at was ruining relationships, and he had a feeling she was the same. She had a goal to build this place up and he could help her with that, nothing more.

He leaned close to her ear. "Unless I'm mistaken, boss, I don't think you have to worry about the 'no boobs' problem any longer."

She pulled away suddenly.

"I may be tired, but a man knows when he's hugging a woman." Even in the shadows he swore he could see her blush.

She slapped him on the shoulder and rolled next to him again, shoulder to shoulder. "All right, cowboy. Now you. Tell me about your first love."

He thought of lying, but they'd become friends. "Her name was Sharon. I was seventeen and she was sixteen. I had wild dreams of going to college, getting a degree and managing the family ranch. She had wild dreams of being with me. We went all the way on our first date and I thought I was the luckiest guy in town. By the time I left for college she was like a drug. I came home every weekend just to be with her. Sometimes we didn't even talk, we just had sex. Before the end of my freshman year, her dream came true. She was four months pregnant when we married that summer.

"I thought I could finish college, we'd move back to the ranch and have a few more kids, but I guess marriage and motherhood wasn't what she wanted. She left Lillie and me three months after Lillie was born. I stayed in school, working thirty or forty hours a week, and rocking a baby at night. My dad was so mad he almost disowned me then. He didn't make it easy on me, but at least he paid tuition."

He'd never been so honest with anyone in his life. Most folks didn't really ask. They thought they already knew the story of his life.

"Did you love her a great deal? Did her leaving break your heart?"

He pushed his palms against his eyes and decided to be truthful with himself for a change. "I don't think I ever loved her at all. I loved what we did on our first date. All I could think about was doing it again. I thought I loved her when she was carrying my child, but when she didn't love Lillie things changed. I found it hard to look at her and there was no way I could make love to her when she just let Lillie cry and never bothered to change her."

He kicked at the hay. "One of the last things she

ever said to me was that she thought I loved Lillie more than I loved her. She was right. I didn't blame her for leaving."

Jubilee looked at him. "How many women have you slept with?"

"Not many. Sharon, one married woman I shouldn't have and maybe a half dozen girls I've picked up in bars where we were drunk and both knew it was a one-night stand. On those nights I was so drunk we may have only slept."

"I've slept with four, all nice guys I drifted into relationships with. Friends who filled in as lovers."

"How many did you love?"

She shook her head. "None. Something is broken in me. At least you thought you loved Sharon. I never even got that close. I'm messed up."

"Me, too," he said. "We're the kind of people who give loving a bad name."

She giggled. "Isn't that a line from a song?"

"Probably. I sometimes think my whole life is a country song."

"Maybe it is. Trust me. I'm older than you and for a year or two I was big into country music. I even kissed Willie Nelson at a concert."

"I got a feeling thousands have done that. And I figured out you had to be at least a year, maybe two years older than me. But, boss, being around you, I'm aging fast."

They were both laughing when Destiny stepped up to the open barn door. "I can't sleep," she announced, as if it was a global problem someone needed to solve. "For no reason at all I seemed to be missing Mason."

Charley stood, pulling Jubilee up with him. "Sorry about that, lady. The best cure for sleepless nights is a long ride. You want me to saddle up a horse?"

Charley wondered why he ever thought Destiny was pretty without her makeup. From what he could tell by the clinging silk robe, a few pounds had joined the wrinkles crawling up on her while she slept.

"You have got to be kidding." She made a face that caused an outbreak of new lines.

"I wouldn't mind a ride," Jubilee said from behind him.

Charley did his best to ignore Destiny's complaining as he saddled two horses.

When he walked them between the two sisters, Destiny was saying that she'd made a few calls today and things around here were about to change.

"Help me up," Jubilee whispered to him as she put her foot in the stirrup.

He placed one hand on her knee and the other on her backside, smiling as he boosted her into the saddle. When he looked up she was grinning down at him and he knew they were both thinking of the first time he'd helped her up.

"All right?" he asked as his hand moved along her leg, checking that her boot was firmly in place.

"I'm fine. Let's ride."

She was out the barn door before he could swing into the saddle. Neither looked back at Destiny. Neither cared. At this moment they just wanted to leave everything behind them and simply ride the wind.

He caught up with Jubilee halfway to Lone Heart Pass. She'd learned to ride over the weeks she'd been here and he'd found he enjoyed watching her moving so gracefully with the horse as she rode.

The night was cool, but he barely noticed. She looked so beautiful with her long blond hair flying like a mane. He could hear her laughter in the wind. Her bad day was disappearing under the pounding of hoofs over grassland.

She slowed when they reached the rocky entrance to the pass. The tall pillars of rock looked milky white in the moonlight, and the entrance was completely black.

As he pulled up beside her, he said, "The old timers called this Lone Heart Pass because only one man can ride in at a time. I've always thought the name had a lonesome sound to it. Kind of sad. Haunting."

Jubilee slid off her horse and walked to the entrance. "Wish we could go in, but it's so dark. Too bad a full moon isn't high over the top."

Charley climbed down and reached into his saddlebag. "No bright moon crossing tonight. What was it Lauren said, something about a heart's wish coming true when the moon shines down from the opening above the pass?"

"It's still beautiful. A passage guarding an opening to the canyon. I love that this place is on my land."

Clicking on a small flashlight, Charley said, "How about we go in just for the fun of it? There's no full moon tonight, but we should be able to see enough to walk the pass through. On the other side we'll have a great midnight view of the canyon."

He took her hand and they moved slowly up the rocky trail to the opening. Once inside the passage, they moved into a long roofless opening just wide enough for them to walk through together.

Charley gave her the flashlight and raised his arms wide. His fingers brushed along rock washed by oceans for thousands of years before the sea that had once covered this land dried out. He could feel her excitement, and hoped that whatever was torturing her earlier would leave her alone in this quiet place where ghosts seemed to whisper and heart dreams were believed to come true.

They made it to the other side and stood silently staring as moonlight danced over the stillness of the canyon at night. It was like a stunning oil painting done in black and shades of blue and gray.

"It's beautiful," she whispered.

He rested his arm lightly across her shoulder. "That it is. The evergreens look almost black in the night, like a ragged line of ink running the canyon walls. The tumbleweeds near the bottom almost seem to be dancing in the shallow water."

She moved closer to him for warmth and they stood in silence for a while.

Then, without a word, they turned around to walk the passage back toward her ranch.

Halfway through, he whispered, "Turn off the flashlight. I want to see how dark it is."

She did and suddenly it was so black she seemed to have disappeared at his side.

She giggled. "It's a level of dark I've never seen."

"You vanished, Jubilee, but you left your laugh."

Her hand touched his chest. "It's like we fell out of the world. I only wish it was that easy to step out of my life sometimes. It's so silent here. So dark. I've disappeared from my life and I'm floating free."

"What would you do if you really could disappear from all your problems? Become an only child? Fly away on a moonbeam? Live in a daydream?"

She was silent, but he could still feel her hand resting on his chest. She was right in front of him. He could hear her breathing, feel it against his collar. He could smell the light, fruity smell of her hair.

"What would you do right now, invisible lady, that the world would never know about? No one would see. No one would remember."

Her hand started at his heart and moved up his body until she brushed the day's growth of stubble along his jaw. "I'd kiss you," she whispered. "I'd kiss you softly, gently, like I think a man like you has never been kissed."

Charley couldn't have moved if a dozen rattlers circled suddenly around his boots. He'd known passion and he'd tasted wild sex just for the excitement of it, but she'd just named the one thing he'd never experienced.

She leaned slowly against him and moved her lips along the path her fingers had just traveled from his jaw.

When her mouth moved over his, he drew in a breath, but didn't move.

Soft, full lips began at the corner of his mouth and gently planted feather kisses across his bottom lip. There was no race into passion. No attack. No fevered assault. Not a beginning or an ending. Just a tender, loving kiss as fleeting as a butterfly, as beautiful, as priceless.

If he hadn't already been leaning against the passage rock, he had no doubt that his legs would have buckled.

When she kissed him with only the slightest pressure, and then pulled away, he whispered, "Again. Dear God, you've got to do that again."

He felt her smile as she brushed over his mouth once more, this time welcoming him returning the kiss. Any other time and he would have advanced, turning the slow burn to fire, run full force into what he had no doubt would be an earthquake of a climax. But this was Jubilee, his friend, and she was offering him what he'd longed for.

Her open mouth moved to his ear. "When we leave this place we'll never speak of this kiss again. I want to hold the tenderness of it in my heart."

He turned and buried his face against her throat, drinking in the feel and smell of her skin.

When she rested her cheek against his shoulder, he could feel her heart beat against his. Her words came out like a thought she let slip away. "If the moon really granted wishes in this place, I'd wish your heart wasn't so broken and mine wasn't so cold. Tonight, in the darkness, I can almost believe I'm worth loving."

He kissed the top of her head, seeing her scars in the darkness as he'd never seen them in the light.

Then they shifted away and all he held was her hand in his.

"We'd better get back." Her laugh seemed nervous now. "My sister's probably had us both declared dead."

She clicked on the light and they moved along the passage. Just before they stepped out into moonlight, she turned. "Thank you for this. No matter what happens tomorrow, I'll hold this one moment close."

"Anytime," he answered, trying to understand what *had* happened. Nothing really, just a gentle kiss, but somehow he knew the truth. It was more. Far more.

CHAPTER TWENTY

Lauren
March 27

LAUREN COULD NOT believe she'd let Tim talk her into coming to the Two Step Saloon on a Saturday night. Over the years half the times her father had been called out after midnight on weekends was because of trouble at the Two Step. It was a local place that didn't even post hours. The floors were sprinkled with sawdust and the whiskey was probably watered down. It was every bit as dingy as she thought it would be.

But Tim was convinced that every drunk and pothead in the county circled through the Two Step. People looking for a new high, others looking for a low to help them forget. He decided if the burlap man went anywhere in public, it would probably be here. So he talked her into coming home for the third weekend in a row saying she'd be his cover tonight.

"We'll do research. Ask around. Someone has to know the guy," Tim had promised when he called.

When she still didn't want to go, he'd added that they'd only stay an hour. That should be long enough to find out a few facts.

Three hours later they were still hanging out in a place she didn't want to be. She might be legally old enough, but she told herself she was also far too smart to be bumping elbows with this crowd. If the people in this place had any brains before they came in, they'd drowned them in beer by now.

Lauren was beginning to question Tim's logic. He'd been ordering them fresh rounds of beer as soon as the bottles were half empty and didn't seem to be aware that he'd been the only one drinking since the first round. The first hour he'd made up stories about everyone who walked in, but either it had gotten too crowded or his brain had gotten too foggy to keep it up.

She'd tried feeding Tim, but the food was so spicy he'd downed a bottle in just a few gulps.

He'd stopped talking twenty minutes ago and seemed lost somewhere in his own mind, or what was left of it anyway.

She thought of calling her pop, but that would make her sound like a kid. In a few months she'd graduate from college. She was an adult.

Looking around the room, she realized she didn't fit in here. Not one of the groups would welcome her. She didn't blend with the ranchers, or the suits obviously celebrating a business success, or a group of women in scrubs who looked tired from working a twelve-hour shift. There were a few tables of couples her age. They looked years married and probably got a babysitter for their one night out. It was getting late: women in boots and short jean skirts were coming in to dance. They were made up, their hair curled high, and looked far too tan for March.

Lauren laughed. She was starting to look like the before picture. If she got any plainer she'd be in the

Franklin sisters' category. Even if she had tried getting dressed up tonight, maybe put on a little makeup
before she left home, no drunk was likely to dance
with, much less try to pick up, the sheriff's daughter.

"I'm going to the ladies' room," she mouthed and
pointed.

Tim nodded. The second time his head went down,
it stayed on his chest.

Lauren walked to the back of the bar, thinking she'd
wake him up and somehow get him to his Jeep when
she came back to the table. She'd seen him slide his
keys into his jacket pocket, so all she had to do was
retrieve them.

Great date tonight! They didn't even find a clue.
Putting a drunk Hemingway to bed would be her only
entertainment for the evening.

With the Two Step being the only bar for thirty
miles, all kinds wandered in the place. She passed the
growing crowd of cowboys and several businessmen
near the bar. One tall man with black hair caught her
eye. For a moment she thought it was Lucas Reyes,
the upperclassman she'd fallen hard for in high school.
They'd become friends just before he left for college.
He'd given Lauren her first kiss, her first taste of passion. Half of her dreams had been of him, and the sad
thing was, he didn't even know he'd broken her heart.
She hadn't seen him since he finished law school. In
that last year they were both on the same campus, he'd
texted her once just to let her know all was well. He'd
said he'd see her at Christmas but he hadn't come back
to Crossroads that year, or the next. He was always
working on a big case in Houston.

He must have been because he hadn't bothered to

answer her text when she tried to reach him to wish him a Happy New Year, that year, or the next.

Lucas Reyes was still thick in her thoughts when she stepped from the ladies' room and began down the narrow hallway. The smell of beer and fried tortillas was thick in the smoky air. A few couples just beyond the back screen door were laughing as they shared a joint. She could hear the heartbeat of a bass beating out a song she didn't recognize. This wasn't her kind of place.

When a low voice with just a hint of an accent whispered her name, Lauren thought it was more in her mind than real. No one knew her here.

"Lauren," a shadow in the hallway said again. "Is it really you?" The tall, lean, perfectly dressed dark-haired man materialized as if from a dream. Her one crush. Her one fantasy.

All the old feelings and memories rushed back as Lucas Reyes blocked her path. The memory of the way he'd saved her from falling when she'd been fifteen. The times they'd talked under the midnight stars as friends, barely touching, hearts afraid to open.

How she'd melted when he'd kissed her with passion one night on campus and then crushed her by apologizing. The way he'd drifted away like stardust in such tiny bits at a time that she couldn't remember the day or week he'd gone. No last kiss. No words of goodbye. He just wasn't in her life anymore.

Months had dragged on while she waited for a call that never came. Hope finally died, hardening her heart an ounce at a time.

She faced the handsome man who'd been the boy she'd first loved even though she'd never said the words. His midnight-black eyes seemed hard now. The lines in his face had lost the easy smile. A dark gray suit covered the lean body that had worn Western clothes so naturally years ago. For a moment she thought she was looking at a ghost; then she realized this was the now and her memories were only what had been.

"Lucas." What did she say to the first and only boy she'd ever ached for? What could she say to the man who walked away from her life? He'd done it so gradually she hadn't even heard her heart break when he vanished.

Staring, she tried to remember the last time she'd seen him, heard his voice. A year. No, almost two. He'd called when he was still in law school saying that the semester was hell and they'd get together after he climbed out of all the work. He'd texted that he was going to intern in Houston at a law firm. She'd heard he skipped graduation so he could be in on his first trial. After that, she'd asked a few times about him when she came home. No one had heard from him.

He'd walked away from his life here. He'd walked away from her.

She took a step toward him, this ghost from her past. His hair was shorter now, making him look more than only a little over a year older than she. She wondered if he didn't wear it that way on purpose. He'd always seemed older than his years. Rushing to be grown in high school. Trying to run faster and faster through college.

When she stood close, no words came. Maybe it was that way for him, too. *How you been?* just didn't seem like enough to say and any answer would be too little.

Suddenly, all the loss and hurt she felt hardened into anger. She'd been just a kid to him. Just someone to leave behind.

Lauren, who'd never done anything impulsive in her entire life, placed her hand on Lucas's white shirt and pushed.

The back of his head tapped the wall, but he didn't react as she leaned against him and brushed her mouth over his.

The kiss started out as almost an assault, but quickly exploded with all the desire she'd never let out. He took her advance without retreat and the kiss turned to fire. She felt his breathing quicken as his chest moved against hers. She tasted whiskey on his breath, but she didn't back away. She'd wanted this for years. The passion he never let show. The need. The longing. This might be their last kiss, but she'd never forget it.

She felt him shudder when his last reserve broke. He lifted her off the floor and into his arms with so much power she couldn't breathe and didn't care. Digging her hands into his hair, she kissed him as if it were both of their last moments on earth.

Then, like a far away roar, people began moving toward them, bumping against them in the narrow hallway, giggling, making comments.

Lucas set her down and straightened, but his eyes never left hers. "Lauren," he whispered so low only she could have heard it. "Lauren."

She touched her fingertips to his lips as she stared

up at him. The need to tell him to forget what just happened battled with her desire to beg for more.

Then, as the next wave of bodies passed them in the hallway, Lauren stepped away and darted into the crowd. His hand grabbed at her waist, but he was too late to hold her.

When she glanced back from the darkened bar, she saw him searching the crowd for her and for a moment she thought she saw his eyes. They seemed filled with hunger and hurt.

Lauren almost ran to the table where Tim still sat. She pulled his keys from his pocket and tugged him up. With his arm over her shoulder, she led him through the bar and out into the night. He didn't seem to have enough brain cells left even to ask where they were going.

Thirty minutes later she dropped him off at his house and walked along the shoreline to her home. She could still feel Lucas's chest pressing against her breasts, his warm breath on her throat, the taste of their kiss in her mouth.

Finally, in the silence of the abandoned deck, she stopped long enough to think.

She'd come face-to-face with raw need for another tonight. Not a slow warming of her body or a longing for more, but red hot, all-out passion. If they'd been alone she had no doubt they would have made love. Who knows how far they would have gone in the hallway if they'd had longer. She'd dated several guys in college, but Lucas's kiss was far above anything she had imagined.

For the first time in her life, Lauren had lost control and she didn't like it.

Barely saying good-night to her pop, she walked to her room. Tomorrow she'd go back to school. Maybe with time she'd be able to make sense of what had happened.

Lauren lay down in the darkness of her room, knowing sleep was a million miles away.

Her phone blinked. Lucas was calling. Only what could she say?

Ten minutes later, it silently blinked again. Then again and again.

Lauren reached across the bed and turned it off. She couldn't talk to Lucas until she figured out what to say.

Shrugging, she decided that might take more than one lifetime. She might as well start believing in reincarnation.

The old dead guy's tattoo came to mind. *Surrender to the Void.*

Lauren smiled. She didn't plan on surrendering at all. If anything, she was the aggressor, and if Lucas crossed her path again, she might just attack again.

She felt half drunk with her sudden boldness.

Giggling, she thought of sending him a text. If he didn't want to be attacked, maybe he should consider buying a gun and getting a concealed carry license because one of these days she would find him.

Sweet, shy, brainy Lauren had just discovered she had a wild side.

CHAPTER TWENTY-ONE

Thatcher
March 27

MOVING THROUGH THE weeds that always seemed to grow along trails everyone who lived in the Breaks called the back roads, Thatcher listened. Anyone out this time of night needed to spot another person or animal before they spotted him.

"Stay close to me," he whispered to Tim O'Grady.

"I'm your shadow," Tim answered, his voice higher than usual.

Tim had talked Thatcher into taking him where outsiders never go in the Breaks. Thatcher didn't think it was a good idea, but Tim told him it could help the sheriff solve the case of the body in the canyon.

Plus, he'd added that he needed the exercise, as if taking a chance at being shot would be good for him.

Tim seemed convinced that the body found wrapped in burlap and the shooting of the wild mustangs were related.

Thatcher didn't see how, other than they were both done by idiots. And there were a lot of idiots who hid out in the Breaks, so maybe the college boy was right.

Moving now among the midnight shadows, Thatcher used his ears far more than his eyes. He also carried his old .22 rifle. The strap had long ago worn out and he'd replaced it with rope, but the aim was still true. When he hunted at night, he taped a flashlight to it, but tonight he only carried it for protection.

Tim carried no protection. Maybe he thought he could talk his way out of anything?

Thatcher didn't want to even think about what kind of trouble they'd be in if they got caught tonight.

For the past week, Thatcher had been hanging out at the sheriff's office. It was far more educational than fifth or sixth period.

He'd been traveling around with Tim O'Grady looking for clues as to who killed the burlap man almost every Saturday morning since Tim went to work for Brigman.

No one had turned in a missing person report. Hell, no one even claimed to know the guy with *Surrender to the Void* tattooed on his arm. But when he'd asked a few neighbors, they'd shifted their gaze for a second before they answered.

They were lying. Thatcher felt it all the way to his toes.

He had a feeling the dead guy was one of the crazies that lived off County Road 111. The same general address as his own home. There were at least twenty broken-down mobile homes tucked into rocky crevices that had no address or even a road going near them. Add to that the cabins and dugouts built along the tree lines, and you got maybe forty or fifty nuts living out in no-man's-land that the sheriff couldn't even find.

If the sheriff showed up out here, every cabin and mobile home would be abandoned before Brigman could turn off his engine and climb the path to any front door.

Thatcher's mom, Sunny Jones, had been raised out here by two pot-smoking hippies she'd said were her grandparents. She told him once that they came out with friends to start a pot business, but their profits went up in smoke. Neither remembered where their son, Sunny's father, lived. They just said that their son came home once to drop off Thatcher's mother. She was just a baby then and he'd said to tell her that her parents were dead if she ever asked about them.

Sunny Jones ran off at fifteen and when she came back home pregnant and alone three years later, she had to haul the bones of her grandparents out of their cabin before she could start living there. She didn't have any deed to the place, but if no one had claimed it while she was gone between fifteen and eighteen, she figured it was hers.

No one knew or cared how her grandparents died, and she didn't care about her parents since they dumped her and never came back.

The old folks could have died from bad drugs or asphyxiation from a faulty heater. As far as Thatcher knew, folks rarely bothered with a funeral out here. After she dumped the bones, his mom started common-law marrying and divorcing every few years, but she never did drugs. Whiskey and religion were her addictions. Now and then, she'd pick up a man who'd do some work around the place.

They lived in the middle of the Breaks, so Thatcher figured that made them middle class. The closer to the highway folks lived, the better off they seemed to be.

They had electricity and running water. Near the back, it was mostly outhouses and wood stoves.

The squatters way back were lower class, he decided. Some claimed to be wanted men. A few simply hated people or thought the world was about to end and figured this pothole in Texas would be the last place the zombies would look.

Thatcher knew most of the folks who lived off Road 111 by sight. They were his people in a way. He understood them.

He couldn't take Tim or the sheriff all the way back, but if they were careful, he could show Tim this place. The nuts and drunks got together every week to swap poisons and lies. They called it the Saturday night prayer meeting.

Tonight, with the sheriff asking questions about the horses being shot, everyone in the Breaks would be there with a theory about what had happened. No kids were allowed, but Thatcher had his own private entrance.

Tim bumped into him as they started climbing a rise almost making Thatcher yell out.

"Be careful." Thatcher cut all the cuss words he wanted to say. "We're close."

"Right," Tim answered.

Thatcher leaned close. "When we get there do exactly what I do. No talking from here on. Don't ask questions, understand?"

Tim whispered, "Yes," then slapped his hand over his mouth.

Thatcher rolled his eyes back figuring they had maybe a fifty-fifty chance of getting back to Tim's Jeep alive.

As they neared a dilapidated old barn used to store junk cars, Thatcher slid into the weeds, vanishing like a horned toad in the sand.

Tim followed.

They crawled low and silent until they reached the back of a barn. Years of runoff had washed away the ground beneath one corner of the structure. Thatcher slid under. Tim followed one second later.

They were inside. In the dim light Thatcher touched his lips, silently telling Tim to not make a sound. If they lay on their bellies, no one would see them in the dark corner.

The men were already there, moving around like ants on a mound. They were trading pot for home-made liquor or cigarettes, and talking. If you could cut humankind up as if it was one big carcass, most people would consider these folks the slop left from the butchering.

Spreading out flat on his belly, Thatcher propped his chin on his hands and listened as the shadows of more men moved inside the aging barn. He knew it could be hours before he heard anything worth remembering, but if anyone knew anything about the dead man in the canyon or the men who shot the horses, someone was bound to mention it.

Tim took a while to settle.

Bull, the self-appointed leader who fit his name, stood up on a box that acted as a platform. Thatcher knew the big man had hard liquor in the thermos he held. "We got some talking to do, boys," Bull said, calling the meeting to order.

Folks stopped talking when Bull cleared his throat a few times. "There's someone poking around and the last thing we need out here is a lawman within smelling distance."

Several men swore about how they hated strangers. One even mentioned a redheaded kid asking about a dead man. Another voice from the back said he wondered if redheads had redder blood than most people do.

Tim glanced at Thatcher and he saw fear in the college boy's eyes even in the dim light.

"We don't know nothing about anybody," Bull bellowed. "They need to leave us alone."

"We know they were describing old Hubcap." A voice sounded from somewhere in the group. "Not likely to be another old man with those tats."

Bull nodded. "Anyone know where the old guy lived?"

"Somewhere far back," one said.

Stretch, a tall ex-marine with a scar across his face, added, "This is something that needs to be settled here. I say we post guards to watch the main road. I don't want nobody writing my name down on a report."

Willie's hard laugh shot through the air. "You just don't want any of your wives to find you, Stretch."

"Damn straight," Stretch answered. "I sort of married one every time I came home on leave. After a few years I was safer being deployed than staying in the States."

"I know how you feel," Willie answered.

Thatcher shook his head slightly. Willie was a good guy for the most part, but lying was habit for the crippled up ex-con.

"We all have our reasons for wanting to live out

here in peace." Bull drew the group back to the point of the meeting.

Everyone nodded, but no one volunteered to serve as lookout.

"What about the mustangs that were shot?" Willie interrupted. He was a rabbit of a man who hopped from one topic to the other even on a normal night—and tonight didn't seem normal. There was an electricity in the air, as if a storm was coming in. Thatcher wondered if the others could feel it, too.

A few men Thatcher could make out in the dim light commented that they didn't care about the mustangs or who shot them. One added that the sheriff had more important things to do than look for horse killers.

Everyone seemed to have an opinion on worthless horses and fools who'd waste bullets on shooting them. Now and then, in winter, a herd of mustangs made it down this far south. They were hard to handle and likely to go back to the wild as soon as they downed a fence.

Bull, mostly thanks to his size, stood and took charge one more time. "We all know who shot the horses and it weren't the drunks the sheriff caught. Those who did the killing are the only family not here tonight and they are not our problem. The trouble that can destroy us is the dead man found in the canyon. If the law traces him back to here, we're all in trouble."

Someone in front said that the sheriff wouldn't trace the body here. No one seemed to agree with him.

Bull shook his head. "He's from here. The tats prove it. But there's half a dozen old guys living way back and I'm thinking none of us knows any of their real names."

Thatcher fought the urge to agree with the scared man. Trouble was coming. Thatcher's mother told him once that Bull was the smartest man who lived out here, but being the brightest among rocks didn't keep you from still being dull as dirt.

"Maybe we should have us an investigation," Potter said, surprising everyone. He never talked, but everyone stayed friendly with him because his was one of the few places that got mail delivered. His farm faced Road 111. Anyone who had to have something delivered always used his address.

Potter minded his own business and never gossiped, and as far as anyone knew, he always held the mail in his garage until someone dropped by asking about it. "If the sheriff comes to anyone's door, it'll probably be mine," Potter added. "I'm closest to the main road. We start there and check on everyone out here. We need to find the answers."

Thatcher wanted to yell *Amen*. First, Potter had an idea, and second, it was a good one. It just proved that some people weren't as dumb as they looked.

Bull took over passing out assignments. "The sheriff might have a death wish if he comes in here poking around, but we can check out what's going on. We'll divide up the area and check every cabin, trailer and tent. Someone's got to be missing or know the tattooed man's real name. Surely it's not Hubcab on his birth certificate." Bull puffed up. "Once we find out something I'll let the sheriff know and tell him there is no need in him looking any further."

One of the men up front by the fire whined that if he knocked on doors he'd feel like a damned census taker.

Stretch laughed. "I had one knock on my door and ask if I was married. I wiggled my eyebrows at her and told her I wasn't, but if she was willing I wouldn't mind trying it out for a few nights. She took off running for her car. Didn't even stop when she dropped her pen."

Everyone laughed.

Stretch shrugged. "Closest I ever came to marrying in Texas. I still got the pen."

Thatcher shifted until he could see most of the faces. It had taken him an hour, but he'd just figured out who was missing from the crowd.

The Dulapse brothers. Cajuns who came to live here about ten years ago. They chopped down trees along the canyon rim for firewood in the fall and sold it on county roads. Mesquite trees, not worth anything, and mostly a bother to all, drew a good price as wood for smoking beef. Some of the best restaurants in Austin and Dallas bragged about mesquite-smoked steaks.

"We got what we wanted."

"What did we get, O'Grady? No facts. No proof. Only a nickname that we'd already heard to help us ID the dead guy and two brothers guilty of horse shooting by reason of being absent from the meeting."

"I got more than that," Tim said as they walked away. "I got some great characters. I swear these people don't live in my world. Bull and Stretch are straight out of a novel. In fact if I could think of a plot, I'd put them in as main characters."

They walked in silence until Thatcher passed his house. He pointed further down the road where they'd hid Tim's Jeep in the brush. "Why don't you make notes, Tim, while I pick up a few things at my place and then you can drive me over to the Lone Heart. Charley's probably wondering where I am."

"You living there?" Tim asked.

"No, just visiting."

He turned around and doubled back with Tim still walking and talking.

When Thatcher made it back to his home, the place was so dark only someone familiar with the path would even try to find it. He opened the unlocked door and turned on the light. Thatcher was surprised the electricity still worked. His mom had been gone long enough to have missed paying at least one bill, but he knew from experience that the power company didn't bother coming this far out until she missed at least three.

He circled around the place. There was no food or money left. Nothing worth stealing. Maybe if he tried not to use any electricity, the power company would forget about him. His mom had left a dozen times before. He knew the signs she'd be gone a while. She'd always buy a dozen cans of soups or beans and leave a twenty under the plastic flowerpot on the table.

She claimed that she'd be back by the time the soup and money ran out. Only she never was. Not when he was eight. Not now.

When he'd been little, he'd knocked on the neighbors' door and asked for a handout. By ten he'd learned to fish and hunt rabbits to supplement the soup. A year later he started catching snakes and selling them.

Thatcher rushed to his hiding place in the corner of his room. He pulled out his moneybag, an old sock, and peeled off two twenties. Since he was meeting with the sheriff tomorrow, he might as well buy a few groceries. Brigman would bring him home. He'd get enough to make it during the week, and on weekends he'd stay over at Lone Heart Ranch. He'd trade work for his keep. They seemed to welcome his help and he needed the company.

As he walked around without taking off his jacket, he started thinking about the ranch, and he decided he wanted to be like Charley and Jubilee. They might not have much, but they didn't seem to worry about having food. Jubilee had even bought him clothes and Charley worried about him working too hard or not getting to school on time.

His mother would come back someday, probably with a new boyfriend. She'd be all giggly and happy, but she'd never think to ask how he made it while she was gone. The new boyfriend would take her shopping for new sexy clothes and lots of food. For as long as he was around, Thatcher would try to be invisible. The bills would be paid and the refrigerator would be full, at least for a while.

"Maybe I won't buy groceries," Thatcher whispered to himself. "Maybe I'll go live at the ranch for as long as they'll let me." His mother wouldn't come looking for him. After all, he was the same age as she was when she ran away. Sunny Jones would just figure parenting was over.

Smiling, he decided he'd take money he'd planned on spending on soup and buy a real cowboy hat. He'd go to school, stay at Lone Heart Ranch and learn all he could from Charley. And he'd never come back to this place where people had more tattoos than teeth.

The next morning when Thatcher caught the school bus, he had all he valued packed in a pillowcase. The lock on his locker would be his safe.

He managed to stay in school until after lunch with Kristi. Then he walked down the seventh grade hall and out the back door. Ten minutes later, he walked into the county offices.

Pearly was doing her nails on government time. She waved, fingers wide apart.

He pointed at the sheriff's open door.

She nodded.

Thatcher thought of saying that it was nice talking to her, but they seemed to be communicating fine without words.

He silently slipped into the sheriff's office.

Sheriff Brigman looked deep in thought, like a man born to worry. From the door it looked as if he was holding the ad Thatcher had found in the canyon in one hand and a scrap of notebook paper in the other.

"Afternoon, Sheriff," Thatcher said.

Brigman looked up and smiled. "I was just going over some of Tim's notes about what he saw last night. Don't get too close to this investigation, son. It's not safe."

"I tried to tell Tim that, sir, but he's like a bloodhound with two noses."

Brigman stood. "How about we walk over to the café and talk about it over pie?"

"Sounds good." Thatcher didn't mind that idea at all. He guessed he was in for a lecture, but at least the sheriff's talks usually came with food.

Pearly delivered a letter. The sheriff barely glanced at it before he shoved it into his bottom drawer.

Thatcher heard a click locking the letter in his secret drawer.

Before he could ask any questions, Brigman said, "Good to see you, Thatcher—only isn't school still going on?"

"Early release for good behavior." Thatcher followed the sheriff to his car.

Brigman frowned. "You know, if you don't take the classes, you'll have to repeat the grade."

"Yeah. Been there, done that." He'd already figured out that a note from the sheriff might get him out of trouble. "Only I have important news for you, Sheriff."

Brigman might not believe him, but he at least looked interested.

They spent the next hour talking about the Dulapse brothers and how the men living out in the Breaks were going to do their own investigation. Thatcher filled the sheriff in on details Tim hadn't thought to ask about last night.

He ended his report with, "It ain't safe for you to go in there, Sheriff. The brothers are mean as snakes."

"Maybe I'll send word that I want to talk to the Dulapse boys. The drunks I arrested for shooting the horses were so drugged up they confessed, but I still think the brothers had something to do with it. Why else would they have been in such a hurry to visit the drunks?"

"If Bull says they didn't do it, I'd believe him, but don't the Dulapses need to confess?" Thatcher shook his head. "They might connect you and me if you visited with them. Folks see you bring me home now and then. Right now they think I'm just always in trouble. If they thought we were friends, I wouldn't be safe out there."

"Maybe I'll just stop out on County Road 111 at their firewood stand. I know what I'm doing. They'll never know they're being interrogated."

"I need to learn that skill." Thatcher leaned back in what he thought of as his seat in the patrol car.

Brigman smiled. "You thinking of going into law enforcement, son?"

"No, but I think Kristi Norton might be. She's real good at talking about two things at once. Like at lunch. I thought we were discussing how a necklace was made and it turned out we were talking about what she wanted for her birthday. I didn't even know I was supposed to get her a present. Never got anyone else one." He laughed. "Never got one, either. You may find this hard to believe, but I'm not sure my mom knows my birthday. She's never mentioned it."

Brigman didn't seem to think his confession was funny. "I need to make some rounds. You want a ride home? I'll let you out at the turnoff."

"Nope. I'm going over to Lone Heart. I'm staying there for a while, helping them out." He thought a moment before adding, "You might want to keep my location between us, Sheriff. I don't want any Cajuns showing up looking for me."

"You have my word, son, and if you're ever in trouble, remember, you can always come to me. I've got your back."

Thatcher didn't mention that he wouldn't mind if the sheriff would watch his front, too. He had a feeling that if the Dulapse brothers knew he was poking around in their business, they might come after him, and it would be head on.

CHAPTER TWENTY-TWO

Lauren
March 28

LAUREN FOUND TIM O'GRADY in the back of her father's office frantically writing every detail of his adventure with Thatcher down on an old laptop he'd carried through college.

"This is what I'm looking for, L. This is it. Life. I was wrong about hiding out to write. I got to live before I can write."

"Take a break, Tim. The Franklin sisters want to talk to you." She offered her hand.

He frowned as if planning to refuse, but reconsidered. "Sure. Maybe they'll confess to something now they know I work for the sheriff." As he stood, he took her hand. "I know it's hard to understand a writer, L, but you've got to try. You're my best friend, you know."

"I know." She thought of adding that if he didn't get out more she'd soon be his only friend.

They walked across to the Franklin sisters' antiques store.

Both sisters smiled at her when she stepped in and then quickly forgot her when they spotted Tim.

"He's here," Rose shouted as if her sister wasn't standing six inches away.

Daisy pulled out her phone, dialed a number and said one word, *bingo*, then ran to meet Tim as if she hadn't known him all her life.

Lauren moved aside and fought down a laugh as the two middle-aged women made over Tim as though he really was Hemingway. They wanted to know all about what he was writing, where his ideas came from and had he found his voice yet.

Tim loved the attention and within minutes molded into an author dealing with wild fans even though the sisters had never read anything he'd written and hadn't been wild a single day of their lives.

Lauren stood by the door watching the show.

Faster than a professional kidnapping, Rose and Daisy whisked Tim outside and into their van. If Lauren hadn't run to keep up, she would have been left behind.

"We have someone you have to meet. She's very interesting." Rose backed the van out of their spot and floored the gas pedal as she headed toward Ransom Canyon. "If she'd lived in another time, another place, she would have been known as a sage. She's very reclusive, but she said she'd meet you as soon as we told her you were destined to be a great writer."

Tim was almost drunk now on the flattery. "What's this person do now?"

"She collects things."

"What kind of things?"

Lauren leaned near Tim's ear and whispered, "Bones of would-be writers."

Tim's eyes widened as if, for a second, he believed her.

Rose answered his questions. "Books. She has thousands."

A few miles outside of town they pulled off on a dirt road that led to a house near the canyon. The stucco home looked as if it was balanced on the edge.

Tim said he'd seen it for years, but never knew who lived in it.

Lauren had also seen it from the bottom of the canyon, but never knew how to get to the house from the road.

Rose and Daisy stayed in the car as they pointed Tim toward the front door. "It's okay, Tim, she's expecting you. We'll wait."

Not wanting to wait in the car with the sisters, Lauren followed Tim.

As they walked up the path, Lauren was fascinated by all the wild native flowers, Indian paintbrush, sunflowers, bluebonnets, and many more she didn't know the names of. Whoever lived here knew the land and what would grow along this windy shelf.

A woman dressed as if she belonged more in Santa Fe than Crossroads answered the door. She was in her thirties or maybe even early forties, and her eyes danced with intelligence and life. There was something in her gaze that told Lauren she'd seen the world and that she didn't tolerate fools.

"Come in," she said without asking who they were. "I've been expecting you, Tim O'Grady, and you, too, Lauren Brigman. The sisters have been telling me about you two for years."

Lauren wondered who the woman was. How could she have lived so close to town without Lauren knowing about her?

The foyer of her home opened up to a huge room that was bright with natural light and rich in color. One long wall, maybe thirty feet, was lined with shelves, all stuffed with books. As they moved through the rooms, she saw that all the walls were bookshelves, as though the house had been built that way.

"My name is Terry Handley," the woman said. "The Franklin sisters may have told you that I read."

"What do you like to read, Miss Handley?" Tim asked.

"Everything," she answered. "And, it's Mrs. Handley, but you may call me Terry."

That was it, Lauren thought. This woman who looked as though she'd traveled the world must have simply read thousands of books.

Terry went about making tea as if there was no hurry.

Lauren looked around at the counters and shelves. Thick sticks of paper bound with rubber bands lay everywhere. Manuscripts? One pile was stacked so high by a chair that the paper could have served as an end table.

Tim wasn't so patient. "The Franklin sisters thought you might have the secret or maybe some advice."

The lady finally looked at him and smiled a smile that seemed ageless. "I've known many writers. For a few years I was an editor in New York, but lately I'm a ghost writer."

"Really?" Lauren found that fascinating. The ghostwriting obviously paid very well. She studied the woman, realizing she had a full rich life right here in what some would call the middle of nowhere. She didn't have to be in public. She wasn't fighting her way to the top of some ladder.

"Would you like some tea?" she said as she turned from Tim and looked straight at Lauren.

"I'd love some. I want to hear all about you, Mrs. Handley."

The lady laughed. "An interest in others is the first key to a rich life. Why they do what they do. Why they love whom they love. Know a man's secret and you'll understand him."

Lauren could almost hear Tim's breath leave his lungs. He had never had patience and didn't want it now. He'd come to talk about his writing.

But he obviously didn't want to be rude. He waited as she poured the tea and asked Lauren how her father was doing.

Lauren was surprised Mrs. Handley knew her father, but then everyone knew the sheriff. If she knew the Franklin sisters, she'd probably heard the backstory on everyone for a hundred miles around.

Slowly, as they talked, Lauren realized the woman not only knew about the people in town, she cared about them. Only she had a strong feeling they didn't know much about her.

Tim finished his tea and shook his head when Mrs. Handley offered more. He seemed to have lost interest in the conversation.

Lauren found the lady interesting. They talked of nothing and everything while Tim perused the shelves as if he thought her home was a public library.

Finally, Terry Handley walked them back to the door. She took Tim's hand and looked up at him. "Your gift is laughter, Tim."

His laugh held little humor. "I think the Franklin sisters thought you might help me get published."

"I'd be happy to do what I can. Write a thousand pages and come back. I know a few publishers who would be interested in looking at work from someone as serious as you."

Tim tried to grin. "So you see something in me that tells you I might just have what it takes?"

"You're curious about the world and you run full out to find the answers. I think you'll travel far in life, but..." Terry patted Tim then turned to Lauren before she added, "She's the writer."

A few minutes later, Tim climbed into the car. He didn't say a word until they'd said goodbye to the Franklins. Then he complained that he should have known the Franklin sisters wouldn't know anyone who could help him get published. "All I need is a break. It's not just talent, it's who you know in the publishing game. A great teacher, someone who knows a publisher or a movie producer. I could write a script."

Lauren didn't say a word. The woman had missed the mark completely. Tim would be the writer, not she.

CHAPTER TWENTY-THREE

Charley
March 29

CHARLEY TRIED TO act as if he'd slept when he entered
the ranch kitchen. In truth, he didn't think he'd closed
his eyes for more than an hour since he and Jubilee
had gone to Lone Heart Pass. He must have relived the
kiss in the darkness of the passage a hundred times.
The memory haunted him, possessed him. The way
she'd touched his chest, as if her light contact could
hold him back. Then, how they hadn't even hugged,
making the touch of their lips electric.

They'd simply kissed. And now he couldn't even
tell her how one kiss had changed him. She'd said
they'd never talk about it. *Never.* Holding it inside
made the memory too real to allow sleep, made seeing her and not touching her almost painful. The only
cure he could think of was work.

Yesterday they'd been too busy, so neither of them
talked much. He had little hope that today would be
better.

"Morning," Jubilee said, without turning around
from the stove to look at him.

She sounded as tired as he felt. "The coffee's ready."
Her hair was in a ponytail now and she already had her

boots on. She looked as if she should be catching the
school bus, as if she wasn't old enough to run a ranch.
But if he'd learned one thing about Jubilee Hamilton,
it was that she could do anything she set her mind to.

He poured a cup and sat down, wondering if he
could focus enough to carry on a conversation. Something had to give between them. At this rate they'd
either die of overwork or kill each other making love.

She set down his plate of bacon and eggs.

He managed to thank her before he ate.

"Sorry I burned the eggs," she said when she refilled his cup.

"I hadn't noticed." The food could have been made
of mud and he would have simply salted it before shov-
ing it into his mouth. "I thought I'd plow the wheat
field today. Weatherman said high humidity but no
wind."

"Do you need any help? Just tell me what to do."
Unlike him, she simply stared at her plate of food.

"No, I'll be finished by…"

They both turned as a van came roaring up the
dirt drive.

Charley stood and reached for the rifle above the
door, but he didn't pull it down. Unwelcome strangers didn't always mean trouble. But being alone out
in the country did mean caution.

They both waited in the doorway as the van pulled
near, then swung sideways.

Almost before the huge vehicle stopped, a stout
woman dressed in white jumped out of the passenger
seat and stretched as if she'd been trapped inside for
hours. Then both side doors slid open. A thin girl in
skin-tight stretch pants and an oversize sweater that

hung off one shoulder, crawled out of the back. Only unlike the first woman, she moved fluidly, as if someone had told her to pretend to be a willow.

"These people look like they work for my sister," Jubilee whispered. "I think I've seen the one in white at her house before."

"The first one's a nurse, I'm guessing," Charley said. "But what does the other one think she is?"

"Maybe she's the cook. Or the yoga instructor. If we're lucky, they've come after Destiny. I heard her say she keeps a yoga instructor on speed dial and yesterday she swore to me that things were about to change around here."

Charley turned his head sideways, still looking at the thin girl. "Her pants look painted on and someone forgot to finish knitting her top. I don't know much about yoga, but if she keeps doing that 'willow in the wind' imitation, someone around here will probably plant her."

"Stop acting like you've never seen clothes like that. I know what you're doing, practicing for laying on the hick act."

"It usually works." He frowned. Jubilee was finding it far too easy to read him lately.

The driver came around to the side of the van that faced them. He looked as if he played walk-on parts in *The Sopranos*. Beefy. Probably armed. A wanted-poster smile. He marched to the back of the van and began unloading boxes and cases. The two women made no effort to help him; they just stared at Charley and Jubilee.

"You have any idea what to do, boss?" Charley's

voice was low as if he might frighten them off with any noise.

"No. Since they probably work for Destiny, maybe we should wake her. Who knows, if they're her staff maybe they missed her so badly they tracked her down."

"Well, if they are," Charley said, "I think they may be moving in. From the look of them, that's more likely than they made a wrong turn and think we're the dude ranch north of Crossroads."

Before Charley could ask any questions, the thin woman leaned back into the van and pulled out a screaming toddler she must have woken up. A few seconds later the stout woman lifted out another one, who looked just like the first, only if possible, he was screaming louder than his brother.

Charley debated stepping out, rifle in hand, and demanding whoever they were that they get off the property at once. "You're running out of bedrooms, boss, and I don't think one bathroom is going to be enough."

"It's the twins." Jubilee's face went white just as a scream, coming from upstairs, drowned out both the babies' cries.

Charley tugged Jubilee out of the way as Destiny bolted through the kitchen and onto the porch.

"No, you don't," she shouted. "You take them right back. I told Mason not to even think of sending them to me."

"We can't take them back. He told us to drop them off." The thin girl shoved her charge toward Destiny. "He says if you don't come back home, the twins are staying right here with you."

Destiny set the baby down immediately and stormed

off the porch, ruining her perfect pedicure. "You two are not leaving. I'll need a cook and a nurse with me. You wouldn't believe how rough it's been for me here with no help. I've had to do everything myself."

The stout lady skirted Destiny and plopped the second baby boy on the porch. As she walked backward, she let out a cry. "Sorry, we were told we'd be fired if we stayed." All three ran for the van like bandits and drove away with the back doors flapping.

Destiny turned toward Charley. "Well, don't just stand there. Help me get all of this inside. Jubilee, pick up your nephews and follow me in."

Charley shook his head. "I don't work for you, Destiny, but I'll be happy to help out for a few minutes. After that, you're on your own."

Jubilee took the hint. "Me, too. As soon as I get them inside, I have to find my hat and get to work."

"You two are not leaving me alone with these babies."

Her words came out like a general's, but unfortunately, Destiny no longer had any troops.

Charley got all the baby stuff inside, including high chairs and what looked like hundreds of diapers. Then, just to help out, he dragged a line of chicken wire to the porch and nailed it in place outside the slats. It didn't look very good, but the porch would now serve as a big playpen.

He saw Jubilee put both boys in their chairs and give them a handful of Cheerios to play with. Then, like lightning, they both disappeared, with Destiny's voice rolling like thunder behind them.

When they reached the barn, both folded over laughing.

Jubilee gained control first. "Do you think she'll be all right alone with the boys?"

"If she survives, she'll be a different woman by afternoon. I'll call Ike at the Two Step and see if his daughter can bring a few friends and come babysit after school. By then Destiny will probably need a few hours to have a nervous breakdown."

"She says she came out to help me get rid of this ranch. She seems to think I'm trapped here."

"Are you?" Charley was surprised how much it mattered.

"No, of course not, but I can't get through to her. She's determined to do what she thinks is best for me." Jubilee smiled. "That and I think she wanted a break from being a wife and mother."

"How long a break?"

"Maybe forever. She said once I came to my senses and sold this place she'd move to DC and help me find a place."

He began loading supplies into the pickup. "You never did say what upset you so a few nights ago. Something she said, I'm guessing."

Jubilee nodded. "She wants half the ranch. Told me she wouldn't leave until I signed it over to her." Jubilee glanced back toward her house. "I'll never sign anything, no matter how long she stays."

"Sounds like her husband wants her back. Maybe if we stay out of sight, she'll make up her mind to go back to him."

"I think she loves him and the babies. It's just too much right now for her."

Charley shrugged. "She's about to find out how much harder it's going to be alone."

"My sister usually gets everything she wants, but she won't get this ranch."

"She's got her hands full now. I have a feeling if we stay around the house, I'll be wearing a white apron and you'll be doing yoga to stay sane. If Mason wants her back, he's picked the perfect weapon to make her crawl back. Hope someone in that van heading to Dallas has a cell phone. I have a feeling they'll be turning around before dark and coming back to pick her and those babies up."

Jubilee giggled as she climbed into the truck. "We've got farming to do."

"Right." He jumped behind the wheel. "With your help, we'll have the field plowed by noon and can make the lunch special at Dorothy's in town."

"Sounds like a plan as long as we stay away from the house."

He grinned. "We need to give her time to make her decision."

CHAPTER TWENTY-FOUR

Thatcher
March 29

LILLIE LEANED OVER the porch railing and stared at the two tiny toddlers now caged in by chicken wire.

"Walking babies," she said as if identifying the species. "I've never seen two that look so much alike."

Thatcher stared at them, not getting too close to the porch. "Maybe they're from the same litter."

Kristi Norton giggled as she stepped out of the house with two bottles. "Lillie, would you go ask your father and Jubilee if they have thought about supper? Destiny says if she cooks it will be the same menu as lunch—Cheerios."

"Sure." Lillie bounced down from her viewing spot and ran toward the corral where she knew her father would be working with the horses.

Thatcher grinned at Kristi. "I've heard," he said, trying to sound knowledgeable, "that twins happen when a woman hiccups during sex."

Kristi laughed. "You're so funny, Thatcher. I love that you say crazy things just to make me laugh."

He'd thought he was being serious, but now he realized he'd probably been given faulty information. "You want me to feed one of them?"

"Sure. Daniela's cleaning up the mess they made in the kitchen, and the twins' mother is taking her second nap since we got here. You know how to feed babies?"

Thatcher swung over the railing. "It couldn't be much different than feeding a calf."

Kristi smiled. "Right."

CHAPTER TWENTY-FIVE

Charley
March 29

A LITTLE AFTER TEN, Charley took Daniela and Kristi home. The girls had babysat for six hours and were tired but happy. Destiny had paid each a hundred dollar bill and made them promise to come back as soon as they got out of school tomorrow.

Since he couldn't leave Lillie at the house alone, Charley had helped her into her pajamas and wrapped her in a blanket. With luck, she'd go to sleep on the way back.

Thatcher insisted on riding in the back of the pickup for the journey. He'd decided, sometime before dark, that he should stay the night at Charley's just in case there was trouble at the main house. "I got this picture of Destiny bolting out of the house screaming before dawn. I don't much care if she runs off, but I worry about them walking babies that Lillie seems to think are puppies."

Charley laughed, but the scene might not be far from a foretelling of what was to come. Jubilee's sister's reaction to any cry of her offspring was to order someone else to take care of them, and tonight she'd be alone with her children for the first time.

On the way back from town, while Lillie slept between them, Thatcher told Charley what he'd heard at the Saturday night prayer meeting. Charley never questioned a word. In his teens, he'd worked with cowhands who'd lived out there, and knew they had their own kind of law along the Breaks. No county claimed them. No lawmen went in unless absolutely necessary.

Charley was silent for a minute, then said, "One of the cowhands who had a place in the Breaks said he knew a man by the name of Bent who beat his wife every weekend for years. She was so worn down she wouldn't even look at people."

"I've seen men like that." Thatcher shook his head. "It ain't right to hit women or kids."

Charley nodded. "Did your mother tell you that?"

"No," the boy answered. "I seen it firsthand."

Charley didn't want to bring up bad times, so he continued his story.

"The cowhand I worked with one summer claimed Bent missed poker one Friday night so a few of his drinking buddies went out to check on him, guessing he'd gotten drunk without them and passed out.

"Bent was in bed so bruised he looked like he'd been dipped in black-and-blue dye. Both eyes were swollen shut and one of his ears had doubled in size. They said even his toes were bruised and broken at odd angles.

"His wife said she'd found him that way when she got home from her monthly trip to town. Bent never said a word about who beat him up, but they say he walked a wide circle around his wife's grandmother for the rest of his life."

"An old woman beat him up?" Thatcher asked.

"That was the rumor. The sheriff never investigated." Charley pulled up to his place. "Maybe I should go with the sheriff if he decides to start asking questions. I know a few of the men from the Breaks."

"You might want to do that. I want to help the sheriff but I haven't figured out how."

Thatcher ran inside when they stopped. He'd already made up his bed on the couch and was neatly folding his new clothes over the back of one of the kitchen chairs when Charley carried Lillie sleeping in his arms.

Charley walked past him, feeling dead on his feet. It had been three hard days and two sleepless nights since he'd closed his eyes. He mumbled good-night to Thatcher and carried Lillie to her room.

She opened her eyes when he laid her down; she wanted him to hold her until she drifted off again. By the time he crossed the living room, heading toward his bedroom, Thatcher was snoring and Charley felt as if he was sleepwalking.

He was so tired he felt like a drunk trying to prove he could still walk straight. When he closed the door and turned around to face his bed, the shock of what he saw rendered him wide awake.

Jubilee lay curled up on top of his grandmother's quilt that served as his bedspread. She still wore the clothes she'd worked in all day. She hadn't even removed her boots.

It registered in his tired brain that if she'd come to sleep with him, she would have at least undressed or put on something clean like a nightgown or even a T-shirt. He didn't know much about women, but he'd noticed they tended to spend time dressing just right for a romantic evening. Men only tended to be interested in undressing.

Her hat lay on the floor as if it had tumbled off when she'd collapsed. Her hair was tangled across her face. Her mouth was open as she snored lightly.

"Boss, if you're going for sexy, you missed the mark." Leaning down, he brushed her hair off her forehead and kissed her cheek. "You gave it your all today. I have to admire that." She'd worked right beside him, pulling her weight the entire day.

He had no idea what to do with her so he sat down on the corner of his bed and tugged off her boots, then his own.

She mumbled something about just wanting a little nap before she had to go back to the house.

Charley didn't answer. He knew she'd probably had the same amount of sleep he'd had in the past two days. He leaned back, almost touching her shoulder, and closed his eyes.

He was asleep before he let out a breath.

Sometime during the night he rolled over and managed to pull the quilt over her. She'd turned away from him, but her nicely rounded bottom pressed against his side, reminding him she was there.

At dawn, he opened one eye, trying to think of what to say to her. If she'd noticed how often he'd patted her last night, she'd be yelling before he could get a word in. Not that he had anything to say for himself. He had no defense.

He'd worried for no reason. She was gone. Boots, hat and nicely rounded bottom.

Charley got up as if it were an ordinary morning.

He showered and shaved. Woke Thatcher up. While the kid showered, he dressed Lillie and started breakfast.

"How many eggs can you eat?" He yelled though the bathroom door at Thatcher.

"How many you got?" the kid answered.

Charley laughed and made six.

"Morning, That," Lillie said when he appeared at the table. "Will you stay with us for a while?"

Thatcher looked at Charley. "I could help out around here. I could pay for what I eat."

"You're welcome to stay as long as you want and you can help me build a chicken coop this weekend. I have a feeling this ranch is going to need eggs."

"I saw lots of wood in the back of the barn. Levy must have never thrown a board away. We could use the wood and an old drawer for the nests in a coop."

"You plan it, kid, and I'll help you build it. How about we surprise Jubilee?"

After he shoved the last bite in his mouth, Thatcher offered to walk Lillie down to the bus stop. Only when they got to the porch, he offered to carry her on his back so she wouldn't get her tennis shoes dirty.

Charley heard him ask Lillie what she thought a chicken house should look like and she said, "A castle."

Charley was smiling when he turned and saw Jubilee walking around her almost-garden. She'd gotten so excited when the first plant broke ground. He couldn't wait to see how she'd act when she saw it ready to harvest.

If she saw it. If either one of them was still around by fall. Every day he watched her charts—money in, money out. It was going to be close. If they had to sell off the cattle early they'd lose thousands. If the crop didn't make it, there would be little cash left to buy feed. If the barn didn't stay full of borders. If one of them got sick.

There were too many ifs.

This wasn't just a job anymore. He cared about this place. He cared about her.

The realization hit him hard. He cared about her.

CHAPTER TWENTY-SIX

Lauren
April 2

ON FRIDAY LAUREN finished her last class, clicked on her cell, picked up her books and began the mile walk back to her dorm. The Texas Tech campus was beautiful. April green with the sun shining bright. She was almost finished, but she felt more fear than anticipation. In six weeks she'd graduate without a plan of what to do next.

Polly suggested they move to Dallas, still be roommates and have a wild time. She had a friend who owned a coffee shop. They could both work there.

As Lauren walked, she pounded out the reasons why that plan would never work. Her mother lived in Dallas, so it was not the place to be. Working in a coffee shop would be wasting her degree in history. And last, she hated coffee.

Her cell sounded about the time she passed the statue of Will Rogers riding his favorite horse, Soapsuds. Lauren smiled up at him as she pulled out her phone. There was a legend at Tech that if a virgin ever graduates, Will Rogers would get off his horse. "Get ready to step down, Will," she mumbled as she flipped open her phone.

She thought it might be Lucas. Tomorrow would be a week since she'd seen him and she couldn't help wondering if he thought of her as much as she'd thought of him. Maybe she'd gone nuts in the back hallway of the Two Step, and maybe she didn't have much experience compared to most, but the man kissed like liquid passion.

Only the phone number wasn't Lucas's—it was Pop's cell number. Knowing him, Pop probably wanted her to drive home this weekend. He'd been putting in extra hours lately.

"Hi, Pop," she answered as she moved away from the statue and headed across the grass toward her dorm.

There was a long pause. "Lauren. This is Tim O'Grady. I'm calling on your dad's cell." His words came slow. Sober. Rehearsed.

"Hi, Tim. Why don't you drive to Lubbock this weekend? We could haunt a few of the bad restaurants you hung out in while you were here."

"No, Lauren. I'm heading toward Lubbock, but not to party." Another pause, when he returned he sounded as if he was fighting back sobs. "I need to tell you about your father before you hear it on the news. He's been hurt, Lauren. He's been hurt bad."

She froze, books tumbling around her. The call every person who loves a lawman fears, waits for, prays will never come. "An accident?"

"No, L, it wasn't an accident."

"Give me the facts, Tim. All the facts." If it wasn't an accident and the news might be involved, Lauren knew it was bad.

Her hand was shaking so hard she could barely hold the phone.

"All right. First, he's alive and on his way to the hospital in Lubbock." Now Tim's words came fast and hard. "I'm right behind them. The EMT says he's stable but he'll need surgery as soon as possible. We've got a police escort and are going eighty out here on the open road. Our estimated time of arrival is less then thirty minutes. I've been calling you for over an hour."

She'd turned her phone off for class. "I'll meet you in the emergency room." She picked up her books and walked toward her car. "Talk to me, Tim. Tell me what's happening. Where was he? Was anyone else hurt?" She couldn't bring herself to ask if he'd been attacked. All her life she'd heard people talk about how lawmen are sometimes targeted just because of their badges. But not Pop. Not in a tiny place like Crossroads.

"I'll tell you all I know." Tim's voice was high again. "None of this seems real yet. I can't get my head wrapped around it, L. I'm in the car following the ambulance and I still can't believe it."

She waited for him to get control.

Finally, he began. "They think he was ambushed out on County Road 111 where the road winds in between shallow canyons. Thatcher found him. His patrol car had been shot up. Tires flat. Windshield shot out."

Lauren knew exactly where Pop must have been. He'd taught her to drive on that winding road. The shallow box canyons had once been used as makeshift corrals during the cattle drives. The hills weren't more than twenty or thirty feet high.

Tim continued when she was silent for a while. "Thatcher said he found your dad lying flat in the dirt beside his car. The kid was loading the sheriff in the back of his pickup when he heard rounds that seemed to be coming from nowhere. He jumped in the truck and was a mile down the road before he realized he'd taken a bullet in his leg just above the knee. Somehow he drove to town with your dad bouncing around in the truck bed and his leg dripping blood.

"The clinic isn't open on Friday, so the kid took your dad to the school. The nurse started care while the principal called an ambulance. The last bell had sounded thirty minutes earlier so most of the students were gone, but I bet the main office was chaos."

Lauren climbed into her car feeling cold inside. "Where is he hit? How deep? Are any bullets still inside?" She doubted she'd remember the details, but she had to keep talking or she'd start screaming.

"One shot to the left arm. Bullet may have broken his bone." Tim's voice was calm again. "He was hit twice in his left leg and once in the shoulder, but that one looks like it might have grazed him or maybe the bullet passed though. Three of the bullets are still in him, I think."

"Four times," she whispered. "Pop has been shot four times." She couldn't close her eyes now. If she did, she'd see the bullets going into Pop's body. See him jerking back and falling.

"One of the Lubbock deputies who is driving in with the ambulance said it looked like the shooter wasn't trying to kill him, just using him for target practice. If he'd been able to stand again and had tried to reach his car, the shooter probably would have shot him again."

There was a long silence, then Tim added, "Lauren, he's lost a lot of blood, but your dad's strong. He'll pull through this. He called the office and I rushed to the school. Four holes in him and the sheriff was still giving orders."

Lauren barked a laugh. That was her pop. Oddly, that gave her comfort.

"While he was bleeding all over the place, he handed me his cell and made me promise to let you know he was all right. Then they put a pressure wrap on him and the sheriff started cussing, wanting them to take care of Thatcher first. The boy would have none of it. He was hopping around on one leg, trailing blood everywhere and saying he was fine. I swear the two of them are just alike."

She started her car. "I'll see you at the hospital, and thanks, Tim, for telling me the details." Dropping the phone in her pocket, she pulled out of the parking lot, even though the hospital was almost close enough to walk to. The day was warm and bright, but she couldn't stop shivering.

Pop was shot. Why would anyone shoot him?

A hundred questions came to mind that she wished she'd asked Tim. Was her father awake when they loaded him for the drive? Did he know who shot him? What was he doing way out on the county road? How was Thatcher? Where was the kid now? In the ambulance with Pop or in the car with Tim?

She calculated the time. Thatcher would have been headed home from school. Or maybe he'd been home to pick up something and was headed toward Lone

Heart Ranch. Either way, he was driving, something her father had caught him doing a dozen times. But, this time, this time…if he hadn't driven by, her father might have bled to death or taken that fifth bullet.

Lauren ran into the emergency room, expecting to see half the town of Crossroads there.

No one she recognized was waiting. She was early.

A nurse at the desk told her the ambulance from Crossroads wouldn't arrive for at least another ten minutes. "We've been in contact. We're ready and waiting."

No one looked up at her as she paced. A couple holding two sick kids sat by the left set of doors. A half dozen middle-schoolers huddled around one boy who looked about Thatcher's age. He had a new cast on his leg. Skateboards were piled high in the chair next to him.

She just stared at them. If Thatcher had to be hurt, it should have happened like this—he should never have been shot. What kind of person shoots a kid?

The answer was simple. The same kind of person who'd shoot her father. Lauren tried to slow her breathing. There was nothing she could do now but wait for the ambulance.

Lauren plopped down on one of the hard plastic chairs as she mentally counted the seconds off in her head. Tim had called twenty minutes ago saying he was thirty minutes out. He'd be here in five minutes, ten at the most.

Hospital staff—doctors, nurses, aides—all seemed to be circling. Also waiting. Through the glass she saw a news truck pull up. The scene seemed as though it belonged in a movie, not in her life.

The nurse from the main desk took a call, then crossed the room and knelt in front of Lauren. "You the sheriff's daughter?" she asked.

Lauren nodded.

"We were told to expect you and to let you walk with him as far as you're allowed." She smiled a sad smile. "The ambulance driver said they had to threaten to knock your father out if he didn't stop telling them how to do their jobs."

"Thanks. Can you keep the reporters away? I don't think he'd want them to film him like this."

"I'll see what I can do, but a county sheriff being shot is big news."

Forcing herself to breathe, Lauren moved closer to the door and tried to remember everything Tim had said.

She held her cell in her hands, trying to think. Should she call her mother? Maybe Tim already had. If Pop was conscious, he'd probably told everyone not to call Margaret. They'd been divorced for most of Lauren's life. Would she come if she knew?

An argument they'd had once when they thought Lauren was asleep drifted through her mind. Her mother had screamed that she wouldn't watch him die. She'd wanted him to change jobs and he'd refused. She'd sworn that she wouldn't stand beside him if he got hurt. She wouldn't be there when they put him in the ground.

Margaret, who always got her way, didn't win that argument. She left and her pop stayed on as sheriff.

Putting her phone in her pocket, she decided not to call her mother. Not yet. Not until she knew something.

The Lubbock police must have brought the ambulance in because two uniformed officers passed through the sliding doors first.

She jumped up as four men running with the gurney rushed in. Before they were ten feet inside, a medical team was moving with them, giving orders.

Lauren pushed her way to the gurney. For a second, she couldn't even find her father amid all the tubes and machines and blankets and blood.

"Pop," she said over all the shouting. She'd never seen her father like this. His uniform looked as if it had been ripped off and the white T-shirt, now spotted with red, was cut open. Tubes were running from the arm not covered in bandages. "Pop," she said again as she grabbed his hand.

He tightened his fingers around hers and opened his eyes. "I'm going to be all right, baby. Don't worry. Don't cry."

He hadn't called her baby since she was six.

No words came to her. *I love you* didn't seem enough. She held on as tight as she could, but his fingers relaxed and he closed his eyes.

The gurney hit a set of double doors that said No Admission. Lauren was shoved back out of the way. She lost her grip on his hand in a second and he vanished behind the doors.

"Miss, you have to wait out here," one of the EMTs said in a kind voice as he hung back to block her from entering the last set of doors. "He's going right in to be prepped for surgery. You'll see him in a few hours."

The tiny bit of logic still working in her brain knew the man was right, but she still shook her head and debated trying to bolt past him. Didn't they know she considered him the only family she had? The only one who'd loved her every minute of her life.

An arm gripped her shoulder, turning her into a hard chest. "Lauren. Let them do their job."

She looked up at Tim. "Someone shot my pop," she cried as though Tim didn't already know every detail.

His skin was ghost-white and tears dripped from his eyes unchecked, but he held her tight, as if knowing she was about to crumble. People moved around them in the middle of the hallway, but Tim didn't budge. He'd been her best friend forever. He could read her mind and he wasn't going anywhere. He'd stand in the storm with her.

Lauren didn't know if they were there for a few minutes or an hour. Finally, she asked, "Where is Thatcher?"

"He's back there with the patch-up team. Bullet went right through his leg. Someone said it didn't look like it hit a bone or an artery."

"I need to see him. I need to know everything that happened. I need to thank him." Details, she thought. Somewhere in the details I'll find the reason why and how all this could happen.

Tim agreed. "Some kids his age would have run when the bullets started flying. He said when he saw the cruiser, for a second he thought it was a trick your dad was pulling to get him to stop so the sheriff could yell at him for driving."

They began walking back up the hallway to the main emergency room. Tim's arm was still around her shoulder as she talked. "While I'm waiting on Pop, I'll make notes of everything Thatcher remembers," she said, thinking she sounded like her father.

No matter what, he always wanted to know every detail as if he could figure out the logic of it all if he only had the facts.

"You do that, L. I think I'll find a comfortable chair and collapse. I've had an overload of reality today." He kissed her cheek. "If you need me, I'm right out here in the lobby."

She nodded and walked into the emergency area, totally ignoring a sign that said Staff and Patients Only Beyond this Point.

She had to do what her pop had taught her to do. Think of all the might-bes and then go down each road, considering what would need to be done. Then, no matter what happened next, she'd have at least the beginning of a plan.

CHAPTER TWENTY-SEVEN

Thatcher
April 2

THATCHER HAD NEVER had so much attention in his life. He tried pulling away, thinking he'd just hop out of the hospital and catch a ride back to Crossroads. Only the vampire in white wanted blood. And the tall nurse, with an evil glint in her left eye, kept telling him he'd have to have shots. Then there was the chubby woman in an old wool suit. She kept asking him where his mother was, as if it was his job to keep up with Sunny Jones.

Finally, Mr. Norton showed up. Thatcher had never been so happy to see the principal.

Mr. Norton managed to calm everyone down. He said that Thatcher's mother was on vacation and would be flying in soon, but the boy needed attention now and he was sure that the law required a minor, even without consent of parents, to receive emergency care. As a representative of the school district, he was fully prepared to authorize consent for care, if needed.

Thatcher didn't understand half of what they were talking about, but he got the shots and the bandage while Mr. Norton told them all about how the boy was a real hero, facing gunfire to save a sheriff's life.

Thatcher didn't want to tell them all that it didn't exactly happen that way, but he'd had enough pain-killers to decide Mr. Norton's account of the afternoon sounded better than his.

When the staff finally moved on to the next screamer a few curtains away, he asked Mr. Norton, "Any chance Kristi came with you?"

Norton smiled a kind of smile that said he could read Thatcher's thoughts. "She wanted to, but I wasn't sure what shape you were in. She was upset that you were shot. When I left, she said she planned to make you a poster."

Great! Just what I need, a poster.

Thatcher tried not to look too disappointed that she wasn't outside the door waiting. "We're friends."

The principal probably knew that he'd looked at Kristi's bra that night her blouse was wet. Thatcher was about to confess to all his wicked thoughts when Mr. Norton spoke up.

"She told me you two eat lunch together." Mr. Norton sat down on the bed. "She said you are one of the brightest, funniest boys she's ever talked to. Is that true?"

Thatcher shook his head. "No. Half the time she's so smart I don't even know what she's talking about."

"Well, son, she is a grade ahead of you."

"It's more than that, Mr. Norton. I've figured out that girls talk about and worry over things that guys don't even think about."

"You're telling me. I live with three of them."

He couldn't believe he was sitting there talking to the principal of the school, as if they were just regular people. If he'd owned a cell phone, he would have taken a picture. The principal even offered to take Thatcher's truck to the one-eleven turn-off where it could be picked up later. Thatcher knew the old piece of junk would be as safe there as it would sitting in the school parking lot.

"Kristi tells me you've been staying out at Lone Heart Ranch while your mom has been gone. That true?"

"Yep. I've been helping out some. We're working on a chicken coop that looks like a castle. I drew it up and Charley Collins showed me how to make it happen."

"Tell me about it," the principal said.

Thatcher started talking. He knew Mr. Norton was just trying to get his mind off being shot, but he didn't care. For once, he was talking about something he understood.

Mr. Norton told him the design sounded great and he should think about being an architect.

Thatcher said he'd give it some thought, but coroner and law enforcement were still on the table. Leaning back, he closed his eyes. The sounds around him made any hope of sleep impossible. People talking, carts rolling, machines beeping. This would be the last place anyone would think of coming to rest.

Lauren Brigman rushed in. She hugged him so hard he thought about asking for another X-ray. Finally, she let go and patted him.

She sat beside him and asked him to tell her every detail. "I have to write it down for Pop. He'll want to know what you saw when he wakes up."

Thatcher tried to tell her everything in order, just like he'd told the highway patrolman who rode with him in the ambulance and the cop who came in after they finished doctoring up his leg.

"I'd been out at the Breaks picking up a few baby chicks for Charley's daughter, Lillie. I was on my way back to the Lone Heart Ranch when I came up on the cruiser. It was crossways in the road and for a second I thought the sheriff was just making sure I would stop. Then I saw the windshield out and the tires all flat. I pulled up and was counting the bullet holes in the doors when I saw something by the road."

Thatcher didn't want to tell Lauren the next detail. He knew she'd cry. But she was waiting.

"The sheriff was down on the dirt with his arms spread out. Blood was everywhere. When I knelt over him, he looked up at me and said, almost calm-like, 'Get out of here, fast.'

"I figured he was out of his head, so I wrapped the arm that wasn't bloody around my neck and started pulling him up. I told him I wasn't leaving without him. We were almost to my pickup when we heard gunfire. I grabbed his duty belt at his waist and we ran to my truck with him dragging one leg and leaving a trail of blood behind him." He took a breath. "Your dad's real heavy but I made up my mind I wasn't leaving him. Not out in the dirt looking like roadkill."

She stopped writing and looked up. He saw the thank-you in her light blue eyes; she didn't have to say a word.

Thatcher straightened, knowing he'd done the right thing. "There wasn't time to get him inside the cab. Bullets were popping all around us. I just helped him into the bed, jumped in and hit the gas."

"You saved his life," she whispered.

Thatcher watched her. "You're not going to hug me again, are you?"

"No." She smiled. "When Pop gets out of surgery, he'll want to know if you saw anyone or anything."

He shook his head. "It all happened so fast I didn't have time to look around. All I could think about was getting the sheriff help and getting us both out of the line of fire."

Lauren put down her notes and said she had to get back to the waiting room to be near her father, but Thatcher could see the tears she was fighting to hold in. Mr. Norton must have seen them, too, because he walked with her to the door.

Thatcher leaned back, thinking how tired he felt. As if he'd run the twelve miles to school and then turned around and run home. He watched them talking, wondering how Mr. Norton knew the right words to say. They must teach that in principal school.

Finally, she turned back and smiled at him. "Take care of that wound, Thatcher."

"One of the nurses already threatened me if I didn't keep it clean. Keep me up on how the sheriff's doing, would you?"

She nodded. "I'll find a way."

"I'm heading out of here tonight. Wish the sheriff was going home, too." He looked at the principal. "Any chance you could cover up that cage of chicks I got in my truck? It's supposed to get cold tonight and I'd hate to disappoint Lillie by bringing home frozen chicks."

Mr. Norton said he had a blanket in his car.

Lauren tugged off her Texas Tech jacket and tossed it on Thatcher's bed. "If it's getting colder, you might need this. Wear it home. I'll pick it up later."

When Lauren disappeared, Mr. Norton did, too. A few minutes later he was back with a file of papers and a box of supplies. "You ready to get out of here? I'll drive you to Lone Heart Ranch. I'll get the truck for you later."

"You bet." He pulled on the Tech jacket.

A guy in white showed up with a wheelchair. Apparently, this was just a "fix them up" room and not a "let them rest" room. Which was fine with Thatcher. This was his first visit to a hospital, and he decided it would also be his last. If you weren't hurting when you went in, you would be by the time you got out.

The evil-eyed nurse was back, rattling off orders. Thatcher didn't even bother to listen. He didn't plan on following any rules.

They tried to hand him crutches, but Thatcher only took one. No telling how much two would cost.

"I can hop out," he said, even if he was feeling sleepy.

Mr. Norton told him he'd have to ride in the wheelchair. It was standard procedure. Whatever that meant.

Thatcher zipped the jacket. It looked just like the one he'd seen Tim wear. They must issue them to anyone who went to Tech. He felt smarter just wearing it.

As he was rolled out into the waiting room, Thatcher noticed all kinds of cops. Highway patrolmen, city police, sheriffs. It looked like a convention for everyone who wore a badge.

As Thatcher's wheelchair moved through the crowd, they cleared a path for him, and then they did something strange. They all stood. Some nodded or smiled at him. A few patted him on the back. But they all looked at him straight, as if they were really seeing him.

Mr. Norton leaned down and whispered, "They are paying their respects. You saved one of their own. Now every policeman and sheriff around will know who you are."

Great, Thatcher thought. All he needed was a hundred guardian cops. This one good deed he'd done would ruin any chance he had of living life on the wrong side of the law. Not that he'd considered it, but the option now seemed to be off the table.

He might as well figure out what it took to be a sheriff because he seemed destined to walk the straight and narrow.

Looking straight ahead, he didn't know what to do. Waving as though he was on a float didn't seem right, and neither did ignoring the lineup of badges. He settled on looking sick. The worse he looked the less likely they were to hug him.

At the end of the line, by the front doors, he spotted Charley Collins. The tall cowboy stood, hat in hand, waiting.

Just as he knew Charley would, he took charge. He thanked Mr. Norton for calling him and said, "Let's go home, That. You've had a long day."

They stepped outside to flashing lights. Then, like a curtain closing, they were surrounded by lawmen. The line of uniforms stretched all the way to Charley's pickup, which was parked illegally in front the emergency room. No reporter had a chance of getting close.

As Charley pulled out, a Lubbock sheriff's department cruiser was in front of him leading the way, and two highway patrol cars were behind them. They stayed with the truck, lights flashing, until it turned off at Lone Heart.

Thatcher relaxed in the familiar feel of the pickup. As he watched the light blinking ahead of them, he drifted in and out of sleep. What happened on the back road only hours ago seemed more like a dream now.

Charley didn't say a word until he opened the door to help Thatcher out. Then he said, "You did the right thing, son. I'm proud of you."

That meant more to Thatcher than anything anyone had ever said to him. Charley was someone he looked up to.

As Thatcher limped inside, he admitted, "I was too scared to think of anything else to do."

Charley laughed. "I think I would have been, too."

As they moved inside, Jubilee and Lillie were waiting with hugs.

Thatcher protested, but not too hard.

When Lillie kept patting on him, he said, "I went out to the Breaks to pick up some baby chicks for you, Flower, but Mr. Norton has them now."

"He'll bring them over tomorrow," Charley yelled from the kitchen. "He said Kristi wants to come by and check on you."

Thatcher was tired and hurting, but the thought of Kristi hugging him cheered him up. Since he hadn't started this boyfriend/girlfriend thing, he had no idea how long it would last, but while it did he planned to collect as many hugs as he could.

CHAPTER TWENTY-EIGHT

Jubilee
April 2

"HOW IS HE?" Jubilee whispered to Charley when Thatcher went in the bathroom to change.

Charley leaned on the counter a few inches away from her. "He's tired. Probably all the adrenaline and painkillers. Norton told me the nurse said he'd sleep solid tonight, but tomorrow he'll be in pain. They gave him some pills if he needs them."

"He won't take them."

"I know. Norton said he never even cried." Charley grinned. "Says he cusses worse then anyone he's ever heard. The kid is more worried about the sheriff than himself."

Thatcher came out of the bathroom in boxer shorts and a T-shirt. "I'm not wearing those pajamas," he mumbled, "and I don't usually wear underwear, but I will since you left them out."

"Good." Jubilee smiled at the kid. She'd expected him to be grouchy as a bear. "I drove to town to buy what I thought you'd need. You're going to stay put for a few days and rest."

"I heard it all at the hospital. The chubby nurse said she'd come out and sit on me if I didn't stay off my leg." He let Lillie help him with his covers. She tucked him in as if he was one of her dolls.

"You are in my hospital, That," Lillie said. "I will take care of you."

"That's fine, Flower."

The little girl put her fists on her hips. "You got to do what I say. I'm the princess doctor."

"Great. I take one bullet and now I have to mind someone wearing Tinker Bell pajamas."

She tucked one of her stuffed ponies beside him.

Jubilee broke into the conversation while she still could. "Would you like some supper, or milk and cookies?"

He leaned against the pillow. "No, thanks. I just want to go to sleep. It seems about thirty hours have gone by since I stepped out of school this afternoon."

Charley turned off the living room lights, leaving only one small lamp on next to Thatcher's couch of a bed. "If you wake up in the night, you yell before you get up. No matter what you need, you call me. That leg may hurt when you put any weight on it."

"Don't think there is much chance of me waking up. I feel like I could crash right here for a week." Thatcher sounded almost asleep. "Wake me when there's news on the sheriff."

"I will."

Lillie crawled up on the chest next to his bed and said she'd tell him a story even though his eyes were already closed.

Charley motioned for Jubilee to follow him out to the porch. The night was cool. They left the door open so they could see Thatcher.

The moment they were alone, she moved into Charley's arms. "He's all right," she whispered. "I've been so worried."

Charley's cheek touched hers as he whispered, "I'm not so sure about the sheriff. He's got some complications. Lauren texted me to make sure Thatcher got home all right and said it looked like they were in for a long night. I should have been with him."

"But…"

"He asked me once if I'd go along as backup and I told him I would. If he'd have called, I would have been with him."

She felt her blood chill. "You might have been killed, Charley."

"Or, I might have been able to help."

Jubilee moved closer to Charley. She couldn't seem to pull away. The thought that he might have been hurt circled in her mind. Over the weeks they'd become a team. She depended on him. "Promise me you won't go out there, Charley."

"I can't lie to you." His muscles tightened as if he expected a blow. "If I'm needed, I'll go. Someone out there may have shot the sheriff on purpose."

She could feel his anger as he added, "They shot at our Thatcher."

For a long while they simply held each other. She could almost hear the words they weren't saying. She didn't want him to go, but she admired him, too.

Finally, they relaxed and talked about what might need to be done. For Thatcher. To protect the ranch. If the sheriff needed Charley to help.

With him pressed against her side, as if the porch were too tiny for them to stand apart, she knew whatever had to be done could be done.

She told him about how the van that had delivered Destiny's twins showed up again right after he left. Any hope that her sister would be leaving had vanished when the cook and nanny climbed out along with the yoga teacher. They'd marched into the house like troops going to war.

"Apparently, Mason couldn't stand the thought of his dear wife suffering here on the ranch. He agreed to send help if she'd just consider coming back to him."

Charley was surprised that Mason wanted the spoiled, self-centered woman back but there seemed little reason when it came to love.

"I joined the cause and promised her I'd try to survive here without her, but I'm afraid she's not finished mapping out my life for me yet.

"The staff will make it complicated here, but Destiny said the nanny and cook cried to come help with the twins and Mason gave in there, too.

"I gave her staff bedrooms, then left, saying I needed to take the babysitters home. Lillie and I went shopping after dropping off the teenagers. Destiny didn't miss me—she's in her element now. She has troops to boss around."

"Good. Stay here," Charley whispered as he nuzzled against Jubilee's neck. "I love the way you smell."

She pushed him away, then laughed when he protested and pulled her back against him. "I'm not finished," he muttered as he kissed the spot just below her ear.

Jubilee giggled, needing this playful interaction as much as he did. They'd both had a stressful day, she told herself. They needed to relax a little.

But she knew it was more even if she didn't want

to admit that just maybe she needed this man as she'd never needed anyone.

After one gentle kiss, he turned her so that her back was against his chest. His arms circled her, cocooning her. They were both aware of Lillie's voice drifting from inside. This was not the time or place to take what they were doing further.

Jubilee smiled, guessing when that time came, she'd be the one advancing.

He told her about the talk in the emergency room. If whoever shot at the sheriff recognized Thatcher, they might come after him, thinking he had seen something. A man willing to shoot a sheriff wouldn't hesitate to kill a witness.

She didn't want to think about it, but Charley was right; they needed to be ready. "Should we leave?"

"That would be a nightmare, with all the people treating your house like a bed-and-breakfast and the horses who need special care, and all the work I need to be doing. Plus, I doubt I'd feel safer anywhere else. The sheriff's office in Lubbock said they'll leave a cruiser at our gate for a few days." He just held her for a while, then added, "We're safer here than on the run."

She agreed. "We stay."

"We stay." He slid his hand across her middle. Feeling her soft flannel shirt, brushing the bottom of her breasts. "The only one who leaves will be Lillie. I'll call the grandparents and see if they can watch over her for a few nights. Then we prepare just in case unwanted company drops by."

"I locked Levy's rifles in the attic," she admitted. "Do you think we need to get them down?"

"Yes. We get them loaded and ready tomorrow. I'll put them all up high so only you or I can reach them. Any stranger passing under the gate will be met with someone with a rifle. I'll hire a few men who can cover guard duty when the Lubbock deputies aren't at the gate."

"It's going to cost."

Charley was silent for a while, then added, "Don't worry about it. We've got enough."

She didn't know if he meant they had enough left over or he planned to spend money they'd need later. Right now she didn't care. The most important thing was protecting Thatcher.

She leaned a few inches and looked inside. The lamp put a soft glow over the corner. Lillie was telling Thatcher a story about a pink pony who loved to cook. As she talked, she patted on his arm. Thatcher didn't seem to mind. He looked sound asleep.

"Don't tell That we're taking extra precautions," Jubilee whispered to Charley. "He wouldn't want to be any trouble."

"Mr. Norton and I already agreed on that. I'll watch over him here and a highway patrolman will be at the school when or if he goes. Until they figure out who did this, we've got to assume he could be in danger. There'll be a patrol circling by the school and our gate several times a day. If there is anyone watching the ranch, they'll see."

Jubilee realized this trouble wasn't over. She crossed her arms over Charley's, holding on to him as he held her.

Charley kept his voice low, but his hand spread out once more over her shirt and his finger slowly brushed just beneath her breasts as if he knew what the light touch was doing to her. "You know, several of the lawmen suggested we lock Thatcher up for his own safety. I had to explain that he's a free-range kid. To him, being locked up would be worse than being shot."

"We need to get Destiny out of here," she said as she closed her eyes and leaned against his shoulder. If they didn't pull apart she wouldn't be able to follow any conversation. He was telling her too much non-verbally and she loved all she was feeling.

"I agree." Charley pushed a loose strand of her hair back behind her ear. "I'll call Mason tomorrow and have a talk with him."

"She won't go. She told me it's her duty as my big sister to get me out of this going-nowhere place."

"Do you feel that way here?" he whispered against her ear as his hand reached her side, just beneath the flannel shirt and tugged it aside. He let his fingers almost cover her breast with a touch so light she almost begged for more.

"No," she answered. "I feel like we're building something."

He pulled slowly away and faced her. "We'd better call it a night."

Jubilee hadn't realized how out of breath she was. How warm.

In the low light she caught his smile and knew that he felt the same. By stopping, she wasn't sure if he was taking his time starting something or planning to torture her to death.

She rested her forehead on his shoulder for a second. "And to think I worried about being bored out here on the farm."

"Ranch," he whispered as he opened the screen door. "It's a ranch."

She laughed and stepped away. "You better get Lillie to sleep."

"You're staying here tonight?" He seemed to be trying too hard to keep it casual.

"I'll sleep in your bed tonight, but I'm not sleeping with you." If he'd just been torturing her with his touch, she could play the same game.

"I understand." His blue gaze seemed to be accepting the challenge.

She moved inside before he had time to say more.

Twenty minutes later when he came to bed, she was already under the covers, pretending to be asleep.

She could hear him moving about, trying to be quiet as he tugged off his boots and carefully lay atop the covers.

"Good night," he finally whispered.

She didn't move. What they were doing was dangerous for both of them. He'd told her a dozen times he didn't want a woman in his life, and she'd told him she wasn't any good at relationships. They'd just end up hurting each other.

However, the memory of the kiss they'd shared in the passage kept drifting through her mind. The best kiss ever. In her brain she knew it was a kiss they should never talk about or ever revisit, yet in her heart a part of her wanted it to be a beginning kiss. Something to build on.

Just before she drifted into sleep, she thought she felt him slide his hand over her back from her hair to her hip. Through the blanket she couldn't tell if it was a caress or if he was simply checking to make sure she was covered.

The memory of his stolen touches on the porch drifted across her mind and she smiled. A caress, she thought. One last caress before they both slept.

He was on top of the covers and she was beneath and that was the way it would stay.

But something was newborn inside her tonight. She knew, for the first time in her life, that she was cherished. His gentle touch. His light kisses. His loving caress. All told her he was taking his time, maybe learning to love for the first time.

CHAPTER TWENTY-NINE

Lauren
April 5

FOR THREE DAYS, Lauren had felt as if she was sleep-walking through the hospital. The people in the halls and cafeteria seemed more like ghosts than real people. She guessed they were doing the same thing she was. Drifting in a fog of waiting. Half alive. Half dead.

Tim made the drive from Crossroads every afternoon, usually bringing memos from the office that Pop never read and sweets someone had dropped off, knowing he'd be making the trip.

"There were three dozen cookies," he'd say, "but I ate half on the way."

He claimed he'd be fat if her dad didn't get out soon. They'd talk for a while with him asking questions and her telling him every detail of what had happened at the hospital. She had a feeling he'd be repeating the facts to everyone who dropped by the office.

Every night, when she'd walk him to the elevator, Tim would give her a hug. He gave the best hugs. They made her feel like maybe, just maybe, everything was going to be all right.

Lauren never ate the sweets, or much of anything else. She lived in the chair by her pop's bed. She rode the roller coaster of hope and fear with him. He ran a fever for a while. One medicine made him sick. The night nurse thought that his leg wasn't healing right, and that he might always limp. The shoulder wound was infected. Too many painkillers one day, too few the next. They didn't know if he'd have full use of his left hand. His condition moved from one crisis to another, with just enough hope mixed in to keep Lauren going.

Some days she swore the doctors told her the worst news first so the reality wouldn't look so bad later. The nurses were good, sometimes going out of their way to make sure she was surviving. Someone in law enforcement was always around. Making sure reporters didn't get in. Watching everyone who went into his room. Simply standing guard over a wounded comrade.

Once they moved him to a regular room, people flowed in and out like a constant drip. Friends from town. Other lawmen asking questions, making promises. Even Polly, her mostly invisible roommate, showed up. She cried and said she loved Lauren's dad like a father, then ate the basket of leftover cookies while she told Lauren every detail of her breakup with her latest boyfriend. He'd been unfair, cruel really, thoughtless.

Polly's life was like a long-running soap opera. It had been on the brink of crisis so long she was circling around to the same plot twists over and over. Even Tim, who'd been one of her conquests their first year, thought she needed to get a new story.

"I can put her love affairs in a very short story," Tim whispered, making sure Polly was still in the restroom.

"He's great. He's complicated. He's sooooo hot. He's mean. He's gone."

Lauren couldn't argue. Polly was a magnet for the wrong kind of guy. If she accidentally dated a nice guy, she'd drop him in a week because he was boring. The bad boys she dated were just that—bad boys— but she usually didn't leave until they hit her, or borrowed her credit card, or both. Then every time she'd claim she should have seen the signs.

When Polly dropped by late one afternoon, Tim asked her if she wanted a ride home.

She surprised Lauren by saying "Sure."

When Lauren gave her a look that said *Why are you doing this?*, Polly laced her arm around Tim and pressed her boob against his side.

Lauren frowned at Tim. Now she'd have to listen to both their break-up stories again.

When Polly ran over to kiss Pop goodbye, Tim whispered, "I know, I know, but I'll recover. I always do. At this point I'm looking at life simply as research."

"Good luck."

Polly led him away. Lauren tried not to think about them as she curled up in her blanket in the chair beside her Pop. "Tell me a story," she said, as if he were awake.

Only the sounds of the machines answered.

She picked up her laptop and began to write—first her feelings, then what might be the future, good or bad. Slowly, the notes became a story, not about her life, but about someone else. A tale of what-ifs about a fictional person who could come back from any tragedy by Lauren simply pressing Delete.

The people in her mind kept her company, made her laugh, made her think during the long silent hours beside her father's bed.

On the fourth night, Pop came out of his fog for a while. "Lauren," he whispered, sometime after midnight.

"I'm here, Pop."

"Write this down."

She clicked on her laptop. She could type faster than she could write. "Ready," she smiled, knowing his mind must be clearing of the drugs if he wanted her to take notes.

"The bullets came too fast to be one shooter." Pop dictated. "They weren't from an automatic, but the two shooters must have been standing close to each other. They were low, too, not high, like they weren't more than halfway up on one of the hills. That must be why they didn't hit me when I was down."

He was silent for a while. Lauren waited.

Finally, he started again. "They shot the left front tire out first. I thought I had a blowout. Just as I climbed out and made it to the trunk, the windshield exploded from another shot and I knew I was under attack."

His voice was so weak she almost didn't recognize it. She gave him a sip of water and waited, knowing that he wasn't finished.

"I headed for the car to call it in when they shot me in the arm, then I took one bullet to the leg. I couldn't reach the radio with my left hand, and my right one wouldn't work. I made it to my feet once more when the third bullet went into my leg."

He swore. "I don't even remember when they shot

me in the shoulder. I just remember rolling off the road and into the dirt, knowing that if I stood again, they'd shoot again. At some point I heard an engine start up. Didn't sound like a car. More like an ATV. It sputtered before firing up."

Lauren typed as fast as she could. Pop had closed his eyes, but he wasn't asleep. His voice was so weak it came in no more than a whisper.

"Get that to the Lubbock County Sheriff's Office. They'll know what to do with it. Maybe it will help. I was too out of my head to remember details until now."

"Got it, Pop. I'll take it over first thing in the morning."

"No, now. I want it on his desk when he comes in at dawn," he whispered as he began drifting off. Half asleep, he asked what he'd asked every time he was awake enough to speak. "How is Thatcher? He's all right, isn't he?"

Her answer was the same as before. "He's fine, Pop. He's with Charley Collins."

Pop shifted, fighting to stay awake. "Tell Charley... Tell Charley..."

Lauren waited for more, but Pop didn't finish his sentence.

She closed her laptop and stood, debating whether to go deliver the notes tonight. She was so tired and nothing would be done about his information until tomorrow. Even if her father's memories led to a search and that led to a clue, no one could go out to the scene until dawn.

After walking to the closet, she stood, trying to decide whether to reach for her blanket. A shadow just inside the door caught her eye. Someone was standing in the black triangle of the slightly open door.

Margaret. Lauren's mother didn't need a pointed hat and broom for her daughter to recognize her. It seemed since high school her mother, who'd always been distant, had hardened even more against her. She'd liked having a little girl now and then to spoil, but a grown daughter only showed everyone her age. She'd sent gifts occasionally but, once Lauren turned sixteen, she'd never invited her to visit her condo in Dallas. Every school holiday there was always somewhere Margaret had to be.

Her mother stepped far enough into the room to see her ex-husband. "He's dying and he still has to be the sheriff. Like anyone cares about those facts he made you write down."

"He's not dying." Lauren didn't look at her mother.

"Well, maybe not this time." Margaret moved closer to the bed. "I told him to give up being sheriff, but he wouldn't listen."

Lauren didn't want to be here with Margaret. "Will you stay with him until I get back? If he thinks delivering his notes is important, it probably is." Driving to the Lubbock sheriff's office after midnight was better than talking to her mother.

"No," Margaret answered. "What if he dies while you're gone? I came to check on you, not see him like this."

A man maybe ten years older than her parents stepped inside the room. "Of course we'll stay, Lauren. If you need to go, go."

She looked up and recognized her mother's partner. He was a kind man whose wife had died years ago. Lauren had been visiting her mother, and Margaret had taken her to the funeral. Lauren was only ten or eleven, but she remembered how Mr. Clifton stood by the grave, his back straight as tears streamed down his face. For no other reason than he seemed so alone, Lauren moved beside him and held his hand.

A few years later Margaret became his business partner. She'd told Lauren they probably would never have gotten to know each other well if he hadn't asked Margaret about Lauren now and then.

"Good evening, Mr. Clifton." Lauren smiled at him, thinking that for a man who ran a huge advertising agency, he always seemed so shy. Maybe that's why the partnership with her mother worked. She was usually a storming general.

"We just heard today about your father. I'm very sorry for his trouble and hope for his speedy recovery." He cleared his throat when Margaret didn't comment. "I flew us here in my little plane. Every time I test my wings I wonder why I don't go up every weekend."

"Are you staying awhile?"

Margaret shook her head, but Mr. Clifton didn't even notice her. "We've got rooms at a bed-and-breakfast down the road starting tomorrow morning, but we've nowhere to go but here tonight. I'll stay right with your father until you get back. Take your time, child. I'm guessing you haven't left this room since he was shot."

She hugged Mr. Clifton. "Thank you." He'd lost his wife to a slow cancer. He knew how time stood still in the hospital.

"Yes," Margaret echoed. "We'll stay with him until morning. It's only a few hours. Maybe after a nap we'll come back again to visit. We're happy to help you, dear, but I'm afraid we can't stay long. I have a big presentation Monday morning."

Lauren reached for her jacket, then remembered she'd left it with Thatcher. "I'll be back soon," she said, thinking there was nowhere she wanted to be but here.

Mr. Clifton sat in the chair by her father's bed. Her mother walked around, looking over the fruit and sweets.

Lauren realized she wouldn't have left just her mother alone with her father, but she trusted Mr. Clifton. She had no doubt Margaret would lecture Pop even if he was asleep.

When she'd been small and visiting Margaret in the summers, her mother often took her to the office and ignored her the moment they arrived. Mr. Clifton would take the time to play a card game with her, or fix the TV in the break room so she could watch a movie. That one time at the gravesite when she'd held his hand had somehow bonded them. They were friends and that fact hadn't changed even though it had been a few years since she'd seen him.

She was almost to the elevator when the doors opened and a man stepped out. The hood of his coat hid his features but something about him was familiar.

She froze as he walked slowly toward her, more and more of him moving into her line of vision.

When he was a foot away, she saw his face. "Lucas," she whispered. This businessman was a long way away from the boy she knew in high school, but she would know him anywhere, dressed any way.

He stood almost close enough to touch her. "I just heard about your dad tonight. It was on the Arlington news. I finished up a case there and came as fast as I could drive. How is he?"

"Better, I think. Still drugged up a bit, but the doctor says he's healing."

She stood, staring at Lucas's expensive suit beneath his raincoat. His tie had been pulled loose at his throat, and his hands were shoved deep into his pockets.

She looked anywhere but his eyes. After how she'd attacked him in the bar that night she wasn't sure she could ever look him in the eye again.

"How are you, Lauren?" His hand brushed her arm.

She snapped like a sapling in winter. She wasn't sure if he reached for her or she fell into his arms but one moment they seemed a world apart and the next he was holding her close.

For a while he just held her as she cried on his shoulder. She'd been so strong. A rock, just like she knew her father would want her to be, but now she had someone to lean on.

This was Lucas. The kid who'd saved her life in an old rotting house when she was fifteen. The boy who showed her the stars one night on a ranch where no lights from town could be seen. This was Lucas, who'd given her a first kiss and hinted that someday they'd be more than friends. This was the man she'd kissed wildly in a bar a few weeks ago just because he'd been the boy she'd dreamed about since she'd been fifteen.

Finally, when the tears stopped, Lucas pressed his face against her wet cheek and whispered in her ear, "Are we destined to always meet in hallways, *mi cielo*?"

Lauren laughed, loving the nearness of him, the smell of him, the strength of him. She'd almost forgotten that he called her "my sky" in Spanish. He told her once that it meant "my all" but she knew it was just his way of saying she was special.

Special, she repeated in her mind. Not special enough to call for almost two years. They were like planets circling the sun. Now and then their orbits crossed and they felt the pull to be closer, but most of the time they didn't seem to even be in the same solar system. In college they'd talked a few times about how maybe there would be a someday for them, but both always seemed reluctant to hope.

"Where were you headed?" he asked as he straightened and pulled an inch away.

"I'm taking notes to the Lubbock sheriff's office. Then I thought I'd find an all-night pancake house and eat my weight."

"Mind if I tag along?"

"Only if you have money to pay."

"I've got money." He slid his hand down her arm and laced his fingers with hers. They walked to the elevator as if the whole world hadn't washed between them since they'd touched.

He drove her to the sheriff's office and stood waiting, silently, while she explained what she wanted to print off for the sheriff. He took her to an all-night pancake house near the university.

They talked about their hometown. They shared each other's meals. She told him all about what had happened to Pop since he'd been at the hospital and how he hated being hurt. She cried when he simply reached across the table and held her hand.

She told him how it felt to be graduating. They even discussed what Tim O'Grady was doing with his life. She never remembered talking so much to one person, and the way he kept smiling told her he loved listening to her.

Finally, when nothing but dirty dishes and coffee were left on the table, they talked about the shooting and how frightened she'd been when she got the call.

The first pink of dawn was glowing in the sky when he drove her back to the hospital and walked her across the parking lot.

"You want me to stay with you today?"

She shook her head thinking of her mother in the room. Thinking of what a scene it would make if her mother thought she'd spent her free time with Lucas Reyes. To her mother she was still sixteen and Pop was still raising her wrong.

As they drew closer to the doors, Lucas held her hand tighter and neither said a word. They'd covered every subject she could think of except neither had mentioned the kiss. The night at the Two Step had been carefully avoided.

When he crossed in the shadows of a walkway over the street, Lucas stopped and turned to her. "I know this isn't the time or the place, but I need to say that I can't stop thinking about you." He seemed to be holding himself statue-still. "I feel like you've been in the back of my mind all my life. You're the person I've always thought of as a someday friend. A someday love maybe. But lately with the caseload I'm carrying and the ladder I seemed to be trying to hang on to, I realized it wouldn't be fair for me to ask you…"

Lauren's mind put the pieces together. "Are you breaking up with me before we even start dating?"

He laughed. "We almost dated once, but you were

too young. Then in college I was three years ahead of you and in too much of a hurry to have time. And now, I've got to give this career a chance. In five years, maybe ten, I might run for office and…"

"You are breaking up with me, Lucas." She would have liked to have had one date before she got dumped. "This is ridiculous."

"But, you make me feel so…"

Anger made her straighten. "I don't want to be someone you pass in the night and dream about. We've already had that relationship when I was sixteen and you didn't even realize it."

"But the way you kissed me?"

It was out in the open finally. One mind-blowing, great, hot kiss that neither of them would probably ever forget.

"It was just a kiss, Lucas. We're just friends and at the rate we're moving that is probably all we'll ever be. I'm not your sky. Go back and fight for what you want but don't expect me to be waiting in the shadows for the one moment we almost had." How could she explain that she wanted to matter to him now? She didn't want to be the second choice. The someday person in his life.

She respected him for being so driven. She'd never let him know how he hurt her. It wasn't his fault. She was the one who obviously thought there was something more.

"I have to get back. We only have a few minutes." He stopped, then tried again. "But there's something that needs saying now."

"No, Lucas," she whispered. "There's not." She ran toward the doors, fighting back tears.

When she stepped inside, she wasn't surprised she was alone. He hadn't followed. Lauren shoved the dreams of a girl away with her tears.

She'd aged again, she thought, just as she had the night of the accident at the old gypsy house. There she'd grown up, not in little steps but in a leap. Now, she glanced back and saw Lucas walking away. The girl inside had vanished, and a woman walked into the elevator.

By the time the door opened on her father's floor, Lauren knew what she had to do.

The room was still in shadow when she made it to Pop's side. Her mother was asleep by the window. Mr. Clifton stood when she entered and hugged her, then insisted she curl up in the chair beside her dad.

He covered her with a blanket. "Sleep, dear," he said. "Everything will be better tomorrow, you'll see."

She closed her eyes and listened to Mr. Clifton wake her mother.

Margaret didn't bother to say goodbye. They just seemed to vanish.

Lauren's thoughts were dark and broken. Nurses came in and out, checking on Pop, but she acted as if she was asleep. One nurse even whispered to another that it was a blessing the sheriff's daughter was finally sleeping.

Lauren mourned the might-have-beens with Lucas. She felt her heart turning cold, drying up like a flower covered in the first snow.

By ten, when she finally opened her eyes, she saw her Pop smiling at her.

"Don't cry, baby girl, I'm not going anywhere for a long time."

The joy of seeing him awake made her smile. "I love you, Pop."

His voice was raspy, but his eyes were clear. "I love you, too." He scratched the whiskers on his chin. "I had the strangest dream last night. I thought your mother was here complaining."

Lauren laughed. "She was, Pop. I should warn you, she's mad about you getting yourself shot. She flew back to Dallas saying she had a presentation to get ready for Monday, but I wouldn't be surprised if she came back soon to finish yelling at you."

"Let me guess. She thinks I got shot just to irritate her."

"Something like that." Lauren shoved her broken heart deep into a corner. She had her pop back. Lucas was someone she'd mourn another day. She tried to act as though his visit the previous night had never happened.

"I'm starving," Pop whispered.

"Me, too," she lied.

They ordered two breakfasts and Pop ate them both. Then, when he dozed off, she opened her laptop and began to write her feelings down as if they were someone else's. Slowly a character formed, stronger than Lauren, braver. An adventure danced through her mind, taking her away from her own feelings, giving her something to think about in the hours of waiting.

CHAPTER THIRTY

Charley
April 7

DAWN WAS JUST peeking into his window when Charley woke. He rolled over slowly and found Jubilee still in his bed. The fourth night in a row. *Man, this could be a great dream if she hadn't set down the rules that first night.*

They'd had Thatcher in the house recovering and decided they both needed to be near, so sharing the bed, him on top of the covers and her beneath, seemed the only solution. Charley thought of mentioning that she could have slept with Lillie. It might be a small bed, but Lillie didn't take up much room. But he wasn't about to suggest something she might consider doing.

He liked Jubilee right where she was. Minus the covers between them, he decided, but he'd never suggest such a thing or she'd be heading back to the big house, even with all the guests staying over.

Destiny, with all her army of help, was still refusing to leave the main house, but the good news was Jubilee was still next to him. Working beside him all day and sleeping beside him all night.

He wrapped his fingers around a strand of hair on her pillow. He could never remember loving to watch a woman move as much as he loved watching Jubilee. She had a grace in motion unlike anything he'd ever seen.

She opened those big brown eyes and stared at him, looking as if she could read his every thought. "Don't even think about it," she whispered.

"What?" He tried to look innocent. "I was just wondering what was for breakfast."

"Right."

"Cinnamon rolls." Thatcher's voice came from the living room.

Charley and Jubilee scrambled out of bed and ran to where Thatcher sat on the couch. Charley plowed his fingers through his hair, thankful that he and Jubilee had both slept in their clothes. *For the fourth night in a row*, he reminded himself.

"You all right, That?" he asked. The kid had had a few rough nights.

"Sure. I've been up an hour. Just before dawn, some lady tapped on the door. I hopped over and let her in the minute I saw she was carrying food. She said she was the new cook and wanted to bring us breakfast before the people at the big house woke up and started their daily round of screaming."

Charley glanced over at a tray of rolls, each bigger than the palm of his hand.

"I already ate two. They taste better than any I've ever had from a package." Thatcher lifted his empty plate. "Wouldn't mind having another couple."

Jubilee took his plate as he added, "I didn't know we had a cook. I've been here wounded for four days and she's just now showing up."

"We don't have a cook. She works for Destiny.

When Destiny leaves, so will the cook." Jubilee stared at Charley. "Right?"

"Right," he answered, but he didn't sound very convincing. "I heard Mason's calling several times a day. She's bound to think he's suffered enough, or you're beyond help."

"Could she leave the cook?" Thatcher asked.

"No," Charley said. "I've been trying my best to get them out but they're worse than a mattress full of bedbugs. All of them. The yoga instructor told me yesterday that she wasn't in the mood to talk to me."

Charley looked over at Jubilee, who didn't seem to think that was odd at all.

Jubilee made coffee while Charley got down plates and cups. Every morning they started out with the same conversation: how to get Destiny off the ranch.

Thatcher seemed to be studying them while they moved around the kitchen, both frowning. "You two sure do wake up on the wrong side of the bed. Might want to think about swapping sides."

Both of them glared at him.

"Just one more question. Are you two common-law married now? 'Cause it's been my observation that condition can start a lot of fights and I'm too lame to run fast."

"No," they both answered.

"Okay, just checking. Think I'll take a little nap before I eat another breakfast." Thatcher leaned back and closed his eyes.

Charley moved over to Jubilee and lowered his voice. "How are we going to explain to the kid that we're not sleeping together?"

"We *are* sleeping together," she answered.

"You know what I mean."

"Of course I know what you mean. I'm the one in bed with you, remember?"

They both smiled and began to talk about all that had to be done before dark. Before Thatcher got shot, they'd decided to bet it all on the ranch, but Charley knew money was already getting tight. The only money she took off the table was his salary. The rest, including her own money, went in.

Charley thought it a little mad, but they'd need every dime, maybe even his salary. Right now the more they put in to kick things off, the better the return in the fall.

Only if he gave up his salary, which mostly went into saving for his own land, he'd give up his own dreams. He'd spotted a small piece of land down the road that would be a great starter place. Natural springs, good grass. No, he wouldn't give up his chance. He'd just have to work harder. Put in more hours. He doubted she'd let him work for free anyway.

As he ate, Charley started the list of what he had to do today. Every day he added *make sure Thatcher is safe* to the list in his mind even though he never wrote it on paper.

Before they finished breakfast, a deputy Charley had talked with in the emergency room knocked on the door. He was so big he blocked most of the sunlight with his tall frame.

The deputy nodded a greeting to Jubilee and Charley, and then went straight to Thatcher.

"How are you doing?" Officer Weathers asked, while Charley watched. "You getting around all right?"

Thatcher shaded his eyes. "Could you sit down, deputy? All I can see is the light bulb when I look up so high."

Weathers sat on the trunk that had seemed so big when Lillie sat on it. "Lauren Brigman wanted me to drop by and tell you the sheriff may be coming home tomorrow. I'm heading up to Lubbock pretty soon to be part of the escort. I've been covering for Brigman here in Crossroads for a few days and plan to stay on until he can take over."

Weathers made Thatcher straighten with pride when he added, "I understand you've been working with the sheriff some."

Thatcher nodded, looking as if he didn't know how to talk to the young deputy. He couldn't be more than twenty-four or -five, but he was so big he obviously made Thatcher nervous.

"Where you staying in town?" Charley moved into the conversation with a silent offer of a cup of coffee.

"Over at the new bed-and-breakfast," Weathers said as he took the cup and thanked him with a glance. "Eating most of my meals at the diner. Great food but small portions."

Thatcher leaned closer as if studying the man. "You eat out much, deputy?"

"Nope. My mom taught all her sons to cook. If I stay here much longer, I plan to talk those two Franklin sisters who are fixing up the place into letting me have use of the kitchen."

Thatcher nodded again as if he'd figured out something. The kid relaxed back on his pillow.

Weathers reached in his pocket and pulled out a small phone. "Lauren said you didn't have a cell phone. Some of the guys in my office got together and decided to get you one. I've already put in my number. All you have to do is hit five and it speed dials me. Lauren's three. Sheriff Brigman will be four."

Thatcher didn't accept the cell. "You're kidding."

"No. We think of you as one of our team now. A cell is standard issue." He lowered his voice. "If you'd had a phone that day, maybe someone could have got to you. You and the sheriff wouldn't have been so alone."

Thatcher took the phone. "What about numbers one and two and six through nine?"

Weathers smiled. "I'll show you how to use it. You can call anyone you want, but you'll want to speed dial the most common numbers. Might want to make the first one your parents and maybe the number two could be your girlfriend."

The kid stared at the phone. "My mom don't have a phone, but my girlfriend might. I'll ask her. Only I don't understand what she's talking about half the time. If I called her, more conversation might just clog up my brain."

Weathers nodded. "I know what you mean."

"One question, Deputy. Why'd you make yourself number five?"

Charley moved closer wondering the same thing.

"My first name's Fifth."

"You're kidding." Thatcher looked as if he was fighting down a laugh.

"No. My folks thought since I was their fifth son, Fifth would be a good name."

"Anyone ever tell your folks that when they run out of names maybe they should stop having kids?"

Fifth shook his head. "You should meet my brother,

Eleven. He plays pro for the Dallas Cowboys. Full-back. I'm the runt of the Weathers litter."

Thatcher passed his cinnamon roll to the deputy. "You know, Fifth, I think we're going to be friends. And don't you worry. If anyone makes fun of your name, you tell me. I've got your back."

Fifth glanced at Charley as if to say no one had ever made fun of him, but to Thatcher he simply said, "Thanks."

Charley picked up a list with items needed from the vet. "If you'll be here a while, Deputy, I think I'll go to town and spend some time with my daughter before she goes to school, then I'll pick up Thatcher's medicine. Should be back by eight thirty."

"All I have to do is make it to Lubbock today. They won't be releasing the sheriff until after ten tomorrow. When I came down, I only brought uniforms. I plan on stopping by my apartment and picking up clothes to wear when I'm off duty if any of that time ever comes along in this town."

Charley didn't like leaving them, but he had a few things to do and they'd seen no one suspicious around. He'd probably bring Lillie home tonight.

After all, sheriff's departments for three counties around were watching the ranch. Weathers would be back tomorrow and the two trusted men he'd hired would be in to start work by eight every morning. They all knew to be on the watch.

On impulse, Charley leaned over and gave Jubilee a kiss on the cheek as he walked past her. He figured she wouldn't try to kill him in front of a deputy.

To his surprise, she just stared at him as he walked out.

He got to Fred and Helen Lee's home in time to talk

to Lillie while she ate breakfast. Then, he took her to school. It felt good to laugh for a while and let the worries go. She wanted to come home with him after school and for the first time in three days, he agreed.

A little after eight he stopped by the bank. He went in just as they opened, and five minutes later he was back in the truck.

What he'd just done made him question his sanity, but he'd had to do it. In one swift move he'd transferred his entire savings into Jubilee's ranch account. Almost forty thousand dollars. Not much money toward buying land, but it might be enough to get her through until Lone Heart started paying.

Since the day his father kicked him out, he'd been saving what little money he could, hoping, planning for someday when he could buy a few acres and start his own place.

Now he was gambling it all on Jubilee's place.

But he'd figured out that Jubilee wouldn't have enough money to make her ranch run if he didn't do something. She wanted this dream and she mattered too much to him to have it fail when he knew he could have helped.

He wouldn't tell her. If she found out in the fall, she could pay him back. If they still failed to make a go of the ranch, his dream would go down with hers. Lillie would probably be in high school before he saved enough for another shot at buying a ranch.

Charley started his truck and drove to the vet. He felt good about what he'd done. Scared, but good.

Jubilee had asked him once if he'd ever been in love. He'd said no. Now, for the first time ever, he knew he'd fallen truly and completely in love and he'd just proved it to himself.

No matter how it turned out with Jubilee and her ranch, he'd know, once and for all, what it felt like to love someone. He'd thank her for that, even if she never wanted their relationship to go beyond a few great kisses in the shadows of Lone Heart Pass.

CHAPTER THIRTY-ONE

Charley
April 7

By the time Charley got back to the ranch, his mind was full of what had to be done. He was working far more than his fifty hours a week, and Jubilee was right there by his side. Now, with a little extra capital, they could hire more help, buy a few more head, build onto the barn and enlarge the corrals.

To his surprise, two vans were parked in front of the big house. Apparently his call to Mason last night had convinced the man to send for his wife.

All Charley had said when Mason answered his office phone was, "I'm loading up cattle now. I should deliver about forty head by midafternoon."

Destiny's husband had asked Charley to repeat what he said, then shouted, "I didn't order any shipment."

"I know, but if I have to take care of your wife and sons, I figured it only fair that you take care of my cattle."

When Mason didn't say a word, Charley added details. "Most of the calves are half-wild, but you'll get them settled down before the next load makes it to you. They'll be grazing on your front lawn in no time."

Mason yelled, "You're insane. I didn't want her to

leave. I can't handle cattle at my office or home. I'll call the police. I'll sue you."

"Why?" Charley said calmly. "I didn't sue you or call the police when you sent me Destiny and the twins."

Charley could hear Mason stomping around as he cussed. Finally, he stilled and said calmly, "I'm coming after my wife."

"Good," Charley answered. "See you soon."

Charley smiled as he parked near the barn.

The minute he stepped out of the truck he saw Jubilee running toward him. "They're packing!" she shouted.

He swung her around, laughing. "Any chance she'll be back?"

"I don't think so. She hated the sight of guns over the doors and having only one bathroom drove her mad. Then last night one of the twins ate a lightning bug. That seemed to be the straw that crumbled her determination to stay. That and Mason calling, begging her to come back. He even promised a vacation. I find it hard to believe, but the man said he missed her."

Thatcher hopped out onto the porch, demanding to know what was going on. "The deputy left as soon as the vans pulled up. I don't have anyone to talk to."

Charley set Jubilee down and turned to Thatcher. "The company in the big house is moving out but you're staying right here."

"In the past four days I've read a dozen Westerns." Thatcher leaned on the porch railing. "I'm bored for the first time in my life. I can't believe I'm saying this but I want to go to school."

Charley knew Thatcher was telling the truth.

It took them an hour to get him dressed and change his bandage, but Charley drove him into town. "It's almost lunchtime, That. Don't you think you could wait one more day to go back to school?"

"No, lunch seems about the right time to get there."

When Charley let him out in front of the cafeteria windows, Thatcher took his time, walking slow, leaning on the crutch.

Some kid came out the glass door on the cafeteria side of the building, took one look at Thatcher and ran back in. A minute later, kids were running toward him as if he was a rock star who had come to visit.

As Charley watched, Kristi Norton ran up and hugged him. Thatcher put his arm around her as if he needed support on his good side, then they were lost in the crowd.

Charley pulled away, smiling, and headed back home. He doubted Thatcher would have any problem making friends now.

Charley turned his mind back to work. They had until fall, and everything needed to figure into the balance. The weather—specifically, the amount of rainfall—the health of the animals, grass fires and a hundred other variables.

For the first time in four days, he had nothing to worry about but getting work done.

At the end of the day, when Thatcher came home in the front of Deputy Weathers's cruiser, Charley had a feeling he probably had Kristi's phone number on speed dial. After supper, he asked Jubilee if she knew how to cut hair.

Charley wasn't surprised when she said, "Sure, how hard could it be?"

She set up her barbershop on the front porch and cut the kid's hair, then they both helped him into bed. He'd been brave all day, but now he was almost asleep on his one good leg.

The house seemed settled that night. Thatcher was healing and Lillie was back home. She'd talked so much about her adventures with her grandparents that she'd fallen asleep at the dinner table. Thatcher looked just as worn out.

"He's a good kid," Charley whispered. "Never complains."

"I have a feeling he was raised where complaining didn't do much good," Jubilee added.

As soon as Charley turned out the living room light, she motioned him to the porch.

"Sit." She pointed to the stool. "You're next."

He thought of arguing, but the minute she moved close, he changed his mind. He widened his legs so she could stand in front of him, loving the way she moved as she worked. Her body brushed his ever so lightly now and then as she played with his hair. He liked having her so close.

Neither had said a word about her moving back to her house. He thought he'd tell her he still needed her to take care of Thatcher, but the kid was like ivy. He didn't seem to need much except water and food.

Charley watched as she circled around him, her hair now down and flowing below her shoulders like a cape. Maybe she'd stay if he asked. He'd do his best to follower her blanket rule. Maybe she'd stay. Maybe not.

A fire was building in him. He had to fight to not touch her as she moved around the stool, playing with his hair, bumping against his leg or arm or shoulder.

"I could do this all night," he whispered.

"You wouldn't have any hair left."

"I wouldn't care," he answered.

A whistling sound came from the direction of the road and Charley knew they were no longer alone. "The men are coming in."

She moved away as he pulled the towel off his shoulders and went to meet the cowhands he'd left on guard at the gate.

"Nothing, boss," one said, even before Charley made out his face in the shadows.

"Quiet all the way to the next ranch," the other added. "No stranger has been on your land tonight."

Charley had been running patrols for four nights now, and they hadn't seen one thing out of place. If someone was coming after Thatcher, they were taking their time. Maybe they didn't know where he was, or maybe they didn't see him as a threat.

"You want us to come back tomorrow?"

"Not to guard." Charley decided. "It's all quiet. I'm thinking we were worried about nothing." He shook the men's hands. "But if you want to keep working for me, I could use a few good men. Daylight hours this time. We're bringing more head in tomorrow and I'll have my hands full."

"I'll take you up on that. My wife says I'm too old to rodeo anymore, and I'm beginning to think she's right."

The other man agreed. He'd take the work whether it was night guard or cowboying for the Lone Heart brand.

"Then I'll see you both at dawn tomorrow. We'll be branding."

"Fair enough," they both said at once.

The men disappeared into the darkness, and Charley heard the roar of a truck pulling away from the side of the barn.

Deputy Weathers said there would be a patrol of the road tonight. That should be enough, but Charley had a feeling he'd still sleep light. If any vehicle crossed the cattle guard turning off the road, he'd hear it from his place. He'd be on the porch with a rifle in hand before they could reach his door.

He walked back to the house thinking how peaceful it was now that all the women in the main house were gone. No walking babies crying. No phones ringing. No echoes of Destiny yelling for help.

He passed the barn, thinking that silence was a great sound.

Movement drew his eye to one of the stalls. He walked over and saw Jubilee brushing down the colt she called Baby.

When she noticed him, she held the brush up. "Show me how to do this again, would you? I'm afraid I'll hurt the colt."

He stepped behind her and reached around to lay his hand over where she held the brush. Slowly, in long strokes he showed her how to work with the tiny colt.

"He's still got his milk coat. You'll want to go easy for a while."

As they worked, Charley almost felt as if he was dancing with Jubilee. Their bodies were touching, their movements in rhythm. He took a deep breath, loving the smell of her soft hair.

Finally, she turned and faced him as she dropped

the brush. She looked up, her brown eyes liquid with a need, her mouth slightly open.

Charley couldn't resist. He touched his lips to hers, lightly tasting her as his arm went around her waist and pulled her closer against him. This time it was his turn to kiss her, and he wanted to take his time.

He felt her chest push against his with every breath, as he kissed her tenderly. If he had his way, they'd have a lifetime, and he planned to take his time remembering every touch, every kiss.

She felt boneless in his arms as she swayed. He moved her arms to his shoulders so he could deliberately slide his hands down the sides of her body. Each time he stroked her, he passed closer to her breasts and lower over her hips. No woman had ever felt so right in his arms.

Another pass down her body. His thumbs brushed over the tips of her breasts lightly and she opened her mouth in a sigh. His hands moved lower, holding her as he kissed her deeper.

Without letting her go, he moved to her ear and whispered, "Sleep with me tonight."

"All right," she answered.

"No, don't just sleep. Make love to me tonight."

She smiled a low heated smile and whispered, "Not a chance. I plan on torturing you for a while. I think you're a man women come easy to, but not this time."

She pressed against him as if teasing him, then kissed him with a passion that made him forget to breathe. He guessed she wanted him as much as he wanted her, but she couldn't know that he wanted far more than just a night.

Maybe she didn't believe in herself when it came to love. Only this time all she had to believe in was them.

Maybe this time she'd commit that big heart she swore she didn't have. Charley had no idea how he'd handle it if she made love to him and walked away.

It seemed all his adult life he'd been fighting to get up to level ground. He'd felt old by the time he turned twenty-one, but not now, not with Jubilee. With her, everything seemed new. He thought in terms of possible. He dared to believe in someday. He longed to taste a passion that would last a lifetime.

When he finally pulled away to look in her eyes, he whispered, "Promise me, if you're not going to sleep with me tonight that you'll keep torturing me?"

"Promise." She smiled. "I've never felt like this."

"Like what?"

"Like I might die if you didn't hold me."

He kissed her cheek. "I feel the same way. And I understand. We wait. We make sure. We let the fire build." His hand spread out over her bottom. "I'm betting you'll be the first to snap and attack me."

Laughing, she pressed against him. "And if I do?"

Charley knew the answer. He might as well admit it. He loved this woman. There was no doubt, but all he could manage to say was, "If you attack, I have a feeling I'll surrender."

He took her hand as he turned out the barn light and they walked toward the house.

Thatcher was asleep. The ranch was alive with only the sounds of the night. The house was full of the smells of home. *This time*, he thought, *this time I'm not going to mess loving up.*

He set her on their bed and removed her boots;

then, fully dressed, she slid under the covers. Without a word, he walked to the other side and tugged his boots off, then lay down atop the blankets.

He couldn't touch her. If he did, he wasn't sure he'd ever stop. He just lay still and tried to figure out what moment he'd fallen for her. He knew she wasn't asleep. Her breathing was quick and every few minutes she shifted as if trying to get comfortable.

"Jubilee," he finally whispered. "I'm not saying this because I want you to answer, but I think you should know I'm in love with you."

"I know," she whispered.

He forced himself not to move for a while, then he added, "And don't even think of giving me any of that crap about you not having a heart. I've seen your heart with Thatcher and Lillie. I've felt it pressed against mine. You're going to wake up one morning and realize you love me, too, and I'll be right here beside you waiting."

She didn't comment. Her breathing had slowed. She wasn't settling.

Jubilee had gone to sleep right in the middle of his declaration.

CHAPTER THIRTY-TWO

Lauren
April 7

WHEN THE DOCTOR said Pop could go home in the morning, Lauren thought her dad would get out of bed and dance. He wasn't a man who took to hospitals easily. Since the day he woke up in his right mind, he'd been working hard to get out of this place he thought of as a prison.

The doctor pulled Lauren into the hall and explained that she'd have to go home today and have everything set up for him by morning. "The trip will be hard on him. He'll be tired and need everything in place when he gets there. If he had one injury, or even two, it wouldn't be such a problem, but he was dealing with four, any one of which could have knocked him off his feet for weeks on its own."

So by noon she was on her way back to Crossroads with a truck following her that was packed with equipment, a hospital bed and everything she'd need to make their living room into part gym and part hospital room.

Pop said he didn't care as long as he could look out the window and see the water.

While the movers set up the bed and all the bars

and weights to help him build back his strength, she cleaned house. When they left, she went to the store and tried to stock up on everything she might need. She bought two of everything, just in case.

Lauren was on a mission. She'd decided she was going to take care of her Pop until he was healed and back at work.

She'd talked to all her professors at Tech. They'd heard about the sheriff on the news and were all happy to help. One said if she'd take a B, he'd count her done with his class. Another wanted her to turn in two more papers before finals. She could email them, and she could finish the other two classes simply by passing the final. For the first time in her life, grades were not that important. She'd have her degree and she'd be able to stay with her pop.

Polly said she'd come down on weekends and help. She'd complained that nothing had happened between her and Tim the night he'd taken her home and she wanted another shot at him. So Lauren hugged her roommate goodbye and left, with all the stuff that had surrounded her in the dorm now packed away in boxes.

By the time Lauren bought the groceries and got back to the lake house, it was almost dark. She planned to get to bed early and then drive back to Lubbock before dawn. She knew an ambulance would be bringing her pop home, but she wanted to follow. Her job now was to watch over him, just as he'd watched over her all her life.

Once she got him settled in, she knew there would be a physical therapist dropping by every other day and a home nurse checking his wounds, and probably every deputy and sheriff in the area would be coming by to talk. Add the townsfolk to that mix, and she might want to think about putting in a revolving door.

When a shadow crossed the window in the back door, Lauren jumped. Her first thought was she wished that huge deputy who always hung out at the hospital was with her now.

Then she spotted the lanky form and the red hair. Tim.

When she let him in, he held up two bags. "Dinner."

She smiled and hugged him, remembering that she hadn't eaten all day.

"I love what you've done with the place," he said as she dug into the hamburger bag.

"Did you bring fries?"

"I did, and malts."

"I love you, Tim O'Grady."

"I know. How could you not?" He sat across from her and they devoured the food. He told her all about what was going on in town. He was now on a first-name basis with a few deputies, but he seemed reluctant to tell her details.

Maybe he had none, she thought, or maybe something was up that Tim didn't want her, or her father, to know about yet.

Tim promised that as soon as he broke the burlap man's case, he'd turn his attention to her father's shooting.

"Crimes are piling up and nothing's getting solved. First, there's a filing cabinet of information on the dead guy, most of it probably worthless. Second, we've found a few footprints and shells from the shooting of the mustangs but nothing that will help us solve the crime. Add the third crime, your father's ambush, to the mess and I've got more than I can handle. I moved my whiteboards into the county courtroom. Judge says I'll have to take it all down if a trial comes along." He took a bite and continued, "That's not likely to happen if we don't solve something."

"So, Sherlock, what is the plan?" She'd always been able to tell when Tim was hiding something.

"I'm not saying, but I'm about to do some serious investigating. Charley Collins and I were tossing around some ideas."

"What?" she asked. "When did you see Charley?"

"I'll fill you in later."

Before she could ask more, he changed the subject. "Did you know there was a hippy colony out there in the Breaks years ago? I talked to a few people who remembered them. All peace and tattoos. Our guy could have been part of them."

"Or not," she added.

"Or not," he agreed. "But it's exciting digging into the history of this place and all the things that happened in the past that no one today cares about."

Once the food was gone and the sun had set, Lauren realized how tired she was. She walked Tim to the back door and pointed him toward his house. "Go," she said. "Work on your novel. I want to say I knew you before you were a big-time writer."

Before he stepped down off the deck, he pulled her into a hug. "You're going to make it through this, L. I've got faith in you. In a few months your dad will be back at work."

"Thanks," she said snuggling into one of his wonderful bear hugs. "I couldn't have made it without you being there every day. You're the best friend anyone could ask for."

Tim leaned down and kissed her lips just as he'd done so many times before. Only this time, Lauren kissed him back. Maybe she didn't want to be alone. Or maybe she just wanted to feel something besides worry. She felt as though she'd been emotionally beat up, and tonight she needed a little tenderness to heal.

He pulled an inch away. "Did you mean to do that, L?"

"I did." She had made up her mind. Just because Lucas didn't want her didn't mean that she had to die inside. She could still feel. She could still react to a man caring about her.

Tim kissed her again, deeper, and she melted against him, needing his warmth after all she'd gone through. She felt as if she'd lived years, and now was an old soul in a young body. It wasn't that she'd learned anything. It was more as if she'd discovered that she knew nothing.

Nothing about life. Nothing about love. Nothing about herself.

Lost in her own thoughts she barely realized she was no longer participating in the kiss until Tim pulled away.

"You're not into this, are you, L?"

"Sorry. I thought I could be, but maybe I'm too tired."

"Or maybe I'm not the right man." Tim's smile didn't reach his eyes. "I probably never will be. With you, I'll always be just a friend."

"Is that so bad?"

He shook his head. "With my track record with

girls, this will probably be the longest relationship I'll ever have. So, being your friend isn't so bad."

She kissed his cheek and watched as he walked away.

Halfway between their houses, she noticed he gave in to his limp. Tim was now only a shadow against the shoreline. She knew he wanted there to be more between them, but she couldn't force something that wasn't meant to be.

She also knew he still hoped. That was why, now and then, he kissed her.

THE NEXT MORNING as she walked toward her Pop's room, all she could think about was that she wouldn't hurt Tim the way Lucas had hurt her.

She'd put her love for Lucas in a box, waiting for him to open it, and she'd put Tim in a box that said he was nothing more than a best friend. Now when she'd reacted to Tim's kiss last night, she'd mixed up the boxes and had no idea how to straighten them out.

When this was over, she'd talk to Tim and let him know how much he meant to her as a friend. A friend. Never more.

Pop was sitting up in bed ready to put his clothes on when she walked into his hospital room. Lauren did what she always did with her emotions. She pushed them aside to think about another time.

"That's impossible," the nurse was explaining.

Pop just glared at her. He had one leg bandaged above the knee and below the knee was a cast. His shoulder was wrapped up and his arm was in a sling. "How do you think you are going to get into your clothes?"

"Well, I'm not going out in a hospital gown." Pop was starting to look like a wild man. "If the nurse hadn't cut off my uniform, I'd be wearing it out. You know, when I got shot I didn't think to take an overnight bag to the ambush."

"We can put one gown on the front and another on the back. No one will see anything."

Pop didn't back down. "Oh, yes they will. They'll see an idiot wearing two hospital gowns."

"Well." The nurse puffed up. "I guess you'll have to stay here until you're healed."

"I'm not staying here one day longer. The doctors say I can go and I'm going. I've got three open cases that need solving."

"In hospital gowns," she added as if this was the O.K. Corral and she wasn't backing down. "Or you will not be leaving."

"No." He stood his ground.

Lauren saw the possibility of this argument lasting all day. Her Pop was off most of the painkillers and was trapped-badger-level angry. She thought of cutting a blanket and putting it over his head, but that probably wasn't much better than the two-gown idea.

The beefy deputy who had been watching over her father for a week finally stepped into the room. Lauren had been falling over his size fourteen shoes for days. She'd asked him several times if he couldn't go back to whatever he did and let some thinner, or at least smaller, deputy cover the hospital.

Deputy Weathers usually just smiled and told her he put in for this duty.

If he was there as guard, she finally rationalized that both she and Pop could stand behind him if trouble stormed the door, so maybe he was worth putting up with.

"What's the problem?" he asked as if he couldn't have heard them from the minute he got off the elevator.

Pop spoke first. "They want me to roll out of here in a hospital gown. I'd rather not see that on the news tonight and the hospital can't promise the cameras outside won't get a shot."

Weathers gave a Santa Claus smile. "I've already thought of that."

"Good," Pop said as if that was all he needed to know. Problem solved.

The nurse wasn't so agreeable. "And what might your plan be, Deputy Weathers?"

The deputy smiled. "I brought him a pair of my sweats from the academy."

He pulled out the biggest navy blue sweatshirt and pants Lauren had ever seen from a bag. "They're big enough to fit over the cast and the bandages. I had to have them ordered special when I started the academy."

The nurse gave up.

Lauren and Weathers slowly pulled the clothes over her father's hospital gown. Once he was in the wheelchair it didn't seem so noticeable that another person could have fit in his clothes with him.

Sheriff Dan Brigman rolled out of the hospital with his dignity intact.

CHAPTER THIRTY-THREE

Thatcher
April 9

AN HOUR AFTER lunch on Friday, Thatcher decided he'd had enough of school for the week. Using his one crutch, he limped out of the back door of the school and walked over to the Evening Shadows Retirement Home.

Cap Fuller was working on his old boat of a car. "Hello, hero," he said when Thatcher walked up.

It seemed as if the old guy was getting shorter every time Thatcher saw him, but he was always friendly. He'd even helped Thatcher get his Ford pickup running when one of his mother's common-law husbands left it parked in back of their cabin.

After that, Thatcher drove it, figuring he'd inherited it in the common-law divorce.

"Hello, Mr. Fuller. I was wondering if I could talk you into giving me a ride." Thatcher guessed the old guy knew he'd return the favor when asked.

The senior citizen straightened. "I heard you got your own private deputy watching over you. Don't you want him to take you wherever you want to go?"

Thatcher shook his head. "Where I'm going, wouldn't be safe for him. I need a ride out to the Breaks, not Lone Heart Ranch where I've been staying lately. I don't think it would be healthy for a cruiser to turn into my old neighborhood."

"I know that place. Used to go out there now and then." Cap closed the hood of his car.

"I know. Folks still know your old car." Thatcher smiled, knowing he'd just got a ride. "They remember how you helped your nephew out when he lived out there."

Fuller nodded. "He wasn't a bad kid, just got mixed up now and then. I couldn't see myself letting him or his family go hungry."

Thatcher knew Fuller's nephew had died in a car crash last year and the family he left moved into Crossroads. The old man was probably still helping them out.

Fuller opened his car door. "I'll take you over there, but you let someone know where you are."

Thatcher pulled out his cell. "I will." He tried Charley's cell but wasn't surprised there was no answer. When he'd left the ranch, Charley was hammering on the frame of what would be another six stalls added to the barn.

Just to keep his word, he dialed the sheriff's office and left Tim a message about where he was heading. Thatcher figured he'd be back before anyone picked up the messages.

Thatcher climbed into the passenger seat while Cap backed into the traffic—two cars—on Main Street. Both cars honked. Cap waved.

Thatcher appreciated the old man talking about cars on the way out to the Breaks.

Thatcher had talked about the shooting enough. Everyone in town seemed to want to hear all the details, just like every teacher he had kept asking him how he felt, as if it was part of roll call each period.

Fuller let him off just before the one-eleven turnoff, since—sure enough—Mr. Norton had left the truck there. That was close enough, Thatcher figured. Any further and the car might have gotten stuck in the mud.

After he got his truck started, he drove to his mother's cabin. It was pretty much the same as the way he left it, only the electricity was off. Thatcher thought his mother might have returned, but no such luck. Who knows—she might be gone for good this time.

He walked around, deciding there was not one thing he wanted to take with him except his .22 rifle. So he wrapped it in one of his snake-killing bags and left a note on his bedroom door telling her that the sheriff knew where he was. Then he walked away from where he'd lived all his life and didn't bother to take one last look.

He'd made up his mind that if Charley and Jubilee ever kicked him out, he wasn't coming back here.

It took him a while to get his old Ford started and driving a stick shift wasn't easy with a weak leg, but he managed. By the time the school bus passed Lone Heart Ranch, he was parking his truck out by the front gate.

He'd passed two highway patrol cars on the way and neither had stopped him.

Charley stepped out of the newly framed barn with a rifle cradled on his arm. "You brought your truck," he said, stating the obvious. "Could have parked it a little closer."

"Thought I'd enjoy the walk," Thatcher answered. "I had to go get it before someone stole it."

Charley looked doubtful but didn't insult his truck. "You feel like working?"

"You bet." Thatcher had decided the ache in his leg was nothing compared to being bored. "How about we finish the chicken coop? I got a dozen chicks from an old neighbor of mine today."

"What happened to the ones you picked up that day you found the sheriff? I thought Mr. Norton was going to bring them over."

"Kristi took one look at them and adopted them. She asked me if she could have them and I couldn't tell her no. The old lady down the road from my mom had a dozen chickens. There's always chicks around her place. Half the time she doesn't even collect the eggs, much less worry about the chicks."

Charley handed him a hammer. "We work until you get tired. Agreed?"

"Agreed." Thatcher grinned. It felt good to be doing something. He'd slept through all his morning classes, so a little work wouldn't bother him.

Three hours later they finished the coop they'd been planning before the shooting interrupted their progress. It did indeed look like a castle, just as Lillie wanted.

Jubilee had picked up Lillie after school and they'd gone for ice cream together.

They showed up just before dark with supper in a bag. The little princess went crazy over the coop and the baby chicks. She insisted two of them wanted to come visit her room.

Thatcher's exhaustion vanished when he saw her joy. "I've missed you this week, Flower. It seems like all I've done is sleep, but from now on, I'm on the mend."

"I missed you, too, That." She wrapped her hand around two of his fingers and told him to come to supper as if she was still the princess doctor.

Halfway through the meal, Thatcher asked when Jubilee planned to move back into her house.

She glanced at Charley and said, "I plan to stay here until you're fully recovered."

Charley kicked Thatcher under the card table and he said, "That could be a while, right, That?"

Thatcher nodded as he tried his best to look weak.

"Then I'll stay for a while," she promised.

It didn't make much sense for them all to stay in a tiny house when a big one was close by, but Thatcher had figured out not much makes sense in the world.

Like why would Kristi like him when even he knew he wasn't worth much and her father kept calling him *son* as if he wouldn't mind having him in the family. Then there was Charley and Jubilee sleeping together with their clothes still on. Either that, or they dressed faster than lightning strikes when he called them during the night.

Also add that Lillie thought chickens should sleep in a castle.

So, why not stay in a tiny house, at least until the smell of diapers vanished from the big place?

The worst thing that didn't make sense was that all the lawmen around couldn't figure out who shot Sheriff Brigman.

Thatcher had heard Charley and Tim say they planned to do some poking around on their own and Thatcher decided he'd help. They seemed to think that locals would be more likely to talk to locals. Charley had helped the sheriff out a few times before and Tim was almost an investigator.

The next night, when everyone was asleep, Thatcher slipped out of Charley's house and walked, ignoring the pain in his leg, toward the main road without his crutch. The sky was alive with lightning and low rolling thunder coming from the west.

He'd left his old pickup parked just beyond the cattle guard. If he let the truck roll downhill for a few hundred yards, no one would hear the engine start or him driving away.

Twenty minutes later he was in the Breaks. Flicking off his lights, he drove the roads by moonlight and memory. When he reached the trees, he hid his truck and walked toward the barn where he knew the men would be gathering. Saturday night prayer meeting. Only he didn't go in or crawl under the back corner of the barn. He stood in the trees and watched until he saw the Dulapse brothers heading into the meeting. Then, he doubled back and drove far into the Breaks to their place.

The road was so full of holes he feared his engine might fall out, but Thatcher was on a mission. He had to find some clue that would help Tim O'Grady before the college boy and Charley decided to come out here.

Thatcher thought, with luck, that he might have half an hour to look around the Dulapses' place. The sheriff would probably call what he was doing breaking and entering, but the old door didn't have a lock so Thatcher decided he was just entering.

He flicked on a flashlight and stepped inside an old cabin he knew he'd never be invited into, or, on a normal day, want to go inside. The place was a dump. Worse than his mother's house ever was. Bear dens were cleaner and smelled better. The table in the center of the room looked to be the place where the brothers spent most of their time.

Trying not to move papers around too much, he started through the stacks. The Dulapse brothers had a map of the county marked off as though they were invaders trying to conquer one section at a time. Thatcher knew the land they'd already claimed; he'd hunted deer near the circle. He'd seen a small pot field out there where no roads cross. Word was the land was owned by an old hippy who came out with his wife fifty years ago. The story was that she left him after a year, but the man stayed because his best friend lived next to him with his wife and daughter.

If the Dulapse brothers were doing drugs, they might be dealing with the owner or his friend. Or— another idea hit Thatcher—maybe they killed the old guy and took over his fields. No one would know. All they'd have to do was get rid of the body. Bury it or leave it somewhere where no one would connect it with the Breaks.

Like maybe on a ledge in Ransom Canyon.

He circled the room with the flashlight. In one corner, a few feet behind the table, was a stack of burlap bags.

He sat down to rest his leg and began studying the lines of numbers that were scribbled on scraps of paper like the free flyers they stuff in bags at the grocery and dollar stores. One of the brothers must be keeping a record of what they were making in profit. Another list looked like supplies they'd need.

The Dulapse brothers could be at the meeting right now trying to take over the drug trade in this area. One on one, they wouldn't have a chance at Bull, but together they might take him down. Once the big man was shoved out of the way, or buried, no one else who lived out here would stand against the brothers. Those in the trade would follow along with whatever the brothers said. Those not in the trade would simply ignore anything they saw or heard. It had always been that way.

Thatcher listened to the thunder and thought it almost sounded like gunfire. He'd heard of bad things happening out here, but it was mostly just whispered. Everyone knew that if real trouble started, the law would move in and their life off the grid would be over.

He had to think. If they'd tried to get rid of the sheriff, Brigman must know something about what was going on here. He'd gotten too close.

An image of the locked drawer in the sheriff's office kept flashing in Thatcher's brain. The flyer found in the canyon right after they found the burlap body had been on Brigman's desk. The same kind of bag stacked in the brothers' cabin was used to wrap the body in the canyon. The shooting of the mustangs didn't seem to be related, but it did happen close to the Breaks turnoff. Maybe the brothers thought killing a few horses would frighten strangers off?

Only why ambush the sheriff on a back road? He wasn't knocking on doors out here. Someone had almost killed a lawman, but why?

All were pieces that had to fit together. But they didn't.

If the brothers were the ones who tried to kill Brigman, they'd also been the ones to shoot him, Thatcher, in the leg. Did they think he was working with the sheriff, or were they just trying to keep him from saving Brigman?

Whatever the truth was, Thatcher knew one thing for sure. This wasn't a good place for him to be right now. He was in the bear den and the time for hibernation was over.

His instincts were screaming at him to run. But somehow he had to have proof or no one would believe him. Just saying the brothers were bad wouldn't work. Everyone already knew that. If he didn't find something, Charley and Tim would probably decide to come out and they'd get themselves killed for sure.

Thatcher told himself he had to find clues. He didn't have many friends and couldn't lose either of them.

Facts kept circling in his mind. The horses. The dead body. The sheriff bleeding on the road. Maybe they weren't related. But, if they were, trouble would find him if he didn't figure it out.

He beamed his flashlight around the room once more. Two rifles rested just behind the door. Carefully, he ejected a bullet from each, then picked them up with a corner of one of the burlap bags. Maybe if he took these to Deputy Weathers, he could see if they matched the bullets used to shoot the sheriff.

He thought of taking more, but if the brothers noticed they'd know someone had invaded their house and go out hunting for the prowler. Thatcher, with his leg feeling on fire every time he put weight on it, might not make it back to the ranch before they caught him.

Just as he turned to leave, he heard footsteps coming up the gravel trail to the house.

Thatcher backed slowly away from the door as he turned off his flashlight. There weren't many places to hide in a one-room cabin. He crawled under the burlap bags behind the table and pulled out his phone.

The Dulapse brothers were close. He could hear them cussing.

Thatcher hit five on his phone and was relieved when Weathers answered on the first ring. The man must really not have a life other than being a cop.

"Thatcher, what's…"

"Don't talk," Thatcher whispered. "Just listen. No matter what, don't say a word. I'll call you back when I'm safe."

The door opened as Thatcher flattened beneath the bags.

CHAPTER THIRTY-FOUR

Charley
April 10

CHARLEY ROLLED SLOWLY out of bed. He couldn't sleep. Maybe it was his tired muscles aching or maybe it was his longing to touch Jubilee sleeping so close beside him.

Or maybe, he realized, it was the sense that something was wrong, hanging in the night like a dense fog.

He crossed to the window and stared out over the sleeping land. The knowledge that he loved Jubilee brought him more worry than comfort. After all, he wasn't any good at love. What if he messed it up? The only thing he'd ever been good at was ranching. Maybe he should just stick to that.

Only how would he survive without Jubilee? She'd become a part of him.

The silence of the living room drew him more than any noise he heard. With his mind full of worry over how to love Jubilee, he walked through the house.

It took him a minute to realize what was wrong.

Thatcher wasn't in his bed.

Charley checked the bathroom, the kitchen, the porch.

When he turned on the lamp by his couch bed,

Charley noticed Thatcher's boots were missing, but his crutch was still leaning against the corner.

He plowed his fingers through his hair. Yesterday, he'd been aware of Thatcher listening when he and Tim O'Grady were talking about how they needed to help out with the investigation. Tim had said something about going back into the Breaks and poking around. Charley had told him it would be too dangerous, but Tim said they had to do something to help.

After Charley waved goodbye to Tim, he'd helped Thatcher in the truck. The kid had muttered something about the Breaks not being safe for either of them.

He'd tried to laugh the boy's warning off. Thatcher was still hurting—he didn't need to worry about them.

Only if Thatcher was missing now, he could only be one place. He must have got it in his head to do the job that he'd claimed was too dangerous for either of the men.

He was going into the Breaks at night with an injured leg not near enough healed to hold his weight.

Charley walked back to his bedroom and collected his hat, boots and a jacket.

"What is it?" Jubilee whispered in a sleepy little voice that made him smile.

"Thatcher's gone. I'm going after him."

She sat up. "He can take care of himself."

Charley stretched across the covers and kissed her. "I'll be back soon. Can you stay here and keep an eye on Lillie?"

"Of course." Jubilee leaned back on her pillow. "Only if you're both not back for breakfast, I'm coming after you."

He took one last look back at her from the doorway, thinking that it was quite possible that he'd love this one woman a little more every day of his life. How could anyone not see that Jubilee's heart was as big as Texas?

A moment later, he was running for his truck as he called Tim. O'Grady had been to the Breaks with Thatcher a few times looking for clues about the burlapped man—maybe he'd have some ideas about where they should look first. Waiting until morning would have probably made more sense, but Charley needed to know Thatcher was safe now.

The wannabe writer didn't sound as though he was asleep when he answered.

"Tim, meet me at the turnoff to the Breaks. Thatcher is missing. I think he's gone to do what we talked about doing yesterday. He may need help."

For once, Tim didn't talk. He simply said, "I'm on my way."

CHAPTER THIRTY-FIVE

Thatcher
April 10

THE SMELL OF decay and dirt almost choked Thatcher
as he tried to breathe beneath the layers of burlap bags.

The brothers were in the house, cussing, snorting,
and passing gas like cows who'd eaten far too many
dandelions.

Both men also sounded drunk. They were bragging
about how they'd put old Bull in his place tonight. One
said he was glad they didn't have to stuff the big guy
in a bag. The other claimed Bull wouldn't fit.

As they sat down at their table, one began arguing
about how they should have just clubbed the sheriff
when he was up here snooping around and bagged
him. It would have been a lot cleaner than shooting
him. Since they didn't kill him they'd have to go back
and finish the job now.

Thatcher tried to hold the phone still, but it wasn't
easy. He'd never been so afraid in his life. He was three
feet away from two killers. Correction: drunk killers.
They passed a jug of homemade whiskey between
them as they relived how they'd stormed into the Saturday night prayer meeting and taken over the crowd.

Thatcher didn't hear Weathers say a word. The deputy must know that if he'd made a sound, Thatcher would be the next person killed. He had no idea how much the deputy could hear. Probably most of the shouting and cussing.

An hour dripped by. One of the brothers had passed out and the other seemed determined to finish off the jug.

Thatcher waited. He'd clicked off the phone when they stopped talking, only he couldn't move until he had an opening. His injured leg was cramping, but he didn't dare move.

Finally, the only brother awake staggered out the back door, unzipping his pants as he walked.

The moment Thatcher heard the back door pop closed, he thought of darting for the front door. But, what if he made a sound and woke the other brother snoring three feet away?

His leg was throbbing in pain, but his heartbeat drowned out reason. This might be his one chance. Run or die. The thought that his body would fit in one of the bags that now covered him was no comfort.

Just as he managed to collect his courage, the back door opened and the wandering brother staggered in.

Thatcher's chance was gone. He'd have to stay put until the brothers left in the morning. If they left in the morning.

A sound of whistling came from outside. Then the crunching of steps coming toward the cabin.

The brother who was awake hit his sibling on the shoulder so hard he almost fell out of the chair. "Wake up. Some drunk's come up our path."

"He'll be sorry he bothered us this time of night," the sleepy brother said as he cussed his way to the door.

Both brothers laughed, excited at the thought of having a victim showing up at their door.

"Hey, Dulapse brothers!" A man's voice yelled from outside. "You got any moonshine for sale?"

Thatcher almost swore aloud. The drunk storming the gates was Tim O'Grady.

Both the brothers managed to stagger to the door. They must have realized they were too drunk to fight, so they took turns cussing Tim out and ordering him off their land.

Thatcher was just thankful they didn't shoot him, especially when Tim started asking questions like where could he get some pot this time of night.

Both brothers moved outside and started yelling that they'd kill him if he ever came near their place again.

Thatcher saw his chance. He climbed out from under the bags and limped to the back door. His weak leg didn't seem to work at all. With one hand braced against the wall, he hopped, dragging his injured leg like dead wood behind him.

Fear overrode pain in his brain.

A foot beyond the back steps, he spotted a lean shadow coming toward him. Before he could scream, Charley whispered, "I got you, That."

He looped his arm around his ribs and Thatcher decided if they lived through this night he'd take on religion because right now the rancher was as close to being an angel as Thatcher would probably ever see.

Half carrying him down the rise, Charley ran toward what looked like his pickup parked just beyond the tree line.

"My truck?"

"We'll get it later," Charley said. "Right now we're getting you out of here."

Thatcher's leg couldn't keep up. About the time he thought of telling Charley to go on without him, he felt Tim's arm lock around his other side. Together the two men ran, with Thatcher hanging between them like a rag doll.

They were in the truck and flying down the road before Thatcher could take a full breath.

A minute later a line of patrol cars blinked on their lights. They looked like Christmas lights decorating the lane from the Breaks to County Road 111.

"That'll be Weathers and his buddies. He called in for backup while he was recording everything coming through on your phone. They are going in as soon as we're out of the way." Charley laughed. "You cracked the case, kid!"

"What about me? I was great back there," Tim added as they passed the line of patrol cars.

When he reached the county road, Thatcher hit five on his phone.

"Thatcher!" Weathers answered before the phone even rang more than a beep.

"I'm out. Charley said you heard everything?"

"I heard it all." Weathers sounded as if he might have a heart attack and he hadn't even been in the cabin. "Get your ass to the sheriff's office as fast as you can. I've called in backup from every county around. Sheriff Brigman said he'll be waiting to take your statement personally once you're safe."

"Will do."

A few miles down the road, a highway patrol car

swung in behind Charley's pickup with lights flashing, and Thatcher relaxed.

By the time they reached town, another cruiser had joined them.

Charley and Tim both helped him out of the truck when they reached town. "You did good, That," Charley said. "But, when we get back home Jubilee and I are going to want to have a long talk about you sneaking out. You scared us to death."

Thatcher smiled. "I never had nobody who cared before."

"I know. How about we settle on you leaving a note next time? We're not trying to cage you, That, just keep up with you."

"Fair enough." Thatcher didn't care if his leg hurt or that he almost died tonight. It just felt good to know someone worried about him.

As they walked into the sheriff's office, Tim looked at Charley. "You know, Collins, you're not old enough to be the boy's father."

"I know." Charley laughed. "But he's aging me fast. Between him and Jubilee I'll be an old man by the end of the year."

Brigman looked up from his desk. He looked pale, maybe even a little green around the edges, but the sheriff was back where he belonged and Thatcher didn't care how many lectures he had to sit through.

Within half an hour, the office was packed with lawmen. Everyone in the room had heard the brothers talking. They'd gone in and arrested the Dulapses as soon as they knew Thatcher was safe. And without a shot being fired.

Thatcher sat back, relaxing. Trying to take it all in.

Brigman had been collecting evidence on them, but he couldn't get enough for a case. Someone had even sent a few notes telling Brigman to stay out of the Breaks if he wanted to stay healthy. Once the search of their cabin was over, Thatcher had no doubt the sheriff would have plenty of handwriting samples to compare. Highway patrolmen had been watching the road in and out of the Breaks since the sheriff was shot. They saw Cap Fuller take Thatcher in to get his truck. They saw him go in alone after dark.

Like guardian angels, they'd been at the county line waiting for him to come out. He didn't know it, but they were making sure he'd be safe from then on.

So many facts were flying, Thatcher couldn't keep up. All the clues were falling into place. The Dulapse brothers had killed the tattooed man in order to take his land. They'd shot Sheriff Brigman for getting too close. And Thatcher was shot because he was in the wrong place at the wrong time.

Charley handed him a can of Coke, then sat down beside him.

"Did you know about all this investigating that was going on, Charley?"

"I knew some. That's why I put rifles above every door. That's why we tried to keep an eye on you. We don't want you hurt."

"Oh, I thought the rifles were some kind of strange decorating habit you had." Thatcher laughed at his own joke.

When he looked down he noticed the leg of his jeans was wet. As he pulled the denim up, he saw that the bandage over his wound was more red than white.

"Oh, hellfire and snot," he muttered. "I'm dripping again."

Charley didn't say a word; he just stood and caught Weathers's eye. "We're on our way to the hospital again."

Weathers stepped away from his fellow officers and picked Thatcher up as if he was no bigger than a baby.

On his way to Charley's truck, Weathers said, "We'll take the case from here, but I talked to Brigman and he wanted me to make sure you know that what you did was foolish and dangerous. It also cracked the case."

As he sat Thatcher down in the pickup, he added, "One of the guys will lead you in. You're about to make the trip to Lubbock faster than you ever thought possible."

"Could you do me a favor, Fifth?" Thatcher figured they were friends now. "Could you not tell anyone about this? I don't know how much hugging and patting I can take. I'm injured, you know."

"If that's the way you want it."

Charley started his truck, and in minutes they were on their way back to the emergency room.

Thatcher worried that the chubby nurse might sit on him like she promised if he didn't take care of his leg. The vampire would probably want more blood and the one with the evil left eye was probably waiting around just to scare him.

He was relieved to find only an intern who cleaned up the blood, checked the wound, added a few stitches and wrapped him up. He also handed Charley more pain pills and antibiotics.

"Now stay off that leg for a while, kid," the intern lectured.

"All right, I'll try. But I was running for my life."

"Sure, kid," the intern answered, looking terminally bored.

Charlie and Thatcher laughed all the way home about how the intern thought they were kidding.

CHAPTER THIRTY-SIX

Lauren
April 10

LAUREN GAVE UP trying to keep her father in bed after Weathers called. She helped the sheriff dress in one of the jogging suits she'd bought him. It was still two sizes too big, but it fit better than Weathers's sweats.

She drove slowly to the office, with Pop complaining all the way. He wanted in on the action. If he could have, he would have packed his walker and gone out on the arrest.

When they arrived at the office, it looked more like a big city precinct than Crossroads county offices. Even Pearly's desk had been taken over, along with a few from the other offices.

Pop let her use the wheelchair from home to roll him in. Once he was behind his desk, he was back to being a sheriff in his element.

When she bumped into Weathers, he looked as if he was having a ball. His first big case—no, two cases—and he was in the center of the wheel.

"Sorry," he said as he tried to step away, only to bump into someone else.

"It's okay, Weathers. Make sure the sheriff doesn't overdo it."

"I'll watch over him." Weathers saluted as if she were a general. "This is the most exciting thing that's ever happened to me in my career. No, ever. I felt like I was right there listening to the killers confess. I was right with the kid. Worried about him. Not believing what I heard. Fighting not to make a sound."

Lauren backed a step away, half expecting the big guy to explode with excitement. "Any idea if Tim O'Grady is around?"

"He's in the courtroom. It seems several of the facts he found about the burlap man are proving very interesting. And get this, the old hippy with the tats actually owned the property up there in the Breaks. He didn't have any relatives, but he left his land to Thatcher's mother. Isn't that a kick? Seems he was friends with her parents."

Lauren gave her father a warning look and headed up to the courtroom on the second floor.

Tim was there, moving around a long table of notes. Putting all the pieces together in his mind.

When he saw her, he froze, then smiled. "Good morning, almost."

He leaned down and kissed her lightly. "You okay?"

She nodded. "I'm worried about Pop."

"I'll watch over him while he's here. I'm part of the team. Weathers told us we'll be working all weekend sorting this mess out. The Dulapse brothers apparently were starting their own little crime spree. When they were arrested Weathers said one of them cried like a baby. Folks from the Breaks are calling in with information and complaints about them. They've got two guys on the phones just taking complaints." Tim's words came fast and high with excitement.

"I thought no one talked to the law in the Breaks."

Tim laughed. "Apparently they do when they find out that the brothers shot Thatcher. He was born and grew up out there. He's one of their own. One woman called to say we should turn the brothers loose at the turnoff on County Road 111. She said they'd take care of them."

"I'm so glad it's over." Lauren leaned against Tim, needing one of his wonderful hugs.

"Me, too," Tim whispered as he held her tight. "I'd like to get back to writing. All at once stories are dancing in my head."

"I kind of feel the same way. I started writing my thoughts and feelings down at the hospital. Do you think the lady living out by the canyon was right? I might just become a writer."

Tim shook his head. "It's not that easy, L. I've studied for months. Some days it's like bleeding just to get a few pages."

"You're right. It sounds too hard. Maybe I should just be happy being the friend of a writer."

He nodded his agreement, totally unaware that she was mentally trying to think of a pen name.

CHAPTER THIRTY-SEVEN

Jubilee
May 15

JUBILEE STOOD ON the porch of her big old house. She could still sometimes feel the presence of Levy in the place. She could almost see him sitting at the kitchen table having his morning coffee or standing on the corner of the porch looking out over his land as if it was the most priceless painting in the world.

For a month now she'd been remodeling the old place on a shoestring. She'd painted a few rooms and even some of the furniture. She'd added bold colors in spots and taken down most of the drapes that hung over windows never opened.

This was home now. This place was hers and she never planned to leave.

So why am I still sleeping over at Charley's place? she asked herself.

She couldn't believe how the ranch had changed in three months. Cattle roamed the grassland and wheat as high as her knees grew in once-bare fields. Even the garden was growing. It wouldn't be long until they'd be picking their supper fresh every night.

So why am I still sleeping at Charley's place? she asked herself again.

The way she felt about him took her breath away. In a life of never letting any man matter to her, she'd somehow found the one person she couldn't resist. He mattered.

She watched as he pulled up to the barn with one of the hands he'd hired. In the months since he'd taken over as foreman, he'd changed. He'd come into the role he was born to play. He knew what he was doing. He treated this land as though it was his. He loved it.

When he saw her, he waved and headed toward her.

She watched him coming closer. Unable to look away. When she'd been younger, she'd sometimes imagined what her perfect man would be like. He'd never been wearing boots and jeans. But here he was. Walking straight toward her.

She'd heard him say he loved her once, but she'd never said the words back and he hadn't said them again. Now and then in a few stolen minutes, they'd share a passionate kiss or he'd hold her as though he'd never let her go, but most of their days were full of life on the ranch. Thatcher had become part of their family and Lillie now held Jubilee's heart.

"You up for a ride tonight?" he asked. "Lillie's staying over at the Lees' and Thatcher reluctantly agreed to take Kristi to a dance, even. He says he can't dance, but I'm guessing Kristi will teach him what she can, since his leg is still healing."

Charley reached the porch and pulled her into his arms suddenly as if he had to hold her even for a moment. "If you like, we could ride out to the pass. There's a chance, if the storm holds off until after midnight, that we might have a full moon."

She smiled, remembering the story Lauren told

her about a heart's wish being granted if the moon passed over the open space in the passage. "I think that would be fun."

"Good," he said. "I'll be working late, but I'll try to be back and have the horses saddled by nine."

Jubilee thought about the ride all day. As always, she'd made a list of all she had to do. The bank. The store. The vet.

Charley usually added to her list. Probably afraid she'd get bored. Which wasn't likely to happen.

When she finally took a minute to balance the ranch accounts, she noticed something very wrong. The balance was almost twice the money that should be in the account. She went all the way back to the day she'd decided to put in her own savings. She'd kept a running total in her checkbook every week, but hadn't had a chance to balance her account, to make sure her numbers matched the bank's.

They didn't, now. The bank must have made a mistake. Maybe they'd accidentally logged her deposit twice?

She called the bank, and a few minutes later she sat very still in her little office area just left of the kitchen. The teller had said simply that Charley had transferred his savings into the ranch account. They didn't see any problem; after all, he was a signer on the account.

"Nothing wrong," she managed to say to the teller. "Thank you. I was just checking."

Tears threatened to fall. He'd told her he'd been saving to buy land. He'd even said once that every tip he made at the bar went into a jar to take to the bank.

All he wanted, all he'd ever dreamed of, he'd once told her, was land.

He must have put all his saving in the Lone Heart Ranch account, just like her, on the chance of making this place go. Not for him, but for her.

By late afternoon she knew, moon or not, she'd share another kiss in the passage with Charley. She had something very important to tell him.

It was a little after nine by the time Charley walked out of the barn leading two horses.

Jubilee smiled. Knights in shining armor sometimes wore cowboy boots.

"Still up for a ride to the pass?" he asked when she met him.

He looked tired but happy. A few hours alone might be all they'd ever have, slices of time, but it would be enough.

When she moved to her horse he was there to help her up. His hand patted her bottom as he lifted her into the saddle and she looked down at him. "Did you do that on purpose?"

"You bet." He winked.

They rode over the dark land toward the passage. Neither said a word. It was funny how they talked of other things all day, feeling as if they never had time to talk about things other than what needed to be done on the ranch. Now, when they had time alone, there didn't seem to be a need for words.

He helped her down at the entrance and took her hand. With one thin flashlight beam, he led her into the darkness. The air was cooler there and silent. The magic surrounded them as it had before.

Halfway through, he stopped. "If you could do anything or say anything in the silence of this place, what would you do?"

Moving her hands up his shirt, she felt the warmth of him just below the cotton of his shirt. "I'd kiss you."

He leaned down and she kissed him as softly as she had that first time.

He kissed her back without holding her. When he moved to her ear, he whispered, "I've only been kissed like that once before and it was the best kiss I think I've ever had."

"You're not sure?"

"Maybe we should try again so I can be sure."

She kissed him again, loving the way he accepted her kiss, not as the start of something but as a gift all by itself.

Slowly, as if they had all the time in the world, he leaned her against the cool wall of the passage and whispered, "Look up."

The moon was just beginning to peek over one side of the passage opening.

They held each other, watching it move across the open space above. When it was full, she asked, "What would you wish? Your heart's desire? Your one wish for a lifetime?"

He smiled down at her in the moonlight. "I'd wish that we'd be together, really together, forever together because I'll never love another the way I love you, Jubilee."

She forgot all about the moon and kissed him the way she'd been wanting to kiss him every night they'd slept together.

When she finally stopped, he tugged her farther into the passage. "I want to show you something."

"But it's late."

"We've time." He stepped out on the canyon side of the passage. The night was midnight blue and the remains of a campfire burned low near the edge of the canyon wall.

The firelight danced off the colors of the rocks, making the world warm with hues of the earth. "It's beautiful," she whispered as if afraid she'd disturb the wonder of the place.

Charley stared down at her. "Yes, you are," he answered. "I wanted to see you like this tonight. I wanted to hold you so close right here that I could feel your heart beating next to mine."

Now his kiss came fast and complete. Full of a wild passion she'd never known to even long for.

When she finally stopped to breathe, he took her hand and slipped a ring on her finger. "Marry me, pretty lady."

She laughed. "According to Thatcher, we already are."

"Then we'll do it again. I want to be tied to you so that you'll never run away from loving me. I want to wake up with you every morning and go to sleep with you every night. I want to build a life with you."

She couldn't stop kissing him. She was addicted to this wonderful, kind man.

When they finally pulled apart, they ran back through the passage stopping every few feet in the darkness to touch. Both were out of breath and hungry for more when they reached their horses and rode the wind home. Both were pulling off clothes by the time they hit the door to his house. When they tumbled into bed they were laughing with excitement.

She felt as if she'd been starving all her life and Charley was the one person who could satisfy her need. Suddenly he was touching her everywhere, kissing her everywhere, loving her like she'd never dreamed of being loved.

They'd put this moment off for so long. Waited for it. Dreamed about it so many nights only to discover that it was so much more than they thought it might be.

A heart's wish that melted her cold heart.

When they were both spent, he held her close, brushing her hair away from her face and asking her if she was all right.

"I'm perfect," she answered.

"Good," he whispered. "You want to do it again? Thatcher won't be home until after midnight. We may not get much time alone, but if it's like this, it'll be enough."

"All right. We do it again." She laughed. "Only after midnight, we're closing the bedroom door. If he needs us for the rest of the night, he's going to have to yell."

"What have you got planned?"

By the time she could pull her thoughts together enough to answer, he'd already lit a fire inside her and she was lost in loving him again.

The second time was slow and tender. He took his time learning her body and she did the same. They kissed deeply until she begged for more.

The third time was white-hot passion rolling over them, then a sweet surrender of two souls.

As she drifted back to earth, he held on tight. "I'll never get enough of loving you, Jubilee."

She stretched against him and whispered, "You want to go again?"

He laughed. "If we do, you'll have to bury me out by Levy because I'll be dead with a smile on my face."

She laughed and climbed out of bed to get a drink. When she came back, Charley was under the covers, finally. She curled up beside him and was almost asleep when she heard a car rattle over the cattle guard at the front gate.

Charley came awake.

"It's okay. It's just Thatcher getting home."

"About time. It's almost one o'clock." Charley sounded exactly like a father.

She giggled. "You'd better be glad he didn't make it in earlier."

Charley squeezed her. "I am, come to think of it. When we get married, how about we move into your house? Then he'll have his own room. Preferably far down the hall."

"I agree. By the way, when is the wedding? Since I know you've already got everything planned out."

"Soon. How about next Sunday," he answered. "I've already booked the place."

They heard Thatcher come in. Then his cell rang. Kristi must have called him while her father drove home from dropping him off.

For a while they could hear Thatcher talking to her, or rather she must have done most of the talking, because all they heard was That saying things like "I agree" and "You're right about that" and "Me, too."

Finally he said good-night to her and they heard him fall into his bed on the couch.

"You all right, That?" Charley yelled.

"I'm fine. Trying to dance is harder than killing snakes."

Jubilee giggled. "Good night, Thatcher."

He didn't answer and she guessed he'd already fallen asleep. She cuddled into Charley's side and let out a long sigh.

"I forgot to tell you," she whispered. "I'm in love with you."

"I know. It was bound to happen." He laughed. "I'm not ever letting you go, Jubilee, so don't even think about walking out on me."

"I feel the same way. You have to stay. We couldn't split the ranch."

He was silent for a minute, then added, "Honey, this land is yours."

"No, it's not. I had the deed changed today. It's ours."

He shook his head. "I didn't want to take your land."

"I know. I didn't want to take your dream. You transferred your savings without asking me so I transferred the deed."

He was so still and silent, she knew he was angry. Suddenly, she laughed. "I'm not sure what you're upset about. We both got what we needed. What we wanted."

She could feel his anger as he moved a few inches away.

Tossing the covers, she yelled, "I'm walking out, Charley!"

His hand shot out and tugged her back. "No. I can't let you go. I love you too much."

Tears welled in her eyes. Finally she'd met a man who wouldn't let her walk away without a fight. "I'm not letting you go, either. I've spent years looking for someone like you. If you leave me, you'll have to drag half this ranch behind you."

"Then I'd better stay."

"And love me the rest of your life," she added.

"And love only you for the rest of my life," he answered.

As she leaned to kiss him, she heard a rattle coming from the other side of the thin wall. "Would you two go to sleep?" Thatcher yelled. "Since you're all loving tonight, are you now common-law married? I'm not exactly sure when that kind of thing happens."

"We're marrying as soon as I can find a preacher," Charley said, realizing he didn't need to yell for Thatcher to hear everything. "And you'd better shower and dress up, because you're my best man."

"Well, finally," Thatcher said. "I'm tired of chaperoning you two."

Charley laughed as he moved his hand over Jubilee's hip. "Go to sleep, son."

There was no answer from the next room. Charley moved close to Jubilee and whispered, "Go to sleep, my love."

She didn't answer. She was already there.

CHAPTER THIRTY-EIGHT

Lauren
May 24

LAUREN STOOD BESIDE Jubilee on the rim of Ransom Canyon. Both wore summer dresses that matched the colors of the canyon wall.

Charley Collins took his bride's hand and they faced the preacher.

It was a small wedding put together with love and laughter. No fancy invitations, no flowers decorating the place, just the backdrop of the canyon and a bouquet of wildflowers.

The groom wore a cowboy hat. The flower girl was dressed like a fairy, and the friends crowded round were all smiling. Lauren decided she'd never seen a more beautiful wedding.

"I'll love you forever," Charley whispered as he slipped a plain gold band on Jubilee's finger.

"And I'll love you the same," she answered.

Lauren smiled. She'd give anything if she could find the kind of love Charley and Jubilee had.

But if it didn't come along, she'd already decided she'd write about it.

* * * * *

Wrangle Your Friends for the Ultimate Ranch Girls' Getaway

Win an all-expenses-paid 3-night luxurious stay for you and your 3 guests at The Resort at Paws Up in Greenough, Montana.

Retail Value $10,000

A TOAST TO FRIENDSHIP, AN ADVENTURE OF A LIFETIME!

Learn more at www.Harlequinranchgetaway.com

Sweepstakes ends August 31, 2016

WCHMR

Same great stories,
new name!

In July 2016,
the HARLEQUIN®
AMERICAN ROMANCE® series
will become
the HARLEQUIN®
WESTERN ROMANCE series.

Connect with us to find your next great read,
special offers and more.

f /HarlequinBooks

@HarlequinBooks

www.HarlequinBlog.com

www.Harlequin.com/Newsletters

HARLEQUIN®

A *Romance* FOR EVERY MOOD™

www.Harlequin.com

HWR2016

HARLEQUIN®

SPECIAL EDITION

Life, Love and Family

Save $1.00

on the purchase of

WED BY FORTUNE
by Judy Duarte, available
May 24, 2016, or on any other
Harlequin® Special Edition book.

Available wherever books are sold, including most
bookstores, supermarkets, drugstores and discount stores.

Save $1.00

on the purchase of any Harlequin® Special Edition book.

Coupon valid until August 31, 2016. Redeemable at participating outlets in the
U.S. and Canada only. Not redeemable at Barnes & Noble stores.
Limit one coupon per customer.

52613685

Canadian Retailers: Harlequin Enterprises Limited will pay the face value of
this coupon plus 10.25¢ if submitted by customer for this product only. Any
other use constitutes fraud. Coupon is nonassignable. Void if taxed, prohibited
or restricted by law. Consumer must pay any government taxes. Void if copied.
Inmar Promotional Services ("IPS") customers submit coupons and proof of
sales to Harlequin Enterprises Limited, P.O. Box 3000, Saint John, NB E2L 4L3,
Canada. Non-IPS retailer—for reimbursement submit coupons and proof of
sales directly to Harlequin Enterprises Limited, Retail Marketing Department, 225
Duncan Mill Rd., Don Mills, ON M3B 3K9, Canada.

5 65373 00076 2 (8100)0 12159

U.S. Retailers: Harlequin Enterprises
Limited will pay the face value of
this coupon plus 8¢ if submitted by
customer for this product only. Any
other use constitutes fraud. Coupon is
nonassignable. Void if taxed, prohibited
or restricted by law. Consumer must pay
any government taxes. Void if copied.
For reimbursement submit coupons
and proof of sales directly to Harlequin
Enterprises Limited, P.O. Box 880478,
El Paso, TX 88588-0478, U.S.A. Cash
value 1/100 cents.

® and TM are trademarks owned and used by the trademark owner and/or its licensee.

© 2016 Harlequin Enterprises Limited

SECOUPBPA0616

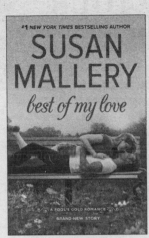

REQUEST YOUR
FREE BOOKS!

2 FREE NOVELS
FROM THE ROMANCE COLLECTION
PLUS 2 FREE GIFTS!

YES! Please send me 2 FREE novels from the Romance Collection and my 2 FREE gifts (gifts are worth about $10). After receiving them, if I don't wish to receive any more books, I can return the shipping statement marked "cancel." If I don't cancel, I will receive 4 brand-new novels every month and be billed just $6.49 per book in the U.S. or $6.99 per book in Canada. That's a savings of at least 19% off the cover price. It's quite a bargain! Shipping and handling is just 50¢ per book in the U.S. and 75¢ per book in Canada.* I understand that accepting the 2 free books and gifts places me under no obligation to buy anything. I can always return a shipment and cancel at any time. Even if I never buy another book, the two free books and gifts are mine to keep forever.

194/394 MDN GH4D

Name	(PLEASE PRINT)	
Address		Apt. #
City	State/Prov.	Zip/Postal Code

Signature (if under 18, a parent or guardian must sign)

Mail to the **Reader Service:**
IN U.S.A.: P.O. Box 1867, Buffalo, NY 14240-1867
IN CANADA: P.O. Box 609, Fort Erie, Ontario L2A 5X3

Want to try two free books from another line?
Call 1-800-873-8635 or visit www.ReaderService.com.

* Terms and prices subject to change without notice. Prices do not include applicable taxes. Sales tax applicable in N.Y. Canadian residents will be charged applicable taxes. Offer not valid in Quebec. This offer is limited to one order per household. Not valid for current subscribers to the Romance Collection or the Romance/Suspense Collection. All orders subject to credit approval. Credit or debit balances in a customer's account(s) may be offset by any other outstanding balance owed by or to the customer. Please allow 4 to 6 weeks for delivery. Offer available while quantities last.

Your Privacy—The Reader Service is committed to protecting your privacy. Our Privacy Policy is available online at www.ReaderService.com or upon request from the Reader Service.

We make a portion of our mailing list available to reputable third parties that offer products we believe may interest you. If you prefer that we not exchange your name with third parties, or if you wish to clarify or modify your communication preferences, please visit us at www.ReaderService.com/consumerschoice or write to us at Reader Service Preference Service, P.O. Box 9062, Buffalo, NY 14240-9062. Include your complete name and address.